TIME OF DEATH

Alex Barclay lives in County Cork, Ireland. She is the writer of three other bestselling thrillers, *Darkhouse*, *The Caller* and *Blood Runs Cold*.

For more information about Alex Barclay and her books, please visit her website, www.alexbarclay.co.uk

Praise for Alex Barclay:

'Right now, she's the rising star of the hard-boiled crime fiction world, combining wild characters, surprising plots and massive backdrops with a touch of dry humour'
Mirror

'Explosive' *Company*

'Darkhouse is a terrific debut by an exciting new writer'
Independent on Sunday

'Compelling' *Glamour*

'Excellent summer reading . . . Barclay has the confidence to move her story along slowly, and deftly explores the relationships between her characters'
Sunday Telegraph

'The thriller of the summer' *Irish Independent*

'If you haven't discovered Alex Barclay, it's time to jump on the bandwagon' *Image Magazine*

Also by Alex Barclay

Darkhouse
The Caller
Blood Runs Cold

ALEX BARCLAY

Time of Death

HARPER

Harper
An imprint of HarperCollins*Publishers*
77–85 Fulham Palace Road,
Hammersmith, London W6 8JB

www.harpercollins.co.uk

This paperback edition 2012
1

First published in GREAT BRITAIN by
HarperCollins*Publishers* 2010

A catalogue record for this book is
available from the British Library

ISBN: 978 0 00 792620 6

Set in Meridien by Palimpsest Book Production Limited,
Grangemouth, Stirlingshire
Printed and bound in Great Britain by
Clays Ltd, St Ives plc

MIX
Paper from
responsible sources
FSC® C007454

To Mary Maddison

ACKNOWLEDGEMENTS

Thank you, always, to my agent Darley Anderson and the fabulous team at the Darley Anderson Literary, TV and Film Agency. Special thanks to Camilla Bolton, criminal mastermind.

Love, thanks and fond farewell to Wayne Brookes, the star who shines wherever he goes.

Thank you to Lynne Drew for her wisdom, insight and thoughtfulness.

Many thanks to Belinda Budge, Moira Reilly, Tony Purdue and everyone at the wonderful HarperCollins.

To Anne O'Brien – thank you for never missing a trick.

I am thoroughly grateful to all the experts who give up their time, share their expertise, and understand that I have to play with the facts. Very special thanks to SSA Phil Niedringhaus and to everyone at The Rocky Mountain Safe Streets Task Force. Thank you to David Aggleton, Aggleton & Associates, Inc.; Cold Case Investigator, Cheryl Moore; Kerry O'Connell; Billy L. Smith Sr.; L.E.T.S. International, Inc.

To Sue Booth-Forbes, thank you always for your kindness, generosity and inspiration.

To Paul, for everything you do, thank you out loud.

Love and thanks to my endlessly supportive family and friends.

NOTE

Eleven years ago, an organized crime operation was dismantled following a year-long undercover operation in which FBI Special Agent Ren Bryce infiltrated the inner circle of its head, Domenica Val Pando.

On the night that Val Pando was to be arrested, the compound was burned to the ground by a rival gang and Val Pando escaped with her husband and young son.

Her whereabouts remain unknown.

PROLOGUE

El Paso, Texas

Erubiel Diaz lay curled on the wet floor of the soiled gas station restroom. He had been violently ill. But to a man with damaged senses, a weakened stomach and voided bowels could never be anything more than a physical condition. It could never be the bad omen that he had been foolish to ignore. As a result, his instinct that morning had not been to turn back, but to hook a fingernail into a small bag of white powder and take in a pure cocaine rush. Outside, a car radio crackled with a thunderstorm warning. Within hours, the searing heat was set to be broken by quarter-sized hail.

Erubiel Diaz now stood in the cobbled courtyard of a million-dollar home on the west side of the Franklin Mountains. Diaz was squat and muscular, short-limbed and heavy-browed. He was wearing a yellow sleeveless T-shirt and black shorts to his calves. His body, his clothes, hadn't been washed in days. He was a dark blot in a space that was filled with light, with flowers, plants and trees that he would have recognized if he was the landscape gardener on his van's fake sign. Only the plant by the living-room window looked familiar to him. Something to do with a bird.

Diaz had a round, lined face, sallow skin, and bloodshot eyes. He squinted against the bright sunshine that bounced off the white walls of the Spanish-style house. He had done what he came here to do. As he made his move to leave, he heard a car pull up outside. The security gates to his left slid slowly open. He pressed himself against the cool stone of the perimeter wall.

The woman who stepped out of the car was nothing like the women he paid for, or took for free, nothing like the worn-out mother of his children. This woman was tall and delicate, with fine blonde hair to her shoulders and a light, freckled tan. She wore a long, flowing skirt, and a white cotton blouse. Three gold bangles shone on her slender wrist. Her polished toenails were the color of the flowers beneath the window. Diaz looked down at his feet. They were wedged into Tevas that were a size too small – their criss-crossed straps digging into his flesh. His toes were short, covered with black hair, their nails caked in dirt.

Diaz checked his watch. It was an absent glance; no matter where the hands pointed, he knew what time it was. What he could not have known as he lurched forward and slammed the woman face-down onto the trunk of her car, was that he had just sent those hands spiraling wildly toward his time of death.

The sound of the woman's breath as it was forced from her lungs died in the rumble of the forecast thunder. The charcoal sky exploded with light. And the woman watched as the quarter-sized hail came crashing down, severing the fiery blossoms of the Red Bird of Paradise.

1

Special Agent Ren Bryce pulled into the parking lot of The Rocky Mountain Safe Streets Task Force office. She reached out to turn off the radio.

'*Coming up next,*' said the presenter, '*we take a look at Denver's Fifty Most Wanted. The list will be released later today by the Rocky Mountain Safe Streets Task Force and the US Marshals office . . .*'

Ren turned to her back-seat passenger.

'Coming up next, Misty – you and me in the office, trying to find these assholes.'

Misty was the black-and-white border collie she had adopted seven months earlier when her owner was killed. Her collar had a special engraving: 'I Smell Dead People'. Misty and Ren were recent graduates of cadaver dog training school – Misty's second time, Ren's first. But there were no plans to put her to work. For now, Misty's skills were on the down low.

Ren's boss, Supervisory Special Agent Gary Dettling, had given Misty security clearance for the week, so she could spend it in the office, instead of Ren's temporary motel home.

*   *   *

When Gary Dettling set up The Rocky Mountain Safe Streets Task Force, the maverick in him chose a building that was a piece of Denver's agricultural history. The Livestock Exchange Building, red brick, four stories high, was one of the few buildings in Denver that had its original interior: polished marble floors and grand mahogany staircases. It started out as home to the Denver Union Stockyard Company and one hundred years on, still kept a link to its roots; the Colorado Brand Inspectors' office was on the second floor, Maverick Press was on the third: cowboys still had a home in the Livestock Exchange Building.

Gary Dettling was the straightest maverick Ren knew. He had created something that shook things up – a multi-agency task force – yet he ran it with a tight grip on the reins. The nine-man one-woman team worked from a bullpen. There were no formal partners, but two years earlier, within months of Ren Bryce starting there, she had fallen into a natural group with the three men who sat around her – Cliff James, Colin Grabien and Robbie Truax. A filing cabinet to Ren's left and one to Colin's right created a subtle break in the room to seal the deal.

Ren secured Misty in her quarters and headed down the hallway to her office. She threw her coat on the stand by the door and hung her gray suit jacket on the back of her chair. Her work wardrobe was always a slim-fit black or gray suit, a top in whatever color matched her mood in the morning, and black three-inch heels. Years earlier, Ren had bought an Armani pant suit after a drunken lunch-time date. She had no idea where it was, but the forgeries – expertly made by her mother, Kitty – were holding up well.

Cliff James was the only person in the office when Ren arrived.

Cliff was ex-Jefferson County Sheriff's Department, fifty-two years old, a big warm bear with a face set to perma-smile. Happy family life, happy man.

Ren turned to him. 'My motel room is the type of place a man called Randy would take a girl called Bonnie in his pick-up on a Friday night when her trucker husband, also called Randy, is out of town.'

'Does it have a heart-shaped bed?' said Cliff.

'To Randy and Bonnie, every bed is heart-shaped.'

'God bless them and the illegitimate offspring Randy-the-husband will unknowingly have to bring up as his own.'

'The good news, however,' said Ren, 'is that I am leaving. I will soon have in my possession the keys to a beautiful home on Mardyke Street, straight out of Olde Denver.'

'How did you swing that?'

'My mom's friend, Annie, is in need of a housesitter.' She paused. 'Desperate need, clearly.'

'What? You'd be a great housesitter,' said Cliff. 'Clean. Rarely home. Avoids the kitchen. Excellent firearm skills . . .'

'I like the way you said "clean".' Ren smiled. 'I note, also, that "tidy" didn't go along with it.'

Cliff glanced at her desk. That was all it took.

'Where is everyone?' Ren checked her watch.

'Two separate robberies in the wee hours.'

'Lucky escape for me.'

'Yeah, because being here today will be a whole lot more fun,' said Cliff. 'Hey, here it is. He pointed at the television mounted on the wall in the corner and hit the volume on the remote control. Gary Dettling was standing at a podium, flanked by officers from Denver PD and the US Marshals Office.

Gary was athlete handsome, taller than all of them, dark-haired, loved by cameras. Ren had read posts on a 9 News forum from women who prayed for him to get a regular slot. Ren worked with him every day. She smiled at the screen. *And you still do nothing for me. And please let it stay that way.*

'*Agent Dettling, can you tell us a little more about The Rocky Mountain Safe Streets Task Force?*' said the reporter.

'Just that it's fabulous,' said Ren.

Gary was nodding at the reporter. '*The Safe Streets Violent Crimes Initiative was set up by the FBI in 1992 to tackle violent gangs, violent crimes and the apprehension of violent fugitives.*'

'Violent, violent, violent,' said Ren. 'Do you have any idea how brave we are?'

Cliff laughed. 'My neighbor's kid, he's about sixteen years old? He thinks we help little old ladies cross the street.'

Ren shook her head slowly. 'Safe Streets is not a great name, though . . .'

The reporter's voice struck up again. '*So, this is about pooling resources?*'

'*Yes,*' said Gary. '*The task force is FBI-sponsored, so we have access to all the FBI's resources, but we also benefit from local law-enforcement knowledge, and we're working together as one unit, instead of each agency taking care of individual cases that may overlap. It saves time, money, and it's proven to be a very successful formula.*'

'You bet,' said Ren. 'Two people at Safe Streets are currently and fiercely protecting the city of Denver and beyond, as he speaks.'

'Three,' said Robbie Truax, walking in and putting his knapsack on the floor beside his desk. Robbie was a former Aurora PD detective. He was Ren's pal; kind, wholesome, blond-haired, blue-eyed, healthy – an elongated boy scout. He was also a strict Mormon – no caffeine, no alcohol, no swearing, no sex before marriage. Robbie was the 30-Year-Old Virgin.

The TV screen flashed quickly across the first few lines of faces on the Fifty Most Wanted list. A stab of anger hit Ren.

When the hell did this change happen?

Gary picked a few fugitives from the list, pushed by producers, as always, to choose the most glamorous cases – the fallen-child-star fugitive, the murderous teen, the homecoming hooker . . . The Crimestoppers number scrolled across the bottom of the screen. Ren stood up and went over to the office gallery of the Fifty Most Wanted, pinned across a huge corkboard on the wall.

Cliff checked his watch. 'Ren, don't bother – Gary will be back in a half-hour. He said he'd go through it all when everyone's here.'

'Well, let me just do this—' Ren began grabbing pins from the photos and stabbing them into the top five faces as she re-arranged them.

'Easy tiger,' said Cliff.

2

Gary slipped quietly into his office without visiting the bullpen, but Ren had seen his car drive into the lot. She paused outside his door. Despite her years at Safe Streets, there were still times when she took a moment before going in. Gary's office was like a Dutch minimalist armchair – handsome and elegant, but you wouldn't want to stay in it for too long. It was as if it had been designed as a quick stop-off on your way to solving a case.

Ren knocked. Gary didn't respond. If someone said jump, Gary Dettling, wouldn't say 'How high?' He would probably never jump again for the rest of his life.

Ren leaned an ear to the door.

'Come in,' said Gary.

He was sitting at his desk. Ren imagined him there on his first day in the job, carefully flattening out a sheet of graph paper and marking in the exact location of each piece of furniture and drawing red circles with Xs through them over any spot that would typically hold a personal touch. But Ren knew that the polished mahogany, the pristine blue carpet, the sharp lines, the austerity did not define the man. It masked him. Gary was not just head of the Safe Streets Task Force, he also trained the FBI's UCEs – undercover employees. He had spent so long in deep-cover assignments that hiding his real life had become a habit. He had a wife, a teenage daughter, a house in the mountains, but his office gave no indication of who Gary Dettling really was.

After her own deep-cover assignment, Ren had gone the other way. Once it was all over, she wanted to reinforce who she was more than ever. The problem was, she had never worked out who Ren Bryce was. And somewhere along the way, she had given up. Now, her workspace was as impersonal as Gary's.

'Hey,' she said. 'How are you?'

Gary looked up. 'What's up?'

'Uh . . . the Most Wanted, maybe?'

'Late-breaking change of play.'

'How did you let that happen?' said Ren.

Gary stared at her. 'It happened. US Marshals wanted it that way. I said, sure, OK.'

'Right . . .'

'Ren, it's done,' said Gary.

'I know, but . . .'

'You still get to highlight the Val Pando three. OK, so they've dropped a few places on the Billboard charts . . .' He shrugged.

'That's not the point.'

'Ren, here's the deal. Last year, we almost had the Val Pandos. And it dead-ended. This new top two have had confirmed sightings in Denver in the last month . . .'

'Ah, meaning it's going to be easier to strike this top two off the list. So everyone looks better?'

'Including you,' said Gary.

'I could give two shits,' said Ren.

11

Gary looked at her patiently. And glanced at the door behind her.

'Fine. OK,' said Ren.

'Where are the others?' said Gary.

'In various states of "on their way".'

Back in the task force office, Ren checked her email, flagged most of the new messages, then ignored them.

'Coffee, anyone?' Colin Grabien walked in the door with an offer he usually didn't make until at least two hours into the day.

Colin Grabien had transferred to Safe Streets from the FBI White Collar Squad and was the task force's IT and numbers expert. He was five foot eight in the flesh, six foot eight in spirit and a ball of latent anger. He was the mosquito – Ren was the citronella candle.

Gary finally appeared in the office as Ren was walking out with her makeup bag hidden by her side. She didn't wear a lot – sheer foundation, brown or gray eyeshadow, black mascara on her poker-straight lashes and clear lip gloss – but she couldn't go without it, even when it meant applying it in the ergonomically challenged Safe Streets ladies room.

'Nice makeup,' said Colin when she got back.

'Fuck you,' Ren coughed into her hand.

'OK,' said Gary, 'everyone's here. I'm going to give the lowdown on one and two on our list. Ren will do three through five.'

'Sure,' said Ren.

Gary's phone beeped. 'Ren, go ahead. I need to take care of this.'

Ren stood up. 'OK, gentlemen: here's the lowdown on the Val Pando posse. If I'm repeating myself, please realize that I don't care. First up, number three – Domenica Val Pando, Latina, DOB 10/02/64.

'Domenica was head of a huge cartel operating in New Mexico in the nineties – people trafficking, drugs, weapons, branching into biological weapons. No one has actually seen her since she disappeared the night the compound was stormed, with her seven-year-old son, Gavino Val Pando and her fifty-year-old husband, Augusto Val Pando.

'Domenica showed up on the radar again last August when she was attempting to set up a lab outside Breckenridge to make H_2S – colorless, odorless, fatal in seconds. We stopped her. But we couldn't make any firm links to her, because she was, sadly, too fucking smart.'

Ren stood back. 'This photo is eleven years old.' The team followed her gaze to the noticeboard. Domenica Val Pando used to have an exotic beauty, but she had Americanized it, tweaked her features with surgery. Her hair was now the yellow-blonde that only very dark hair can be dyed. It was perfectly styled, but wrong. Her eyes were deep brown, slightly protruding, her lips full.

'Not every psycho is dead in the eyes,' said Ren.

Colin stared a little too long at the picture. 'I'd hit it,' he said.

'Your standards are rising,' said Ren. 'Let me quickly give you the lowdown on Gavino Val Pando, Domenica's son.' She pointed to his photo, stapled under his mother's.

Gavino had flawless dark skin and longish black hair that he pulled back off his face. He had strong bone structure and full but angular lips. His eyes were brown and lost. Ren stared at the photo. She had spent one year looking after six-year-old Gavino Val Pando and trying to deny how much she really cared about him.

'Gavino's eighteen years old,' said Ren. 'Our last encounter with him was last year in the Summit County jail, where he was taken in for under-age drinking. More significantly, he was paying for it with bait money from a robbery in Idaho Springs, of which he claimed to have no knowledge. We couldn't prove otherwise, but it was definitely connected with Domenica. There is nothing to suggest that Gavino Val Pando is violent and a lot to suggest he was drunk and stupid that night. We had to release him and we don't know his whereabouts, or whether he has remained in contact with Mommy Dearest.

'His relationship with her is complicated. Her husband, Augusto Val Pando, was not Gavino's biological father, but Augusto probably suspected that – he had no time for Gavino. So, while Gavino may be with his mother and therefore a very effective route to her, he definitely will not be with Augusto.'

'And what about his real father?' said Robbie.

'James Laker – presumed dead,' said Ren. 'It is believed he was killed in the fire that destroyed the compound.' *A sweet, kind man, used and abused, first by life and then by Domenica.*

'Now to number four on our list,' said Ren. 'Another of Domenica's minions: Javier Luis, born 1973, five foot two, one hundred and sixty pounds. First-degree murder, attempted first-degree murder, aggravated robbery; drugs; rape, sexual assault on a minor . . . he went MIA from Domenica's compound in 1998, just before the shit hit the fan.'

Ren remembered Javier Luis. He was always dressed in concert T-shirts for bands he had never seen. He was not tall, so his shorts almost reached his ankles. His voice was nasal and whiny. He would look at Ren in a way that reminded her to shutter the windows at night and lock all the doors. She rarely spoke with him and, when she did, she kept it brief.

'Finally,' said Ren, 'number five, Erubiel Diaz, Latino, DOB 12/10/58, one of Domenica's shit shovelers.'

She pointed at the photo.

'This roidy little man was involved in the H_2S lab – as a gofer, not a scientist, so that qualifies him for our hit list,' said Ren. 'He's violent, a probable rapist and every daytime chat show's favorite – a dead-beat dad. He was ratted out by his ex-wife four months ago for showing up in Denver, penniless, trying to see his kids. And off the record? He tried to assault me late one night in the parking lot of the Brockton Filly in Breckenridge and I—'

'Kicked the living daylights out of him?' said Robbie.

'All the way to Frisco Medical Center,' said Ren.

'Where he told everyone he was attacked by a man,' said Gary.

'He was,' said Colin.

Ren rolled her eyes. 'Diaz obviously didn't know at the time that I was an agent, but I let him know when I paid him a visit in the Summit County Jail, where he was being held for failure to pay child support. I couldn't let the sheriff there know what Diaz had done to *me* because then the sheriff would know what I had done to *him*. So Diaz was released, we had nothing on him. But after he'd gone we found out that he had been working for Domenica Val Pando.' She paused. 'And probably still is. So, right now, although he is a little lower in the pecking order, I believe that Erubiel Diaz may well be our golden ticket.'

3

Gary walked back into the office. 'All done?'

'Yup,' said Ren.

'Number one on our Fifty Most Wanted,' said Gary, pointing to a photo of a man with long, thin, greased-back hair, balding at the front. He had fuck-you eyes and a nose that looked broken, re-set and broken again. His face was hollowed out. He had two shaven patches of white hair high on each cheekbone and a downturned slit for a mouth. 'This piece of shit,' said Gary, 'is Jonah Jeremiah—'

'Jim Jams,' said Ren.

'Jonah Jeremiah Myler,' Gary finished, ignoring her.

'Priiiceless,' said Ren.

'Caucasian, DOB 08/12/57,' said Gary. 'Myler springs up in a different city every few months, preying on vulnerable teens and setting up short-lived "cults". He grooms the kids for sex. He has young followers, so he gets them out on the streets. And he waits behind the scenes for the disenchanted youth to show. They may not always use the same name for their sect. Names to date: Crystal Wakenings, Army of the Risen, The Witness Gathering, Divine Seers of the Watchful—'

'You are making them up,' said Ren.

'You couldn't make them up,' said Cliff.

'And The Watchful what?' said Ren. 'That's a lot of seeing and watching. The Watchful Observers. Divine Seers of the Watchful Crowd of Onlookers. Divine Seers of the Watchful Blind . . .'

Gary ploughed on. 'Don't be fooled by Myler's gaunt face. He's not as feeble as he looks.

'Next up is number two, Francis Gartman, African-American, DOB 01/15/83. First degree murder, aggravated robbery, drugs, sexual assault on a minor.'

Gartman looked like someone had paused while inflating his head to allow him to pose for the photo. Every feature looked like it was about to blow.

'Those eyes are completely vacant,' said Ren. 'Soulless.'

'Gartman is a former boxer,' said Gary, 'which translates in his case into giant man, huge strength. He's had enough blows to the head for his frontal lobe to have left the building.'

Gary stepped back. 'Not as dramatic in my delivery as Agent Bryce no doubt was, but there's our top five. Knock yourselves out.'

'Ren,' said Colin. 'Call for you on one. She wanted to speak with a female. She didn't give a name.'

Ren picked up the phone. 'This is Special Agent Ren Bryce. How may I help you?'

'My name is Catherine Sarvas. I'm calling from El Paso, Texas. I saw your Most Wanted List on line this morning . . .'

Ren slid her notebook across her desk. She picked up a pencil. 'And do you have something you'd like to tell me, ma'am?'

'I . . . yes,' said Catherine. 'Yes, I have. I do. I . . .' She paused. 'I'm sorry . . . I thought I could do this.'

She hung up.

'Short call,' said Robbie.

Ren nodded. 'Weird.'

'What did she want?'

'To give me a little flicker of hope on a dreary Monday.'

'Are you going to call her back?'

'I'll give her a little while. El Paso . . . What's going on down there?'

Ren spent Monday lunch-times in the offices of Dr Helen Wheeler. The psychiatrist all lunatics should have: intelligent, warm, caring, wore great shoes you could admire while avoiding your issues.

Until Ren was diagnosed bipolar at twenty-six, she had never guessed that there was anything wrong with her. Mental illnesses were for the mentally ill. It seemed like one minute she was the youngest FBI agent to go under deep cover and blow apart an organized crime operation and the next, she was lying in her pajamas on the sofa, eating junk food, crying, not answering her phone, drinking, obsessing about all the regrets she had in her life, wondering what point there was in doing anything again. Ever.

Her older brother, Matt, suggested she get help. But he already knew what was wrong with Ren. So he brought her to his computer one evening and gently opened a checklist on a psychiatry website that covered her symptoms: the despair, the exhaustion, the sofa, the hopelessness. Ren had looked up at Matt and shrugged. 'That's just depression, though. Everyone gets like that.'

Matt had scrolled down to the mania checklist: *I have lots of energy. I feel amazing. I want everyone else to feel amazing. I want to go out and party. I love everyone. I know everything. I feel creative. I'm working hard. I'm talking too quickly. I'm loud.*

I'm impatient. I'm exercising. I'm alert. I'm swearing. I'm invincible. I'm hypersexual. I'm overspending. Check, check, check, check, check . . .

Ren had cried her heart out. 'This is so depressing. My entire personality can be reduced to a checklist. If I buy lots of shoes, it's because I'm nuts. If I'm having sex five times a day, it's because I'm nuts. Me and two million other losers. And it's not that I thought I was special or unique, but there is something so grim about fitting into this formula. It's like we're some fucked-up alien race. I mean, did you read all that shit? It affects every part of my existence. And there's nothing I can do about it. I can't be fixed.'

Matt had cried too and explained that it may not be fixable, but it was treatable. He told Ren that she was unique and smart and loving and funny and generous and all women have too many shoes and that she was beautiful and he loved her to bits. And she loved him too. Because Matt had also read that telling Ren all this could come back and bite him. Because there was a high risk that someone bipolar would shoot the messenger; at some point, maybe not the same day or maybe not the same year, they would turn to the person who wanted to help them the most and scream, 'This is all your fault. If you hadn't told me all this, I would never have known, and I would have been happy just the way I was.' And then they would scream, 'You. Ruined. My. Life.'

Before that year was out, Ren had fired every one of those razor-sharp words at Matt and they had struck his heart. Ren did, indeed, shoot the messenger. And with a true bipolar flourish, had come back six months later, laden with guilt and gifts, to apologize.

Ren had tried different psychiatrists and psychotherapists since then, but when she met Helen Wheeler two years ago, Ren knew she had found her savior. Helen was in her early sixties, with a cultural awareness that spanned decades and created a bridge to all her patients. On Ren's first visit, Helen had told her, 'I am a psychiatrist, not a mind reader. What you tell me is what I will know about you. And you can leave your brave face at the door. If you're having a bad day, my office is the perfect place to have it in.'

Ren checked her watch as she waited to be called in to Helen's office.

Hurry up. Hurry up. Hurry up.

Helen leaned her head out the door of her office. 'Come on in, Ren,' she said. 'How are you today?'

'I'm . . . good,' said Ren, sitting down.

Helen smiled. 'OK . . .'

'I don't know,' said Ren. 'Did you see the news? It's Most Wanted time . . . which is fine. It's just . . . this year, it's got Domenica Val Pando on it and I feel I'm being taken back years and . . .' She hung her head.

Helen waited.

'It's just . . .' said Ren, 'I guess . . . I was diagnosed at the end of that assignment and some part of me, I know it's not rational, but some part of me thinks that if it wasn't for that, I would be fine, there would be nothing wrong with me. And then . . . then there's another part of me – and it's so screwed up – that wants to be back there, because I was oblivious, I didn't know how lucky I was to be sane. Or at least to think I was sane.'

Helen smiled at her. 'Ren, you are sane. And those feelings are understandable.'

'But what makes no sense is that paranoia is the worst part of bipolar disorder for me, yet undercover work is a whole world of paranoia. You are lying all day every day

20

and you're never sure if you're going to be found out. Give me depression over paranoia any day. Because I just . . . I feel paranoia is what will ultimately bring me down.'

'Ren, nothing is going to bring you down,' said Helen. 'You are in control of all of this. And you are not alone. You have an entire team working with you. Good people, from what you tell me. So, rely on them, Ren.'

Ren nodded. 'I can't stop thinking about the assignment, though. I told this terrible story to gain someone's confidence and get into her life – I sat on a park bench crying to Domenica Val Pando, telling her I had lost my four-month old baby . . .'

'That is part of undercover work, Ren. You were doing your job.'

'I know, but I look back sometimes and I think "How could I have done that?"' Ren shook her head. 'Nothing to do with Val Pando personally – she's a piece of shit – just, me. How could I have done that?'

'It was your job.'

'I know it's what I signed up to do,' said Ren. 'But I guess I get scared at how easy it was for me to do it. Undercover work is such a rush – the better you are, the greater the high. The more you find out, the more you want to find out. It's addictive. You go to bed at night, you write notes, you give them to your contact agent. He's making a case, he's happy, you're happy. But I was still playing the role of Remy Torres, a fake name in a fake life. She was like part-me, part-stranger. So . . . in a way, you never know what she's capable of.' She paused. 'And when it's over and you bring your real self into the equation, when you're away from whatever group of dirtbags you've been investigating, you're faced with how good a liar you were and how well you manipulated people. And you tell yourself that the ends

21

justify the means. But sometimes the means just make you feel dirty.'

'OK, take some breaths.' Helen handed her a box of Kleenex.

'Thanks,' said Ren. 'Oh sorry, I've pulled out the whole lot. It must be a sign. I'll be here weeping all day.'

'I'm sponsored by Kleenex,' said Helen. 'It's written on the back of my blouse.'

Ren laughed through the tears. 'I honestly don't know why I'm crying.'

'Ren,' said Helen gently, 'Remy Torres did not take you down with her. Here you are, Ren Bryce, over ten years on, successful, stable, still pursuing these people, not turning into them.'

'Still pursuing,' said Ren. 'Exactly.'

'You are so hard on yourself,' said Helen. 'You're doing great. Stop beating yourself up. Get back to that office this afternoon and kick some butt. Like you always do.'

'Thanks. I'll try.'

When the session was over and Ren was driving back to work, she could feel her anxiety drifting away. She smiled.

Helen's room always felt like the furthest room from the crazy house.

4

Ren walked back into the bullpen, took off her jacket and put her purse on the floor.

'Did you all go out to lunch?' she said.

'Yup,' said Cliff. 'Someone's got to feed these investigative brains.'

Ren pointed to a brown paper bag at his feet. 'Did you get anything wrapped to take home to your dog that you would now be willing to hand over to one of your hungry colleagues?'

Colin rolled his eyes. He reached out to answer the phone on his desk.

'Yes, as a matter of fact,' said Cliff. 'It's half a steak sandwich.'

'I owe you,' said Ren.

She looked down at her file tray. 'Hey, what's this?'

'I left it there for you,' said Cliff. 'It's Francis Gartman's alleged lady friend . . .'

'Slash woman of the night.' Ren looked at the picture, scanning the details.

'Yup,' said Cliff. 'We need to find her.'

Ren nodded. 'Sure, I'll take a look at this.' She rested her left hand on the neatly folded waxed wrapping of the sandwich. She could smell steak.

'She's running scared,' said Cliff.

'Did someone call in?'

'Yes,' said Cliff. 'Her broken-hearted mama.'

Ren sucked in a breath. She looked down at the photo of Natalie Osgood, the pretty African-American girl with the bruised, vacant eyes and the tousled red wig. 'Sweetheart, let me find you before that piece of shit does.' Ren pushed her finger under the fold in the paper and slid the sandwich toward her.

'Ren,' said Colin. 'Line three. Sounds like your El Paso woman again.'

I am not meant to eat today.

'Hello,' said Ren.

'This is Catherine Sarvas again.'

'Ms Sarvas—'

'Mrs. I'm . . . married.'

'Mrs Sarvas,' said Ren. 'Are you all right?'

The woman let out a sob. She was struggling to breathe. *Please don't hang up.*

'I'm so sorry,' said Catherine. 'I'm so sorry for this.'

'Please,' said Ren. 'There is no need to apologize. Please, take your time. I'll listen to you whenever you're ready to talk.'

Catherine sucked in a breath. 'Thank you.'

Seconds passed.

'I saw your Most Wanted list on the internet,' said Catherine. 'And I wanted to let you know . . .' She started to cry. 'Oh, God . . . I was raped.'

Ren had heard women say that they were raped before and no matter how many times she heard it, it caused a visceral reaction – a recoil.

'He is number five on your list,' said Catherine.

Number five. Ren glanced up at the board, for a moment forgetting the new order. *Oh my God.*

'Erubiel Diaz,' said Ren. 'Number five, Erubiel Diaz.'

'I recognize his face.'

His hideous face. Ren's hand hovered over the page. Every phone in the office seemed to be ringing. It felt disrespectful, the wrong place to listen to what Catherine Sarvas had to say. Ren pressed the phone to her ear. 'Take your time, Mrs Sarvas.'

Eventually, Catherine Sarvas spoke again. 'Maybe you've heard about my family. My husband is Gregory Sarvas?'

'I'm sorry, ma'am,' said Ren. 'I'm not familiar with your husband.'

'Oh . . .' Another pause. 'Eight months ago, my husband, Greg, was shot dead near our home in El Paso. He had been driving our sons home from school.' She paused.

Ren waited, but all she could hear was Catherine Sarvas' breathing. 'I'm so sorry to hear that.'

She quietly typed Gregory Sarvas' name into Google. *Hundreds of hits.* She did an image search. She clicked on one of the photos. It was a wide shot taken from behind a pale gold SUV with all its doors open. There was something beautiful and artistic in the angles and the light. Then the headlines: *Murder. Shooting. Shot dead. Cold blood. Gunned down.* The beauty and light of the photo was quickly gone.

'Our sons . . . Luke and Michael . . . were in the SUV with Greg,' said Mrs Sarvas. 'They're still missing . . .'

'I'm so sorry, Mrs Sarvas.' She glanced at one of the articles. *Luke, 17, Michael, 15.*

'I can't even . . . I can't talk about my family right now,' said Catherine 'I . . . just wanted to . . . help.'

'OK,' said Ren. 'So . . . were you also there in the SUV? You were raped?'

'No, no. It was two weeks before that.' Catherine sucked in a breath. 'I saw the photograph of that man on your list and I had to call. I came across it by accident. But I knew it was him, right away.'

'Did you report the rape at the time?'

'No, I couldn't bear it. I was . . .' Catherine started to sob.

'That's OK.'

'It was so terrible,' said Catherine. 'He was waiting in the . . . it was so . . .'

Ren waited for her to finish the sentence, but she couldn't.

'You mentioned your husband,' said Ren. 'Did you tell him about the rape?'

'Yes. He was devastated. He was always talking to me about staying safe. Our house had a lot of security. I still don't know how that man got in . . .'

'How did your husband react? What did he do?'

'He . . . was so good to me,' said Catherine. 'He took care of me, he did everything he could. And . . . when I was feeling a little more up to it, I asked him to report the rape to El Paso PD. I couldn't bring myself to do it before then. I didn't want to be . . . I didn't want doctors . . . anyone examining me.'

'I understand,' said Ren. 'And when did he report this?'

'The week he died.' Catherine began sobbing harder. 'You never think it's going to happen to you. None of this feels like it's my life. We're a regular family. Greg's a lawyer, we live in a very nice neighborhood. We have two boys who go to a good high school and have bright futures ahead of them.'

Husband – dead. Sons – missing. And she just used the present tense.

'I think my boys are still alive,' said Catherine, as if she was reading Ren's mind.

Ren could sense Catherine Sarvas' rising panic. She had just revealed her terrible secret to a stranger and had heard for the first time how her story sounded out loud. Catherine Sarvas' surge of courage had hit its peak and was starting to waver. She was like a bird paused in mid-flight.

'Please, can you help me?'

Ren paused. 'Mrs Sarvas, I am so sorry to hear what you've been through. I can't imagine what it's been like for you. And we will do everything we can to apprehend this man.'

'And my boys?' said Catherine. 'My children. The rape doesn't even seem important compared to getting my boys back.'

'Are you happy to make a full statement? Would it be easier for now to get the statement your husband made to El Paso PD?'

'I can talk now,' said Catherine. 'I can talk to you. I don't know who else to turn to. I'm not comfortable going to El Paso PD.' She paused. 'I think they think that Luke and Michael had something to do with Gregory's death . . .'

'I'll go through everything they've got.'

'Thank you.'

'It was very brave of you to call,' said Ren.

'What have I got to lose?' said Catherine. 'But you've been very kind, thank you. You made it easier.'

I have no idea how.

'Can we still do this over the phone?'

'Yes,' said Ren. 'Whenever you're ready.'

'OK.'

Thirty minutes later, Ren put down the phone. She turned to her computer and read ten different articles on Gregory Sarvas' murder. The lead investigator was a man called Kenny Dade from El Paso PD. Ren called him and asked him to email her everything he had on the Sarvas family.

She pushed back from her desk and shouted out to the rest of the team.

'Hey,' she said. 'I just got something on Erubiel Diaz.'

Colin put down his phone. 'And I got a sighting on our number two, Francis Gartman: around midnight last night, waving a gun at a bar in Five Points.'

'Any sign of Natalie Osgood?' said Ren.

'He was alone,' said Colin.

'And Erubiel Diaz?' said Cliff, turning to Ren.

Ren let out a breath. She picked up her notes and recounted the harrowing details of Catherine Sarvas' violation, the pages and pages of notes on what Erubiel Diaz did to a kind, gentle, mother-of-two in the walled-off courtyard of her quiet suburban home.

5

A Denver winter stretched on for months and March was its snowiest. Blizzards whipped up out of nowhere, plans were ruined or stalled or put to bed under a blanket of snow. But it could make everything beautiful. And for a place like Mardyke Street, lined with hundred-year-old homes and towering oaks, a thick layer of snow, glowing under the streetlights, created a special kind of magic.

Ren pulled up outside Annie Lowell's house. It was eight p.m., she had taken a break from the office. There were appointments you could bend or break, but calling on a beloved eighty-year-old woman was sacred.

Annie welcomed Ren with a hug that brought a rush of memories from a time when their height difference went the other way. Annie was five feet tall; Ren was five seven.

Everything about Annie Lowell was warm and pastel-colored and soft-focus.

'I'm sorry I didn't get to see you before now,' said Ren.

'Sweetheart, do not give that a second thought,' said Annie.

'Thank you,' said Ren. 'I am so honored you asked me to do this. The motel is killing me.'

29

Ren took in the house: a William Lang, designed in the late 1800s. One of Denver's most famous architects, he had built the homes of the rich and famous until the Silver Crash swept their wealth away. Lang fell from such a height that he never recovered and died a pauper, a thousand miles from the city where he had made such a mark.

Annie led her into the formal living room and sat on the hardbacked sofa with her legs crossed at the ankles and her hands in her lap. Ren smiled.

What a lady. And what an uncomfortable sofa.

Annie had bought the tumble-down house and restored it with money from a life insurance policy she didn't even know her late husband had. She had been widowed as long as Ren had known her and in all that time she had never looked at another man. On her ring finger were the same three beautiful rings she had always worn – engagement, wedding and eternity.

'Did you know that this home was Edward's last gift to me?' said Annie. 'I feel as though he led me right to this door. In the jacket pocket he was wearing when he died, there was a little ticket for a yellow tie he had left at the laundry. I loved that yellow tie, so I went to pick it up. I know that sounds a little silly, but I didn't want to leave it there. On my way back to the house we had been living in, I took a wrong turn and I ended up outside here.' She stared off into the past. 'It looked as broken as my heart.'

'I never knew all this.'

'I think messages are around us every day – you just have to be open to them.'

'I must have been sending one out to you from my motel room,' said Ren.

Annie smiled. Her gaze wandered to a spot on the wall opposite them.

'Oh my goodness,' said Ren, getting up and walking over to the faded photo. It was Ren, her parents and her three older brothers, Matt, Beau and Jay.

'You must have been five years old there,' said Annie. 'Look at you.'

'Look at the boys,' said Ren. 'All sandy brown like Dad. And then me. Do you know, when I was in school, the kids used to tease me. Not in a bad way – it was funny. They'd say, "So . . . your mother obviously had a visit from the mailman – Big Chief Little Stamps."' She pointed to her mother in the photo. 'I mean, even Mom hasn't really got my eyes.'

Ren was an ethnic mystery to most. She had passed for Hispanic, Italian and French. But in the shape of her striking brown eyes, the one heritage no one could deny was Native American – from a distant Iroquois past somewhere on her mother's side.

'You were such a cutie,' said Annie, 'and those boys adored . . . adore you.' She squeezed Ren's hand.

'We always loved coming here.'

'And I loved having you.'

Ren's cell phone rang. She glanced down. 'Oh, I'm sorry, Annie. It's work.' *It's always work.*

'Go ahead, take it,' said Annie.

Ren went into the hall and took the call. She came back in to Annie. 'I am so sorry. I wanted to spend more time with you.' *I always want to spend more time with the people I care about.* 'But I have to go,' said Ren. 'There's this guy we're trying to track down, he's a nasty piece of work and—'

'Ren, you've an important job, you're a busy woman. I wouldn't expect you to have the time to spend here.'

'But you're being kind enough to give me your house, and I feel I've just come in and out.'

'Oh, it's only me,' said Annie. 'I understand. You are so dear to me. I would be happy to have five minutes with you.'

'Good Lord, I can't think why.' Ren squeezed Annie tight. As she was pulling away from the embrace, she could see two places set for supper on the table behind her. Her heart sank. She hoped it wasn't meant for her. But she saw a brand-new bottle of her favorite hot chili sauce. Annie pressed the keys of the house into Ren's hand and hugged her again. Tears welled in Ren's eyes as she rushed to the Jeep and drove to a part of town that hadn't quite got the same kind of history.

Five Points stands where the diagonal grid of downtown meets the rectangular grid of East Denver. It's one of Denver's oldest neighborhoods, known more for what it had been – the Harlem of the West – and what it wanted to be – a triumph of gentrification – than what it actually was – a neighborhood that fell between two stools. The high crime rate had fallen since the nineties, but it still struggled with gangs, drugs, and convincing people that its beautiful Victorian renovations and stylish lofts were in a safe setting.

Robbie and Ren were parked outside a Five Points' alleyway dive, waiting for Francis Gartman. He had been drinking there from noon until six p.m., but had left. The barman's girlfriend had called in the tip, and said that she expected him back.

Ren looked at the time. 'This has been a most pleasant five hours, thank you for coming, but y'all are going to have to make your way home now.'

'I know,' said Robbie. 'This feels a little . . . over.'

'He's not going to come back,' said Ren. 'He sat in that

32

bar watching the pretty snowflakes pile halfway up that tiny barred-up window and that was his cue to leave.'

Robbie's cell phone rang. 'Gary,' he said.

'Let this be *our* cue to leave.'

Robbie listened as Gary spoke. 'Gartman,' he mouthed, then shook his head slowly. He nodded, took down an address. 'We'll be right over.' He started the engine and turned to Ren.

'Aw, fuck Gartman,' said Ren. 'What did he do?'

'He shot dead a fourteen-year-old deaf girl who didn't drop to the floor when he tried to hold up a convenience store. And shot her ten-year-old brother a few aisles down who, with his hands in the air, tried to explain why she didn't.'

'God, why were those kids out so late?'

'So *early*. The family were on their way to the airport to catch a flight. The girl was going for surgery to—'

'No, I can't even hear that,' said Ren. 'That is just too much.'

'And,' said Robbie, 'when Gartman walked in to the place, he was already soaked with blood.'

6

The Safe Streets team were back from the convenience store crime scene by eleven a.m. Ren sat at her desk with a half-full coffee pot. *Coffee pots are half-full. Beer bottles are half-empty.*

'Gartman does not give a shit,' said Ren. 'He just walks right in there, covered in blood from God knows what, kills a little girl, puts her brother in the hospital . . . and does not really care who sees his fucked-up face.'

'When this gets out, there'll be a bunch of people he's screwed over who'll want to hang him out to dry,' said Cliff.

Ren's computer pinged with an email. 'Excuse me,' she said, turning to her screen. 'I just got my email from El Paso on the Sarvases.'

She clicked on the jpegs first. Rows of photos popped up in iPhoto under her brother Matt's wedding photos.

A beautiful day that happened under black clouds and rain.

She looked at the destruction of the Sarvas family.

A terrible day that happened under a blue sky and a hot Texan sun.

The first photo was similar to the one of the SUV that Ren had seen online. But when you looked at the driver's side, something was clearly wrong: Gregory Sarvas' limp left leg was hanging out the open door. Ren continued through the sequential photos and focused on the car's interior and the melting corpse of Gregory Sarvas. He was a big man with a full gray beard; more lumberjack than lawyer. He was dressed in a pale blue shirt with sleeves rolled up to the elbows and beige shorts to his knees. He was slumped across the passenger seat, his face turned toward the glove box. The gun had been fired point blank through his left temple. The hole ripped in his skull was filled with flies. The windscreen was spattered with red, like an exploded dye tag.

The next photo was of the back seat, an eerie reminder of the two people now missing. It was an incomplete picture of a terrible day.

Ren wondered what the chronology was. *Did Luke and Michael Sarvas watch their father die? Did someone tell them to run before it happened, so that they wouldn't have to? Did one of the boys pull the trigger? Did they plan this together? Are they lying dead somewhere else? Are they on a beach in Rio?*

The last photo attachment was of the two boys. Luke Sarvas, the seventeen-year-old, had a surfer-dude look, messy blond hair, tanned, healthy, lean, smiling. His arm was resting around fifteen-year-old Michael's shoulder. They were so clearly related, yet styled by a different hand. Michael was brown-haired, wore metal-rimmed glasses and had a more reserved but genuine smile as he looked up at his brother. The only concession to his age was a black long-sleeved T-shirt with skulls down one of the sleeves. Luke and Michael Sarvas looked like regular, happy kids.

Ren often wondered about mothers and whether their instincts about missing children were right. She had so often heard them say 'I know he's still alive' or 'I know she's still out there' even when there was no evidence, even when years had passed. Was it instinct? Was it denial? Or was it just hope? Fathers would usually stand quietly by, slow to comment but reluctant to hurt their wives by focusing on the facts.

Was Catherine Sarvas right? Were her boys still out there? Or was it the talk of a woman desperate to believe that, in the space of a few minutes on a beautiful summer's afternoon, God would not choose to wipe out her entire family?

Ren went through the rest of the email. There was something missing.

She dialed Kenny Dade's number. 'It's Ren Bryce again from Safe Streets in Denver. Thanks for that email on the Sarvases. Just one thing – I can't see the original report on the rape, filed by Gregory Sarvas. All I've got here is the statement taken from Catherine Sarvas after he was killed.'

Dade paused. 'Uh . . .'

Uh, what? 'Yes?' said Ren.

'There was a slight problem with that request,' said Dade. 'See, Gregory Sarvas never filed a report.'

'What?'

'There was no rape reported.'

'But . . . I spoke with Catherine Sarvas yesterday and she told me that her husband had reported the rape.'

'I know,' said Dade. 'But the first we heard of Catherine Sarvas was when we found her dead husband. Then, when we were interviewing her, out of the blue she asked could his murder have been anything to do with her rape. We were kind of confused at this point. She said that her husband had reported it to Detective Juliana Hyde in our office. We kind of all looked at each other, because Juliana had been on maternity leave for three months at that point. So . . . well, I figured we would just get the details of the rape from Mrs Sarvas all over again, which we would have done in any case. She would have been able to give us more details than her husband.'

WTF? 'Does Catherine Sarvas know that her husband didn't report the rape?'

'Well, we didn't tell her,' said Dade. 'What was the point? He was dead. She couldn't get any answers from him.'

'Jesus, didn't you find the whole thing a little strange?'

'Of course we did.' Dade sounded irritated. 'But at least *we* knew he hadn't reported it. We could factor that into our investigation. We weren't the ones in the dark about it. So, yeah, we've been looking into whether there was any connection between the two things.'

'Or the three things,' said Ren: 'the rape, the non-reporting of the rape and the murder.'

'Well, we haven't been able to connect them, either way.'

'I'm going to have to tell her.'

'What?' said Dade. 'And she'll know we all lied to her? No way. No way.'

'Trust me,' said Ren. 'She really won't give a good goddamn about that. This is a woman whose two teenage sons are missing right now. She will want to know everything that has gone on, so that she can do everything she can to get those boys back. If they can be gotten back.'

'Do you have to give her this information?' said Dade. 'Her whole family is gone. She—'

'I have no choice,' said Ren. 'Because if she realizes that her husband did not report her rape, her brain might take another route, she might start thinking why and maybe we'll all get something we want out of this.'

'What's that supposed to mean?'

'You want to get your guy. I want to get mine,' said Ren. 'And Catherine Sarvas wants her boys.'

'Your guy – is that the Erubiel Diaz you mentioned yesterday?'

'Yes. Catherine Sarvas ID'd him.'

'Any idea where he's at?'

'Not yet,' said Ren. 'We're working on it.'

'If you know anything more about the Sarvas family, I'd like to know,' said Dade. 'Our case dead-ended.'

'I'll keep you posted.'

'OK,' said Dade. 'I appreciate it.'

Ren put down the phone.

Gregory Sarvas did not report his wife's rape? WTF?

7

Ren re-read everything she had on the Sarvases. *How did this all work?* She thought again about the good neighborhood Catherine Sarvas said she lived in, the security at their house. Why would Erubiel Diaz choose to rape someone with those odds stacked against him and – of all the houses on that street – why did he choose the Sarvases? Had he been watching her? And could it really be a coincidence that, two weeks later, her husband is killed and her teenage sons go missing?

Why would Gregory Sarvas not report his wife's rape? Ren flipped to a new page in her notebook and began writing the first string of questions that came into her head.

To protect her? He was ashamed? He was angry? He blamed her? His reputation would be tarnished? Or . . . he planned to take care of the problem without any police involvement? She underlined the last question. Had he already done that? Had he been killed in retaliation? Had he killed someone's son and now his own sons were taken away/killed? Rape . . . Murder . . . Abduction???

Ren picked up the phone and called Catherine Sarvas. There was a depressingly hopeful tone to her voice.

'I'm sorry, Mrs Sarvas,' said Ren. 'I'd just like to go over a few things from our conversation.'

'Yes, no problem. And please, call me Catherine.'

'OK,' said Ren. 'You told me that your husband took care of reporting the rape.'

'Yes, he did . . . I couldn't bear going through all the details with a stranger . . . I mean, I knew I would have to talk to the police in the end, but at that time, I guess I was afraid that if I did nothing, if I waited too much longer, that he . . . the rapist . . . might . . . he . . . I just couldn't bear the thought of one of my friends or my neighbors having to go through—' She broke down.

'I understand how difficult it would be to talk about.' Ren paused. 'So . . . you asked Gregory to take care of it, and he agreed that he would.'

'Yes.'

'And it was El Paso PD?'

'Yes, it was El Paso PD. He said that he spoke with a Detective Hyde.'

Ren paused as if she was writing the name down. 'Catherine, what was your husband's demeanor before his murder?'

'Well, he was concerned for me. He was worried. He didn't want to leave me alone. But he had to work, too.'

'What was his reaction to your rape?'

Catherine paused. 'Well, he was devastated, like any husband would be. I'm not sure I know what you mean . . .'

Here goes. 'I don't know how to tell you this,' said Ren. 'But your husband didn't report the rape to Detective Hyde.'

'What? Who did he report it to?'

'I'm afraid he didn't report it at all.'

'But . . . he did. That's ridiculous. Of course he did. He came home and told me that evening. He even passed on a message from her, saying that I could speak with her in my own time.'

'And did you speak with Detective Hyde?' said Ren. *Which I hate to ask, because I know the answer is no.*

'No,' said Catherine. 'But . . . but . . . why would Greg not report it? I don't understand. There would be no reason not to. I asked him to. He had my permission.'

'Maybe he wanted to protect you,' said Ren. 'What was your state of mind at this time?'

'I had just been raped.'

'Had you seen a doctor?'

'No.' Her voice fell to a whisper.

'Could your husband have been worried about your mental health – worried about what reporting this could have meant for you?'

'But . . . I told him to report it. I was traumatized. I didn't want to report it myself. But I was adamant that he should.'

'Did your husband override your wishes before?' said Ren. 'Did you ever ask him to do things and he ignored your wishes, maybe for what he felt was your own good?'

'I'm sure every husband does that at some point.'

Not about reporting a rape, I would venture.

'Catherine, can I ask you a few more questions?' said Ren. 'I know we've been over some of this already, but I'd like to make sure I have everything straight.'

'OK.'

'Who had access to your property?'

'We each had a set of keys – Greg, Luke, Michael and I.'

'What about tradesmen, a gardener . . . ?'

'No,' said Catherine. 'We hadn't had any work done on the house in over a year. The boys look after the garden.'

Ren looked back at the notes she had taken when Catherine

had described the rape. 'You mentioned you had been shopping at The Homestore. Were you taking any delivery items in?'

'No. I was just buying small things. I . . . just wanted to make the place nice. Greg had brought up the idea of us moving house, nothing concrete. I wasn't interested, but I guess even the thought of moving made me want to dig my heels in a little more . . .'

And I'm sure you'd rather be any place but home right now.

'So, no delivery people had access to your house.'

'No.'

'OK, Catherine, I'm going to go away with all this and start making enquiries. Thank you for taking my call.'

So Gregory Sarvas wanted to move house. His wife didn't. If someone was hoping to sell their house, the last thing they would want to do is report a rape and stamp a black mark on the neighborhood.

Could a husband be that screwed up?

Gary walked into the bullpen. 'Hey,' he said. 'Can I get an update?'

'This Sarvas case is getting weirder,' said Ren. 'Erubiel Diaz rapes Catherine Sarvas. A week goes by, and her husband tells her he will report it on her behalf to spare her the trauma – yet he doesn't. Within days, he gets murdered. And his two teenage sons go missing.'

'Do you think it's all connected?' said Gary.

'I can't see how it wouldn't be,' said Ren. 'Even though it makes no sense.'

Colin shrugged. 'It does if the kids are screwed up. They rape their own mother – which is why she doesn't want to report it – their father finds out, they kill him and run.'

'But she called and ID'd Erubiel Diaz,' said Ren.

'Picked a random rapist from the internet?' said Colin.

'That can happen. People lie. People get desperate. She wants to find her boys, doesn't care what they've done, plans to forgive them, but needs someone on the case with the resources to track them down. And maybe someone who will believe her sorry tale.'

Oh, like me, maybe? Screw you. 'Of all the people in all the gin joints?' said Ren. 'No, her sons did not rape her. That's not what any of this sounds like. I'm not sure what the hell is going on, but I know it's not that.'

'Do you think we need to look at the husband?' said Gary.

'I'm thinking, why not?' Ren shrugged. 'His behavior is off. Not reporting the rape rings serious alarm bells. She also said he talked about moving house around that time.'

'I'd want to move too,' said Cliff.

'This was before the rape.'

'Ah,' said Cliff. 'And did she want to move?'

'No.'

'Maybe he hired someone to scare her out of the neighborhood, to make her feel unsafe there, so she'd want to move, but the guy went too far?' said Colin. 'Sarvas tracks him down to beat the shit out of him, but the guy gets in first, blows him away?'

Cliff sucked in a breath. 'You'd have to be seriously desperate to get out of your neighborhood to go that far.'

'Maybe the man had every reason to be desperate,' said Gary.

'Maybe he was boning one of the hot neighbors and she turned psycho on him,' said Colin.

Ren looked at him. 'Always quick with the fucked-up scenarios.'

'Did you get everything from El Paso PD?' said Gary.

Ren nodded.

'Split it up between you and see what you can come up

with,' said Gary. 'No one's to neglect Gartman in all this. All eyes are on us. And the Gregory Sarvas murder could be a time-consuming tangent.' He turned to Ren. 'You're looking at this as your route to Val Pando? Via Diaz?'

Ren paused. *The correct answer is* ...

'Be careful,' said Gary. 'Don't put all your eggs in one basket.'

8

That night, Ren and Misty walked out the motel-room door for the last time. Ren smiled.

Who could ever be sad, leaving a motel?

She thought about that: *husbands going back to their wives, wives going back to their husbands, people who have had bad sex, guilty people, short-changed hookers, Catholic chamber maids . . . who, on reflection, would have been sad going in in the first place . . .* Ren stopped reflecting.

OK, lots of people. Just not me.

Robbie walked behind Ren up the path to Annie's house. Ren was pulling a suitcase, Robbie had a stack of boxes in his arms. She turned the key in the front door and had to push hard with her shoulder to open it. She dragged the suitcase on to the black-and-white tiled floor. Robbie laid the boxes down beside it.

'Do you need me to take these anywhere?' Robbie nodded toward the stairs.

'Here is fine, thank you.'

'Can I do anything else?'

'You have done more than enough,' said Ren. 'Will you stay for a soda?'

'I'd love to, but I've really got to go. I think this should be your night with Misty.'

'You're a sweetheart.' Ren gave him a hug and glanced out to the Jeep. 'I hope she likes it.'

'What's not to like?'

Ren walked down the path with Robbie and said goodbye.

Misty sat on the back seat of the Jeep and stared out the window at Ren. Then she wiggled back as far away from her as she could.

'Please, baby, do not do this,' said Ren. 'You have to love what Mommy loves. That's the deal.'

Misty's expression was hard to read.

'You used to live in a shack on the side of a mountain,' said Ren. 'Surely a historic dwelling is . . .' Ren paused. 'Oh, is this place too fancy for you?'

Ren leaned in the Jeep door and carefully hugged Misty toward her. 'Come on.' They made their way up the path.

Misty paused on the threshold.

'Hey, get in here, young lady,' said Ren. 'This is your new home.' She crouched down and rubbed Misty's back. 'How do you feel about that?' Ren stood up. 'Misty-fied, clearly.'

Misty walked into the hallway as if to prove a point. Ren closed the door behind them. Silence. For as long as they stood there, there was no sound. No creaking floorboards, no ticking clock, no rattling pipes.

I am completely alone.

Since she turned sixteen, Ren had rarely been without a boyfriend. It was one long relay race where one man was always handing the baton over to another. He just didn't know it. And sometimes, neither did Ren. But something would make her feel safe enough to leave and, if she admitted it, it was knowing that there was a new man waiting in the wings. Even if it never happened with that particular guy, she at least knew he was there. But . . . it always happened.

Ren's men never came without drama. The last person she really cared about was a confidential informant that could have gotten her fired. She had forced herself to walk away from him eight months ago, and for the first time in her life, she'd had no one lined up to take his place. No flirtation to follow through on. No cute guy in the diner. No hot agent on a visit to Denver. Ren Bryce had jumped without a safety net. A few months later, she had a week-long fling with an extreme rider performing at the National Western Stock Show. *A beautiful man. A futureless fling. Endless comedy potential for the guys.*

Ren took a deep breath.

No. More. Men.

The thought made her feel weak.

Misty came and rubbed up against Ren's legs. 'Aw, but I'm not totally alone,' said Ren. 'Come on. Let me show you around.'

Misty clung to Ren's side as she gave her a tour of the house. It was 3,500 square feet; sixteen rooms over four floors. She kept glancing down at Misty.

'I put too much faith in your vibes,' said Ren. 'I have to accept that your reactions are not gospel. It's not all about you.' She kneeled down in front of her and rubbed her ears. 'Even though, really, it is. You are way too cute.'

They got to the bedroom Ren used to stay in as a child. She looked down at the carpet – rose pink, deep and fluffy.

I miss carpet. Carpet has to come back.

Ren took off her boots and socks and walked barefoot across the room. Annie had left the bedside lamps on; warm light through pink pleated shades. The bed was white wrought iron, covered in a faded pink and gray floral quilt. There were two green pillows thrown on it and an indentation where someone had been sitting. When Ren moved closer she saw why. Her old teddy bear – adopted from Annie – was tucked between the two pillows. *Huggy Bear with the stripy legs.* Annie must have sat down to make him comfortable. Ren smiled. *She must know empty beds are not usually my thing.*

There was also a single bed and a bed for Misty in the corner. Ren brought up her suitcase and took out the new pajamas she had packed on top. She got ready for bed, then slid under the flannel sheets. She turned off the lamp and the room was lit by the moon. She looked around at one of her favorite places in the world.

This is not a house for one person. It is totally freaking me out. How am I going to get out of this? I'll die. Annie will be horrified. Where can I go now? My mother will go nuts. Everyone at work will laugh at me. I'll have to find another house-sitter for Annie. I won't have time to do that. This is not a house for one person. It is totally freaking me out. How am I going to get out of this . . .

She picked up the phone and called her brother, Matt.

'Hey, Renald McDenald,' he said. 'How are you? What strange number are you calling me from?'

'Annie's.'

'You're in?'

'I am. In my old bed.'

'Bless your heart,' said Matt.

'How are you?'

'Very in love with my baby-mama.'

'Aw. How's she doing?'

'Thankfully, she's past the *The Exorcism of Emily Rose* phase.'

'Phew.'

'How has Misty taken to her new digs?'

'She paused for effect, then entered as though doing me a huge favor.'

'So . . . you haven't answered,' said Matt. 'How are you?'

'Well, apart from a late-breaking freak-out – wonderful.'

'What were you freaking out about now?'

'*Now*: I like that—'

'But how could someone freak out in Annie's? Even you?'

'OK . . . first of all, there are no limits to where I could freak out. Secondly – remember how huge we thought the house was? Well, it wasn't just because we were kids. The place is still huge.'

'Ren, you're not much bigger than when we were kids. I've grown . . . I might find it very compact.'

'If you put on two hundred pounds, maybe.'

'Does Annie still call you Orenda?'

'Not quite the way you do.' Matt dropped his r's.

'Lucky I have high self-esteem.'

'Vewwy lucky. And no, she calls me Wen.'

'When?'

'Ha. Ha. Do you know what's on the wall in the living room?' said Ren. 'The photo of us outside the zoo. And I'm in that all-in-one short-suit.'

'Ooh, put together from scraps of other material. Your coat of many colors.'

'That my mama made for me,' said Ren. 'And Jay's in his freaky pants.'

'What am I in?'

'Pain, by the looks of it.'

'Mom never quite got the cut of a boy's pants.'

God bless Matt Bryce. He stayed on the phone with Ren for over an hour, listening to everything and saying all the right things. Ren always told Matt that he was who she would be if she was male and sane. Matt always replied, 'You wish.'

There was something wide-eyed about Matt. Like the world was a constant source of fascination to him. In every story he told, there was a dramatic pause, a revelation he wanted you to feel in the same way that he did. Even bleak observations would be delivered in a positive tone. He would talk about a television show he saw where there was human excrement piled up against a crack-house wall, then pause and say, 'It wasn't the shit itself, it was the structural engineering . . .'

He was two years older than Ren, but sometimes she felt like they were twins.

'Now,' said Matt, 'much as I would love to continue to distract you from your freak-out, I have to go and remove my wife's shoes. That's the stage we're at.'

'Poor Lauren.'

'Yes,' said Matt. 'My final word is – there's no need to freak out. You're in a beautiful house, safe and sound with your dog-from-the-dark-side.'

'Stop that.'

'Sleep tight. Call me again if you need me.'

'Thanks,' said Ren.

'And remember one thing . . .' He paused. 'You're an FBI Agent, you loser.'

'Thanks for that.' Ren put down the phone and pulled the covers up around her.

This is not a house for one person. It is totally freaking me out. How am I going to get out of this? I'll die. Annie will be horrified. Where can I go now?

Ren's eyes started to close. She turned over and drifted into the best night's sleep she'd had in over a year.

9

Colin Grabien sat at his desk with print-outs of Greg Sarvas' bank statements and a computer screen with more of Greg Sarvas' bank statements. He had the look of a teenager forced to study for his SATs when all his friends were out to play.

Ren glanced over at him.

'This is bullshit,' he said.

No one responded. He looked up, annoyed.

'What is bullshit?' said Ren. Her voice was flat.

'I don't see Gregory Sarvas' name up on that board—' He pointed to the Most Wanted list. 'Gartman is out murdering little deaf girls, and here I am, going through these boring bank statements. A lawyer with one and a half million dollars spread across four bank accounts. Call *Ripley's Believe It or Not*.'

Grow the fuck up. 'Nothing else?' said Ren. 'Nothing out of the ordinary?' She got up and walked over to his desk.

Colin pointed to his screen and scrolled through a ridiculous amount of data. She rolled her eyes.

'No strange payments in or out of his bank accounts,' said

Colin. 'One property – the family home in El Paso. Mortgage of two hundred thousand dollars outstanding. No other debts. Monthly retainers from five clients, totaling eleven thousand.'

'Ah, but one property he was more keen to get rid of than his wife suspected,' said Robbie. 'I've got his phone records here and it looks like he made several calls to real estate agents in the area.'

'Before or after the rape?' said Ren.

'Both,' said Robbie. 'A little more so after. Ren, can I borrow a highlighter?'

'Sure – in my drawer. Grab one. Not the pink one.'

'I can see why Sarvas would want revenge,' said Cliff. 'I'd want to take my wife the hell away from there.'

'I'm thinking you might be more honorable than a man who wouldn't report his wife's rape,' said Ren.

'Maybe it was the opposite,' said Colin. 'Maybe Sarvas was very honorable. And wanted some old-style vigilante revenge.'

'Pistols at dawn,' said Ren. 'Yes, I thought of that.'

'Since when do you play cards?' said Robbie. 'Ren has a deck of cards in her desk.'

Ren frowned. 'The bottom drawer has the highlighters, you loser. And no, I don't play cards.'

'You never said the bottom drawer.'

'That's not the point. There could have been anything in there . . .'

'I'm going to call these real estate guys,' said Robbie.

'What about Sarvas' clients?' said Ren to Cliff. 'Did you speak with them?' She went back over to her desk.

'From what I can gather so far, Sarvas basically worked remotely,' said Cliff. 'He had twelve clients. Three of them had never even met him. They were a mix – mainly small-business owners, all in Texas. Across a range of businesses—'

Cliff looked up as Gary strode into the office and up to Ren's desk, holding a red Sharpie out to her. She stared at him.

'Your basket is dead,' said Gary.

'Exsqueeze me?' said Ren.

Gary pointed at the gallery.

'Erubiel Diaz?' said Ren.

'Yup,' said Gary. 'How about you put a big red X through that face?'

'Oh my God,' said Ren, taking the pen from him. 'What-whywhenwherewhohow?'

'His headless body was found on a burning pyre in Nogales, Mexico,' said Gary.

'Shit. Really?' Ren stood up.

'Yup.'

She paused. 'Maybe I should wait 'til they find his head before I put the X through it.' She walked across the room and drew an X slowly across Diaz' face. 'What happened?' said Ren. 'Was this a drugs thing? Were there other people being served at this barbecue or was he found alone?'

'Here's what I know,' said Gary. 'Diaz ended up dead as part of a message being sent to the Nogales police. Earlier that day, they arrested the second-in-command of the Puente cartel. The guy's associates tried to spring him from the police station where he was being held, but they couldn't. They shot six officers trying. The station went on lockdown, so the only way these assholes could come up with to get Puente out was by going on a rampage around Nogales. Not just drive-bys – decapitations, everything. They dragged the bodies behind their SUVs through the streets, dumped them in a pile. They came back and forth a couple times and lit that pile on fire.'

'And that's where Erubiel Diaz was found . . .' said Ren.

Gary nodded.

'How did they identify him?' said Colin.

'Dental records,' said Gary.

Ren looked at him. 'You just said he was headless.'

'Temporarily,' said Gary. 'One of the Puente cartel used his severed head as a bowling ball that night. Rolled it right on to a dance floor in one of the clubs.'

'We need to talk to Colin about this,' said Ren, turning to him. 'He knows what it's like to have no body to dance with.'

Colin rolled his eyes.

'But getting back to Diaz,' said Ren, 'I don't see how dental records could've been any use. I saw the dude – he'd never been to a dentist in his life.'

'Ah, but someone knocked out two of his teeth last year in Breckenridge. And Frisco Medical Center had to X-ray his mouth. The dentist there checked him out, had everything on record.'

'So,' said Ren, 'was Diaz an "innocent victim" caught up in a street war, or was he part of a rival gang or the Puentes cartel or . . . ?'

'I'll call the police chief in Nogales,' said Gary.

'If this wasn't a coincidence,' said Ren, 'if someone really had wanted Diaz to disappear off the face of the earth, decaffeinating him and throwing him in with a bunch of burning bodies would be a good way to go.'

'He could have just been wrong place/wrong time,' said Cliff.

'I don't know,' said Ren. 'Right now, the Mexican border is permanently the wrong place at the wrong time. It's like choosing to go to Iraq on vacation. So is it me or could Domenica Val Pando be back sniffing around what she knows best?'

'She would need some serious connections to break back into that scene,' said Gary.

'Domenica *is* well-connected,' said Ren. 'And what if her H_2S project was for use along the border by a cartel? I mean, there are billions of drugs dollars at stake. What if, knowing she couldn't grab a slice of the narcotics action by the direct route, Domenica tried a side-maneuver: offering up a weapon to the people who need it most?'

They all nodded.

'I'd keep my eyes on the dry-ice machine in that night-club,' said Ren. 'The atmosphere could actually be more toxic than an eighties theme night.'

'Maybe Domenica could have gotten a high-enough price for the gas itself that she could hold back after she was paid,' said Colin. 'Then set herself up quietly when things calmed down. If they ever did . . .'

'But, the H_2S plant was shut down,' said Robbie.

'Yes,' said Ren. 'But we're the only ones who know that. The story that made the news was that we shut down a meth lab. All Domenica had to say to whoever her client was – assuming she already had one lined up – was that the guy working for her fucked up, so she had to kill him. And his death could be confirmed, so the story would hold up.' She shrugged. 'Diaz' death right now can't be a coincidence. I would say that somebody wasn't happy about all the attention being drawn Diaz' way.'

'So,' said Gary. 'The breaking of the news to Diaz' wife . . .'

'Do not look at me,' said Ren. 'I want to meet the wife when she has a clear head. I don't want to be there for the weeping. Or the gathering of her bambinos into her arms. I want the emotion gone. Goodbye. I want to walk right in at a later date and get some informazion.'

'Colin, how about you?' said Gary.

'Hold up.' Ren shook her head. 'I said that I need her to get her emotion *out*. She won't cry in front of him.'

'All I seem to hear about Diaz,' said Colin, 'is rapist, dead-beat dad, dirtbag, blah, blah. Is his wife really going to give a shit?'

'Maybe not,' said Ren. 'But the mother of his children will.' Ren turned to Cliff. 'How about you . . . ? Robbie . . . ?' Everyone looked away.

'Look, I don't care,' said Ren. 'But I'm not doing it. I'm conserving my feminine conspiratorial thing for the real questions.'

'What about continuity of care?' said Gary. 'You're the Diaz guy.'

Ren grabbed her bag from the floor. 'Jesus, fine, then. I'll go. On my way home. Everyone owes me. Every last one of you.'

10

The following morning, Ren walked in to the sight and sound of Colin Grabien, hunched over his desk, hammering his keyboard like a man who had learned to type on a typewriter.

Robbie was sitting at his desk with one shirt sleeve rolled up over his elbow and an ice pack pressed against it. A white fluffy bandage was taped to his cheek.

'Oh, Robbie,' said Ren. 'Could you not find a bigger bandage?'

'It is a massive wound,' said Robbie. 'Do you want to see it?'

'My mind is saying yes, but my stomach's saying no,' said Ren. 'And, as we know, my stomach always wins. What happened? Were you in lukewarm pursuit of a suspect?'

'Yup,' said Robbie. 'Francis Gartman. We got a tip-off he was at his cousin's house. We got there, he jumped from a window, I got out of the car after him, crossed the parking lot, I was nearly on top of him – then, bam, I slipped on some ice, took myself out of the game.'

'Ouch,' said Ren. She moved behind him and gave him a hug. 'And Gartman, I'm guessing . . .'

Robbie shook his head. 'Yup, lives to fight another day.'

Ren let out a breath. 'Can I get anything for the wounded soldier?'

'Well, thank you,' said Robbie. 'Could you play the role of over-functioning Mormon mom?'

'I couldn't think of a role I would be less equipped to play,' said Ren. 'Are you missing yo mama?'

'All the time.'

'How Bates Motel.' Ren straightened up and gave his good arm a squeeze.

Colin stopped pounding his keyboard to check his notebook. Ren took advantage of the quiet. 'And Mr Grabien, you were correct,' she said. 'There was little emotion from Mrs Diaz for either her husband or the father of her children when told that his crispy headless body had been found. Her only surprise was that he had been found in Nogales. Apart from showing up in Denver last November, the only place she knew he'd been recently was Juárez. That was the postmark on the letter that came last month with the measly hundred dollars in it that pushed her over the edge and made her rat him out.'

'So that's all we've got on the whereabouts of Erubiel Diaz,' said Cliff. 'Alive: El Paso, July. Alive: Denver in November. Alive: Juárez in February. Dead: Nogales in March.'

Ren slapped the desk. 'Fuck him for getting killed. We'll have to wait and see what Gary hears back from Nogales. In the meantime, I'm thinking I'll turn my attention to Gavino Val Pando. Might be worth putting in a call to Sheriff Gage in Summit County for the files on that bar raid at the Brockton Filly last year. Maybe Gavino was with friends or involved with one of the girls who was there that night? There were at least twelve kids pulled in for under-age drinking . . .' She shrugged. 'It's worth a try.'

As she reached out to make the call, her cell phone beeped with a text from Matt:

Cnt tlk – at scan. Xpect call frm mom re Louis Parry.

Louis Parry? Oh my God.

The disappearance of Louis Parry was the first case Orenda Bryce hadn't solved. She was nine years old. Her fifteen-year-old brother, Beau, was Louis Parry's piano teacher. Ren remembered that summer like a hazy image from a photo shoot; a pretty neighborhood filled with tanned children, frozen under the sun.

The police had returned missing children to their parents already that summer – kids who had stolen money from their mother's pocketbooks to pay for the amusements in the park. The police thought Louis Parry was just like all the others, even though his mother tried to tell them her son was more thoughtful than that; he was a quiet boy, he liked nature, he liked music . . . But by the time the police started to listen to her, half of the first, precious forty-eight hours had been lost.

Ren had spent weeks looking for the sweet blond boy who used to call to the door with a shy smile and a folder of piano scores. She searched all the places that scared her – abandoned houses, crawl spaces, the woods, the railroad yard – just in case Louis Parry had wandered in there by mistake and that those places scared him even more.

Ren didn't realize that someone could have *taken* Louis. She knew about strangers, never to accept a ride from them, but she never knew why. The world of Ren Bryce was safe and beautiful. And she thought Louis Parry's was the same. But nothing anyone did brought Louis Parry home.

Until maybe now. The police must have finally found him. *Heartbreaking.*

Ren slid open her desk drawer and pulled out the deck

of cards. She opened it and slid out the top card. It was the Ace of Hearts. At its center was the face of Louis Parry, wide-eyed and fragile. And printed underneath:

MISSING PERSON
Louis Parry was last seen at 4.30 p.m.
on June 20th, 1981
on Main Street in Catskill, New York.
He was 10 years old, 4' 5" and dressed in
red shorts and a yellow T-shirt.
If you have any information regarding this case,
please contact
New York State Crimestoppers . . .

The card featured in hundreds of cold-case decks that had been handed out three weeks earlier in Rikers Island in New York, in the hope that an inmate would recognize a victim, see something or hear something during a game of cards and call the confidential number.

During a game of cards.

Her cell phone rang.

She hit Answer. 'Hi, Mom.' There was silence at the other end. 'Mom?'

Ren got up and went into the hallway. She pressed the phone to her ear. She heard a huge intake of breath and a desperate sob. 'Oh, Ren. The police were just here. They've torn the house apart. It's your brother, it's—'

'What? Matt?'

'Beau,' said her mom. 'Beau.'

Ren's stomach heaved. 'Whoa, what? Beau? What the—'

'It's about Louis Parry. They think Beau had something to do with Louis Parry going missing.'

'What? What are they talking about? Why?'

'They mentioned something about cards being sent out to prisons – I didn't understand any of that. All I know is that someone called some number—'

'Mom, Mom,' said Ren. 'Calm down, OK? This is a mistake, that's all. A very big mistake. The cards are cold-case playing cards. They're handed out in prisons, to jog inmates' memories while they're playing poker or blackjack or whatever. The hope is that they might have heard someone talk about having committed one of the crimes. Then they can call Crimestoppers with the tip. All kinds of crazy people call Crimestoppers. For all kinds of reasons. A lot of times, the cops just have to follow up as a formality—'

'You weren't here. You haven't seen what they've done. They are convinced Beau was involved. It's like tearing his room apart was a formality.'

'God, Mom. Beau didn't do anything. We all know that.'

'But Beau is dead, Ren. He's dead. And I'm afraid they're going to blame this on him for closure—'

'They cannot do that,' said Ren. 'They need proof. And they will never find proof. They cannot find something that does not exist.'

'I'm sick, Ren. I am physically sick. People are walking by . . . standing across the street. And what about the Parrys? What are they going to think? After all this time? Your father, your brothers and I were out looking for Louis—'

'Mom, calm down or you will have a heart attack. The Parrys are good people—'

'The Parrys are desperate people. These cards – whatever they are – are their last hope. Maybe a part of them wants to give up. Wants to take whatever means they can sleep at night.'

'The Parrys are good people,' Ren said again. 'They really are. They wouldn't—'

Her mother dropped the phone. Ren could hear it bounce across the floor.

'Mom? Are you OK?'

'I'm sorry. My hands are shaking. I'm a wreck . . .'

'Where is Dad?'

'At the gym.'

Ren rolled her eyes. 'Did you call him?'

'I got voicemail.'

'Call someone, Mom, and get them to come over.'

Her mother let out a breath. 'Is there anything *you* can do?'

'Oh yes,' said Ren. 'You bet there is.'

Ren put the phone down. She could not move. She had reached a sub-setting of numb. For now, her mind was incapable of getting any further than Beau.

11

Ren breathed deeply until she was calm enough to speak.

'Robbie, could you do me a favor, please?' she said. 'Would you mind asking Summit County to send over the files on that Gavino Val Pando bar raid?'

'Sure, no problem.'

She Googled the number for the Catskill Police Department and punched it into her phone as she got up from her desk. The receptionist came on the line as Ren was shutting herself into the conference room.

'My name is Ren Bryce. I'm with the FBI. Could I speak with the lieutenant please?' Ren sat down in the far corner of the room.

'Putting you through to Lieutenant Stroud . . .'

Whoa. 'I'm sorry – which Stroud?' said Ren.

'That would be Lieutenant Daryl Stroud, ma'am.'

Ren hung up.

Daryl Stroud. This cannot be the person I have to deal with here. Daryl Stroud had witnessed Ren's first full-blown manic meltdown. He was the low she rode out of Catskill on. Ren had been nineteen years old when she raised her hand to Daryl

Stroud – her boyfriend of one year – to slap him across the face for a reason she could never recall. He would have taken the slap, but he grabbed her wrist when he saw that Ren had turned the stone in her ring into her palm to increase the impact. As she stormed off, she had turned to throw a can of beer at him. It landed at his feet, burst open and sprayed all over him. Ren had hitched her way home and as the hours passed and the alcohol started to drain from her system, she began calling Daryl's house, weeping, ready to beg forgiveness. It was his mother who answered, so Ren had hung up. She then walked to his house and threw stones at his window. He wasn't home. When he did show up an hour later, Ren roared at him that he had cheated on her, which he hadn't, and told him he was an asshole. His parents came out and his dad took Ren on a wordless journey home. Daryl and Ren got back together the next day after tears and vows of eternal love. A month later, Ren had kissed his best friend, the biggest asshole in town . . . while Daryl Stroud remained the sweetest, most genuine, loyal and honest guy you could meet.

She picked up the phone and dialed again.

The receptionist had already given Ren's name and patched her straight through.

'Daryl, hi, it's Ren Bryce again. I'm sorry we got disconnected.'

'Hello, Ren. How are you doing?'

'Shell-shocked. What's going on, Daryl? You know Beau had nothing to do with this.'

Silence. 'I'd love to agree with you,' said Daryl.

'But I'm at a loss as to how you don't.'

'Because of the tip-off,' said Daryl. 'Because of the fact that Beau knew and was trusted by Louis—'

'OK, let's scratch that last one for a start: the whole town knew Louis. And he was a trusting type of kid. Where did the tip come from? What was it exactly?'

'Oh, come on, Ren. You're an agent with the FBI. You wouldn't tell a suspect's family member what you got.'

'That depends. If it were you, Daryl . . . Come on, this is nuts. Please take a look at this tip and the nature of it, where it came from and what its reliability is. Please, Daryl.'

Stroud's tone changed. 'That's not just an FBI way of handling things, you know. Here in the sticks we think that might be a good idea too. That is, when we're not sitting on our hoods, flirting with old ladies outside the diner.'

'I didn't mean anything by that,' said Ren. 'Here's how it is – I'm not worried, because I know Beau is innocent. But I am desperately worried that it will be pinned on him anyway. It seems so sudden and random.'

'I won't treat this any differently than any other investigation.'

That is not reassuring. 'I wouldn't expect you to. Just please remember Beau and who he was.'

'I really am so sorry for your loss.'

'You know something?' said Ren. 'It's been twenty-four years and those words are still welcome. They still help. So, thanks. But please, please do everything you can. Beau's death was devastating enough. The pain is so . . . I . . .'

She stopped.

'Ren? Are you still there? Ren?' Daryl hesitated. 'Please don't cry.'

There was another pause before Ren answered. 'Thank you. I gotta go.'

Sinking into the chair, she stared at the ceiling, holding her head back to keep the tears from falling. It was a few minutes before she was ready to dial Information for a number she knew she shouldn't call, but would regret if she didn't.

She felt sick as she listened to the pulsing dial tone.

'Is this Ricky Parry?'

'Yes.'

'Ricky, it's Ren Bryce.

Silence. 'Oh. Hi. I . . . should we be talking?'

'I really think we should,' said Ren. 'What is going on, Ricky?'

'Someone came forward with information.'

'Who? And what was this information?'

'Don't you know? Like, with your FBI contacts—'

'They're not going to tell me,' said Ren, 'But I hope you can. We all know that Beau didn't have anything to do with this. Your whole family knows that. Our families are friends, Ricky. I'm in shock here. Why did none of you tell the police that this information was bullshit? What about your mom?'

'Mom has cancer,' said Ricky. 'She's very ill. Not that she's ever really been well since . . . then. And losing Dad last year was . . . terrible . . .'

'I know,' said Ren. 'I understand that. We were all there at the funeral.' *My whole family was there to support you.*

'I know . . .' said Ricky.

'Ricky, this new information is false. I'm concerned that you're latching on to—'

'Oh, come on!' Ricky spat the words. 'Why would Beau kill himself if he was so innocent? There has to be a reason. I'm betting the guilt ate him up and he couldn't take it any more. He checked out because he could not live with the knowledge of what he did to Louis.'

Silence. When Ren spoke her voice was quiet. 'I . . . I am

devastated that you think that. You had all been so good to us when Beau died.' She paused. 'I'm so sorry about your mom. I hope she gets better.'

I know how hard it is to lose someone.

Ren stood up and kicked the chair halfway across the conference room. Then she walked over, picked it up and sat down on it. She scrolled through her contacts to Helen Wheeler's number. When she dialed, it went straight to message minder.

'Helen, hi, it's Ren. Could you give me a call, please, whenever you get a chance? I'd really like to talk . . . nothing urgent . . . just . . . something's come up. But if you're busy, don't worry about it. Thanks so much. Bye.'

I am about to descend into my own private hell and it's 'nothing urgent'. What a loser.

Ren made coffee and went back to her desk. Cliff and Robbie were both on the phone. She sat and listened to them and it calmed her. This was her life, this was normal, these were good people. For several minutes, she just sat and drank her coffee.

Cliff and Robbie had a gift for getting people to talk to them, but their styles were completely different. Robbie would sound eager and excited by any piece of information he was given, making the person feel that they could possibly be the key to solving an entire investigation. Robbie played the role of Robbie. Cliff had an alter ego. He made people feel like he was their buddy, they could tell him anything and nothing would surprise him, that he'd been around the block and, really, the world's a piece of shit and we're all just grinding along. He called his colleagues 'these people'. *These people need to know if you've seen your bank-robber husband any time recently . . .* as if it was all out of his hands and Cliff had

67

as little interest in the whole thing as the person on the other end of the phone.

Ren glanced over at Colin frowning at his screen, the phone clenched to his ear. 'You will send me this – I need these financials – What you're gonna do is . . .'

Colin managed to be an even bigger asshole than he was with her.

12

Ren picked up the phone to do something – anything. She was beginning to get side-eyes from the others.

'Let's hear what Catherine Sarvas has to say about Diaz,' said Ren to no one.

She dialed the number. 'Catherine, it's Ren Bryce. I have some news for you – Erubiel Diaz's body has been found.'

Catherine gasped. 'Oh, Lord. Where?'

'In Nogales, Mexico. He was decapitated and his body was burned.'

Catherine paused. 'That's shocking. But . . . I'm relieved.'

'This is not going to be easy, but I'd like to explore the possibility that your attack was linked to the death of your husband . . .'

Silence. 'Do you think so?'

'I don't have any evidence,' said Ren, 'but your family was targeted twice in the space of two weeks and . . . do you have any links to Mexico? Have you vacationed there?'

'No. The last time I was in Mexico was twenty years ago.'

'And what about your husband?'

'No,' said Catherine. 'And when he traveled for business, it was just within Texas.'

'What about your sons? Did they have any reason to go to Mexico – maybe with friends' families, field trips from school . . . ?'

'No. They always vacationed with us. Luke, our seventeen-year-old, went on his first solo trip at spring break, but that was to San Diego State to visit his college. He's . . . was . . . starting at San Diego State. He's going to study law.' Her voice cracked.

'So he went alone?'

'No, I meant he went without the family, but he wasn't alone – he went with three friends. They were checking out the facilities, the libraries . . . probably a few of the girls.'

'No doubt,' said Ren. 'Can I get his friends' names from you?'

'Sure . . . but I don't see how . . .'

'Well, it won't do any harm. Look, Catherine, Luke's missing, and his friends know him best.'

'OK,' said Catherine. 'His friends are . . . John Reiff, Ben Racono and Mark Bayne. I'll get you their numbers if you'll wait on the line.'

Ren sat staring at the boys' names on the page. Three boys, aged between seventeen and nineteen, with so much of their lives ahead of them. All Ren could think about was Beau.

'Guys, I'm taking an early lunch.' She grabbed her coat. 'Back in a half-hour – I'm just going to let Misty out in the yard.'

Ren barely remembered the drive home. As soon as she got in the door she went straight to the sofa and sat there, staring at the family photo on the living-room wall. Beau with his gorgeous smile and his long sandy hair and his skinny limbs and his piano fingers. And just his goodness. Ren wanted to stop there. Because she always stopped there. But this time, she broke through the pain barrier and she started to think about the rest: rushing to Beau's bedroom when she heard her mother scream, her mother's wild eyes as she turned to her in the doorway, her mother's arm as she reached out and slammed the bedroom door on her hand, her mother screaming: 'Orenda, no!' Every vowel sound was stretched as far as her breath would take it. It was an extraordinary, life-changing scream. Ren's scream fused with her mother's, but it was at the shock of being hurt by her. She could not understand why her mother had slammed the door on her. And it was the searing pain of her crushed hand. Ren remembered looking down at the tips of two of her fingers hanging by an almost translucent scrap of skin and pumping blood on to the carpet.

Her mother was screaming for her son. Ren was screaming for her mother. And as she tried the door a second time, her mother screamed again: 'Orenda, no!'

Ren had run to her parents' bathroom. She had stood, bawling, at the sink, confused and horrified by her mother. There was no color left in the face looking back at her from the mirror, but all around her seemed to be red. Her hand was throbbing, still pumping out blood.

Why hasn't Mom come to help me? What did I do? Where's Beau? Why isn't he helping? He must have heard me. Where is everyone?

She heard her mother call her again: Orendaaa! Orendaaa! Wrapping her hand in a towel, Ren had run toward her. This time, Beau's door was open. She was afraid to walk in, as if it was a trap and her mother wanted to hurt her again. But Ren knew there was a reason why the whole world had suddenly turned upside down. She knew something was terribly wrong. Beau was lying on the bed, staring up at the ceiling. His mother was gripping her dead son by his face, kissing it and sobbing and wiping her tears from it.

'He's dead, Orenda. He's dead. He's . . .'

Ren ran to the kitchen, grabbed their Bakelite phone with the eight-foot cord and dialed 911, pacing up and down the length of the hallway as she told the dispatcher about her big brother. As she put the phone down, her mother was screaming for her again. And from that day on, Ren did not want to be called Orenda ever again.

Beau Bryce was dead. He had taken an overdose. He was nineteen years old, handsome, and smart. He was not selfish. He was not unloved. He was clinically depressed. Some people committed suicide and didn't leave a note: Beau had written a short story, an allegory in which his family were different characters and Beau was the tortured hero on a quest for something that he had never been able to identify, therefore had never been able to find, no matter how much the other characters had tried to help him. He had crossed kingdoms, climbed mountains, searched caves, swum oceans, yet he had finished, hovering at a cliff edge, alone and confused. And he had taken one more step. He had trusted an empty sky more than he had trusted the ground beneath his feet or the beautiful land or the people who lived in it.

Tears streamed down Ren's face. She knew the journey Beau had taken, she knew that beautiful terrain, she knew and loved the same characters.

And her greatest fear was that one day she too would trust an empty sky more.

13

Somehow, Ren made it back to work. Gary was standing in the bullpen with a grim look on his face.

'Not good news,' he said. 'Looks like the blood Gartman was covered in the night of the convenience store shooting was Natalie Osgood's. Her body was found last night in a dumpster off Colfax.'

Ren shook her head. 'That son-of-a-bitch. Her mama's worst nightmare has come true.' She let out a breath.

Robbie called her over to his desk. 'Ren, I spoke with three real estate agents,' he said, 'and Gregory Sarvas *did* talk to them about selling the house. Like, it was more than just chit-chat.'

'Jesus,' said Ren. 'Yet another wife kept in the dark.'

'Who's the other one?'

'I don't know – insert celebrity name.' Ren let out a breath. 'Catherine Sarvas told me that it was a casual conversation about moving – nothing concrete. And Greg goes off and makes formal enquiries? It's so patronizing. Did he just disregard her all the time?'

'It probably worked for them . . .' said Colin.

'Oh, please,' said Ren. 'He's dead, she's raped. That worked real well.'

'You know what I mean,' said Colin.

'I do – keep the little woman in the dark.'

Colin shrugged and turned back to his screen.

'Do you say this shit on purpose?' said Ren.

Colin looked up. 'Some women just want men to take care of everything for them.'

'There's a difference between a husband taking the trash out and other bullshit jobs . . . and not telling you he's trying to sell your house from under you or, let's face it, not reporting your rape,' said Ren. '*Rape*, Colin.'

'I'm not talking about the rape part.'

'Oh, well then,' said Ren. She turned to Robbie. 'Did Sarvas talk to the real estate people about buying another house in the area?'

'No,' said Robbie.

'Did he mention where he was planning to move to, or when?'

'No. According to all three real estate agents, Sarvas sounded serious about selling the house. But there were no times, dates, etc.'

'Could someone be that screwed up that they wouldn't want to lower house prices in the area by reporting a rape – even if it was their own wife who was the victim?'

Ren shook her head. 'Ugh.' She walked out. She didn't want to hear any more of Colin's warped world view. The kitchen was empty, so she took a seat at the table.

What is it with some men? Do they get a high from lying to their wives? Do they just not care? Or is it that they're afraid to face up to the truth?

Again her mind wandered back to Beau and the friends and neighbors who had drifted away from the family after his suicide. They were afraid of suicide, afraid of mental illness, afraid of losing their own mind or watching someone they cared about lose theirs. People looked for someone to blame for Beau's suicide, because if there was no one to blame, then it could happen to them. People were angry at the Bryces for being guarded about the circumstances, as if – had they had heard all the details of Beau's suicide – they could stop it from happening to *their* loved ones. People were afraid to talk to the Bryces about their loss because it would mean confronting someone else's raw emotions and maybe having to face some raw emotions of their own.

It's all about fear.

What would it be like for her parents now? They were the only ones who still lived in Catskill. They were good, kind people. And now, in their late seventies, they would be thrown into having to fight to preserve their son's memory. Even though it was all a terrible mistake, that little idea had been implanted in people's minds and would be hard to extract; Beau Bryce took his own life because he was guilty.

Work. Go back to something you can control.

Ren took her cup of coffee and returned to the bullpen. She stopped dead in the middle of the room.

'Hey!' She pointed at the television. 'Someone – pump up the volume.'

Colin reached for the remote control.

'*The police are seeking the public's help in locating missing Denver psychiatrist, Dr Helen Wheeler—*' Helen's photo in the top right-hand corner of the screen . . .

'Oh my God,' said Ren.

'What?' said Cliff.

'I know her.'

'Yeah, you're obviously her best client,' said Colin.

If you only knew. 'She's a friend of mine. I consulted with her on cases a few times, actually. She's a lovely woman. Shhh.'

'Dr Wheeler was last seen as she left work four days ago on March eighth. She was due to speak at an event in Florida on March ninth, but she didn't catch her flight that morning. Dr Wheeler is sixty-two years old, five-foot three, of medium build, with shoulder-length blonde hair and blue eyes. She was dressed in a full-length dark-gray coat over a pale gray wool pant suit.'

Ren felt her stomach sink. *That was what she was wearing the last time I saw her.*

Ren dialed Helen's cell phone as she stood there. It was the only thing she could think of doing. She got voicemail. She didn't leave a message.

Please be safe, wherever you are.

Two hours later, Ren called Helen's office and spoke with her secretary. There was no update. Helen had been gone four days, that was all anyone knew.

Ren tried to work, but she was flooded with images of Beau. And worried about her parents. And wishing she could discuss it all with Helen, the one person who always managed to break the cycle. Ren felt a stab of selfishness at wanting Helen to be back to help her.

Helen wouldn't take off and desert her patients. Helen Wheeler was sane. She was responsible. But then again, everyone thinks the same about me . . . OK, not everyone. But still . . .

Ren's cell phone rang and she recognized the special ring tone for Matt. Work and Matt – the only calls guaranteed to get picked up.

'Hey,' he said. 'What the hell's going on with the Parrys?'

'I know. It's nuts. I called Daryl Stroud – he's a lieutenant now, can you believe it? – and he's taking it seriously. Going by the book.'

'You have to be shitting me.'

'Nope. I cannot understand all this. It's insane.'

'Mom was saying something about cards in Rikers. Some playing card belonging to Louis—'

'She had it all wrong. They're cold-case cards, given to inmates to elicit tip-offs – I explained all that to her.'

'She's definitely not all there at the moment.'

'While at other times . . .'

Matt laughed. It was short-lived. 'This is so surreal. How does it all work?'

'Catskill PD will investigate it, they have to. All we can do is sit back and wait for them to get a grip.'

'But . . . who would have sent them our way? I can't imagine some big inmate in Rikers saying, "Beau Bryce – that's the guy you need to look at".'

'The tip's not necessarily from Rikers,' said Ren. 'Those cards get posted online too – for years, in some cases – on missing persons websites. I mean, families will always want to know what happened to a missing or murdered loved one, so they're happy to have the details plastered everywhere they can. Just about anyone could have called in the tip. It could be a timing coincidence that the cards came out this month. It could have been the publicity done on the release of the cards that prompted someone to call.'

'What does Daryl think?'

'That I'm an arrogant bitch. And that telling me he would treat it the same as any other investigation was going to reassure me. Yeah, right: "Great job on finding that stolen bicycle, Daryl, please apply those same skills to finding the guy who thinks my dead brother is a child killer."'

'Daryl's one of the good guys, though?'

'He is,' said Ren. 'I'm just being an arrogant bitch.'

'No you're not – everything you've said is what I was thinking.'

'Has Mom talked to the Parrys?'

'No.'

'Oh, thank God. Stop her, could you? Because I already called Ricky—'

'You did not.'

'I had to, Matt. He's the only one who could enlighten me . . . which he did not. In fact, he ended the conversation with "Why would Beau have killed himself if he wasn't guilty?"'

'Has he lost his mind? Am I missing something here? When did he go to the dark side? There I was, thinking he would be as upset as we were.'

'Oh no,' said Ren. 'He's probably just . . . I don't know. Exhausted, at this stage. Quick to grab on to anything. I don't know.'

'It can't have been easy for Ricky. God forgive me, but I think all the genetic blessings went to Louis—'

'Like me in our family—'

'As I was saying . . .' said Matt. 'You know what I mean: Louis got the cute looks, the musical talent . . . and he was such a delicate little thing. Ricky was this chubby—'

'Louis was the piece of china, Ricky was the bull.'

'Yes, Ren, yes. Anyway, look, there we are. The Parrys had their albatross with Louis and we had ours with Beau. Not to sound harsh—'

'I know what you mean.'

'At least we know what happened to Beau, however terrible that is. The Parrys might never know what happened to Louis.'

'They definitely won't know if they're looking in our house for answers.'

Matt let out a breath. 'Ren, I'm going to be devil's advocate here. Or, rather, I'm going to tip-toe across the topic gently before our eldest sibling comes in and dances a jig on it: could this by any chance be—'

'Something to do with my job?'

'You said it! Thank the Lord.'

'No is your answer.'

'You haven't gotten someone sent to Rikers to be ass-raped?'

'Not to Rikers, no,' said Ren. 'But your doorbell could ring at any minute.'

Matt laughed. 'Well,' he said, the laughter trailing off into a sigh. 'At least we can see the funny side.'

'For now.' Ren took a breath. 'Matt, Helen's gone missing.'

'What? When?'

'Last time I saw her was the last day she was seen: Monday, the day of my appointment. She didn't show up at a conference next day.'

'Oh, she's probably running from all you crazies,' said Matt. 'I'd disappear if I had to listen to all the voices talking about all the voices.'

'True.' *Smile through the fear. Smile through the fear.*

'Can you do anything?'

'I'm hearing that quite a lot recently,' said Ren. 'I'll find it hard not to try.'

'She'll be back.'

'She better be,' said Ren.

Because I have no idea what I will do otherwise.

14

Denver's 16th Street Mall was a long, grim shopping street monopolized by cell-phone and electronic stores. Bright lights shone on dark slush. Everyone who passed Ren had their head bowed – a parade of hidden faces. Ren's eyes and nose were streaming. She went into the nearest restaurant and ordered a rare steak and a glass of red wine. She pulled out her notebook and wrote Helen Wheeler on a clean page. She followed it with two question marks and let the pen hover over them.

Stop. Helen has probably broken up with her boyfriend and disappeared to a log cabin to get over it. Away from the loonies.

Then something tugged at Ren.

Her overwhelming compulsion to fix things.

The parking lot at the back of Helen Wheeler's building had a dual role. In addition to accommodating forty vehicles, it marked the boundary between a good neighborhood and a bad one. From the back of the lot eastward, the landscape got more ragged and dirty, like the torn ends of jeans dragged through puddles. The front of the building led on to a street of designer stores, organic food markets, an independent bookstore, a stationery store and a restaurant/bar.

Ren looked around the parking lot and saw three broken security cameras. *Surprise, surprise.* The lot was prime retail space for the local dealers: close enough to drag their saggy asses up off their mamas' sofas and go make a sale, just far enough for chickenshit middle-class kids to wander in the hope of scoring some blow.

When Ren visited Helen, she usually slipped in the back door. Every bone in her body wanted to break in there now. Instead she walked around to the front of the building. The sidewalk was shining, the curbs packed with dirty ice and slush. She circled the block, pausing on each corner, wondering which direction Helen Wheeler could have gone in, wondering how that mattered when there was no other information to attach it to. Wondering what the point of all of this was.

She left.

As Ren pulled up outside Annie's, she caught a glimpse of net curtain flapping in the wind. For a second, she thought she'd left the window open, but as she parked the car, she could see that the window was smashed and the wind was sucking the curtain through a massive, jagged hole into the cold night.

Oh my God, Misty.

As she ran up the path, she could see razor-sharp shards of glass sticking up in the snow under the window. Broken from the inside out. Ren knew whoever did it wouldn't still be in the house. No one would break a front window right on to the street and hang around. But that didn't stop her drawing her gun before she unlocked the door and stepped into the hallway.

Adrenaline had kicked in. Mind-sharpening adrenaline. She took a right into the living room. It was ice cold, the curtain blowing in and out, blackened and shredded on the sharp edges of the glass. Ren felt sickened for Annie. Her antique lace ruined, her pretty picture window shattered. As she looked around the rest of the room – the dresser, the drawers under the coffee table – she realized she didn't know where Annie kept her valuables. She didn't know if she had a safe, if she kept her things at the bank. And it was not a question she wanted to ask Annie. She couldn't let her know that the assumed security of an FBI agent staying at her home had no value.

Ren moved through to the dining room and back into the hallway. She paused and looked up to the second floor. *There are too many rooms in this house.* But she worked through them all and up until the final door, had found nothing changed – a house undisturbed. She had saved the best for last. Or at least the most relevant. She opened her bedroom door.

'Misty!'

Misty lay motionless in the corner. Ren's heart caught. She ran to her and laid a hand on her silky back. Misty woke up, licked Ren's hand and rested her head back down.

'Oh, thank God,' said Ren. 'Thank God. You're safe, sweetheart. You're safe.' She hugged Misty close. 'I wonder did barking cross your mind,' said Ren.

Ren went quiet when she heard the sound of a door banging back and forth. A cold breeze seemed to come from nowhere and whip around her. She stood up from the bed. For a moment she was rigid. Then she walked across the floor to where the noise grew louder. Annie called it the back attic. Ren never knew if it was Annie's own creation or the architect's. She had forgotten about it. She remembered it as being the size of an average bedroom. It had black glossy floorboards and a little window that sounded and felt like it was the source of the noise and cold wind. Ren glanced at the wall beside her and the two-foot-six square door that led to the staircase. She remembered Annie telling the Bryce children that it was magical. Ren had been young enough to believe her, so she had made her tentative way up the stairs and thought yes, magical . . . when magic is black and creepy and has tentacles that wrap around your head, poke into your eyes and snake all the way up into your brain.

'Misty, they must have come right by you,' said Ren. 'You poor, gentle soul.'

Ren glanced at the curious door. Thirty years on, she told herself: *Do it.* She opened it and crawled through, then crawled back out for a flashlight. *Chicken.* She had dealt with all kinds of crime scenes and tuned out the filthy conditions, but the ingrained childhood fear of the back attic was stalling her. She started over and went up the stairs. The light illuminated faint traces of footprints in the dust on the treads. Ren kept close to the wall to avoid them, pausing to shine the flashlight on one and get a picture with her cell phone. Just in case.

The closer she got to the top of the stairs, the colder the air. She took a chill breath before she climbed up into the room. The small casement window – banging back on its hinges. Ren looked around the room. It was a Victorian time-warp, as if Annie herself had been living in this house for over a hundred years.

To Ren, attics had always been eerie: dark, overfilled, disordered, but necessary. People discovered all kinds of things in attics, wanted and unwanted. But you had to be willing to explore an attic, because it was never inviting.

A bolt of panic shot through Ren. 'The attic' was the term she used for her mind. The attic: dark, overfilled, disordered, uninviting. And unknown as Ren's metaphor to anyone but one woman.

Ren ran to the window and looked out as if she would see Helen Wheeler running across the rooftops with a black cloak spreading behind her into the night sky.

15

Everyone in the office wanted to know why Ren hadn't called them after the break-in.

'You egomaniacs,' she said.

'But . . . anything could have happened to you,' said Robbie.

'I checked the house, there was no one there.'

'Someone might have seen the moving truck,' said Colin. 'Thought they'd get some nice boxes, ready to go.'

'Hey, I know I'm a hoarder, but there was no moving truck,' said Ren. 'Just me and Removal Robbie.'

Robbie laughed as loud as Robbie ever would. 'Oh, you have no idea.'

'Is there something we should know?' said Ren.

'It's a Mormon thing,' said Robbie. 'If you're in the Elders Quorum, basically, you move people . . .'

'What – emotionally?' said Ren.

'If you break their good china, yes,' said Robbie.

'You mean you literally help people to move house?' said Ren.

'Yup. It's all part of being an Elder.'

'Yet being elderly isn't,' said Ren.

'No,' said Robbie.

'Wow,' said Ren. '*Having* to help people move. That's very nice. And slightly weird. But, to your credit, you were very efficient with my boxes.'

Colin gave Robbie a sucker look. 'I'd say you were broken into, Ren, because someone was watching the house. Maybe someone walking by noticed that sweet little puppy following the lady around—'

Ren frowned. 'Misty's a grown dog. She—'

'He's not talking about Misty,' said Robbie.

Ren stared at Colin.

'Misty . . . Robbie – what's the difference?' said Colin.

You dickhead.

Ren's gaze wandered to the television and the Breaking News scrolling across the bottom of the screen. A male reporter was standing, mic in hand, his blue and red ski jacket and fur-lined hood protecting him against the falling snow.

He raised his voice over the wind: '*The warehouse you see behind me is the controversial "Gitmo on the Platte", if you remember – a building that first hit the headlines two years ago as what some called a primitive holding cell for potential protestors at the Democratic National Convention . . .*'

'Yup,' said Colin, 'protestors outside the building before the DNC even started, protesting against the conditions that they would have to endure if they were arrested for protesting . . .'

Ren nodded. 'Those kind of people, as soon as one avenue is exhausted, they're on to the next thing they can misdirect their anger at. It's why they—'

Oh. My. God. Ren had just registered what the Breaking News was.

'*And today,*' said the reporter, '*the building is once more in the spotlight with the discovery early this morning of the body of missing Denver psychiatrist, Dr Helen Wheeler, several blocks from her downtown office. We understand Dr Wheeler was the victim of a gunshot wound . . .'*

'Oh my God,' said Ren, standing up. *Helen.*

'That's your friend,' said Robbie.

'I know . . .' Ren raised her hand to her mouth. 'I can't believe it.' Tears streamed down her face. Instant, reflexive tears. *Helen cannot be dead.*

'Are you OK?' said Robbie, going over to her. 'Sit down. Sit down.'

They both watched as the gurney with the body bag was loaded into the back of the coroner's van. Ren sat at her desk. Robbie pulled open her drawer and handed her an unopened packet of Kleenex.

Ren's body started to tremble. *Helen is dead. I'm going to be sick.*

'Let me go make you some tea,' said Robbie. 'With sugar.'

'Sorry, thank you. Two . . .'

'Sugars?'

'Yes.' Ren was trying to stop crying. Colin was across the room hovering, embarrassed.

'I'm sorry,' he said. 'I . . . know she was your friend.'

'Thank you,' said Ren. 'I can't believe it . . . Who would kill Helen Wheeler? You should have met her. She was . . .' *Oh, God. How did this happen?*

Ren heard Gary heading down the hallway and into his office. She got up and followed him, closing the door behind them both.

'Helen Wheeler's been found dead.'

'What?' said Gary.

Ren nodded, fighting back tears.

'Where? What happened?'

She filled him in.

'Sit down,' he said. 'Are you OK?'

'No,' said Ren. 'I'm not. I'm in shock. Why would someone murder Helen Wheeler?'

Gary nodded.

'We can offer Denver PD all the resources they need on this, can't we?' said Ren. 'I want to do absolutely everything I can.'

'Yes,' said Gary.

'Thank you.' Ren hung her head. 'Helen gets me, Gary. *Got* me. Hardly anyone gets me. And just as she was starting to make me face shit, she's gone.'

Gary handed her a Kleenex.

'I'm sorry,' said Ren. 'I don't know what to do.' She let out a ragged breath. 'And thank you for letting me stick with Helen . . . instead of the agency shrink. It . . . meant a lot—'

'Well, continuity of care,' said Gary. 'I guess Helen's behind your new ability to cry too?'

Ren laughed briefly through the tears.

'I have no idea what to do with Weeping Ren,' said Gary.

'I'm sorry,' she said. 'I don't know . . . I was totally . . .' She shook her head. 'You don't need to hear any of this.'

'Ren, take the rest of the afternoon off, OK?'

Work – Gary's only currency. 'OK,' said Ren. 'Thanks.'

She walked to the door and turned back to him. 'We both know that's not going to happen, right?'

Gary nodded. 'Yup. Let me call Denver PD.'

Cliff James had arrived in the meantime. The moment Ren saw his face, she knew he had already been told. He was still in his parka, on the phone, listening carefully, saying very little. He looked up at her. His expression was so kind it went straight to her heart.

'I am so sorry, sweetheart,' he said, standing up, shrugging his jacket off. He walked over and gave her a hug.

'Thank you,' said Ren.

'OK, I just got off the phone with Denver PD,' said Cliff. 'My buddy, Glenn – Glenn Buddy is his name, actually – is heading up the case. So, obviously I let him know we're all here for whatever he needs.'

'Thank you so much,' said Ren. 'I think Gary has just made the same call.'

'Ah, but he's not in the inner sanctum. Glenn Buddy was my best man.'

'And, therefore, witness to your best move,' said Ren.

Cliff smiled. 'Indeed. He'd do anything for me, or for anyone I'd do anything for.' He hugged Ren again.

Ren sat at her desk beside the can of Red Bull that Robbie knew she really wanted, running ideas through her head.

'What could have happened?' said Ren. 'Helen left work, didn't make it home? Helen left work, was abducted outside? Carjacked? Walked home and was attacked? Helen made it home, was abducted there, taken to the warehouse? What the fuck?'

'It could be anything at this stage,' said Cliff. 'Glenn's going to drop by later. See if you can help in any way.'

'Psychiatrists know a lot about a lot of people,' said Colin. 'Maybe someone felt she knew too much. Or had stored something on her computer that could compromise them.'

'It's pointless guessing,' said Ren, 'because we have no real details yet.'

'Mmm . . . I do,' said Cliff. 'If you feel able to hear them . . .'

Ren put a hand across her stomach – the first place her emotional pain ran for.

'Do you want me to talk through this in private?'

'No, Cliff,' said Ren. 'Everyone will hear it anyway.'

'OK. Ren, I'm afraid your friend was tortured . . .'

'Oh my God – in what way?'

'She was beaten. And she had fingers broken. And finger-nails . . . removed.'

'I'm sorry . . . what? I . . .' Ren ran to the bathroom and threw up. She stood up slowly in front of the mirror. Her head swam. She pressed her forehead against the cold tiles.

Sixty-two-year-old women don't get tortured. They don't get shot and thrown into a warehouse. They read literary fiction, crime novels, discuss world events, take long walks, spoil their grandkids, garden, meet their friends for coffee . . . help people.

Ren sat down on the slatted bench by the wall. Her entire body felt hollowed out. Helen had once said to her, 'You work from the neck up, Ren, you never go below.' She had put her hand to her heart and said to Ren, 'You need to start going below – to what's inside.'

Helen had led Ren to the place Ren had never wanted to go – the black hole where everything she had never wanted to face was awaiting her. Helen was the one guide she had trusted. And now she was gone.

And now I really am all alone.

16

Glenn Buddy and Cliff James must have drawn attention whenever they went out together. Cliff was six foot four, Glenn Buddy was six foot six. They both had huge guts – Glenn's looked like it was from beer, Cliff's looked a little softer.

Glenn had brought a sandwich and chips with him to Safe Streets, apologizing for having to eat while he was there. His sandwich was over-filled, so he had to open his mouth too wide to fit it in. He threw the chips into his mouth as if he was trying to stone his larynx. Ren tried to focus on the words, not the pictures, but her stomach was tightening.

'OK,' said Glenn, shifting his food to one cheek and speaking out of the corner of his mouth. 'Here's what we got. She was tortured . . . like someone was trying to get information out of her . . .'

Dr Helen Wheeler, attractive, intelligent psychiatrist . . . and suddenly she's in a warehouse being tortured.

'Are you sure?' said Ren.

Glenn glanced at Cliff.

'It's just totally . . . surreal,' said Ren. 'It's like a different

91

world.' She struggled to avoid welling up. *Stay composed or they'll keep you out of the investigation.*

'It sure is,' said Glenn, shrugging again, taking a bite of his sandwich.

'Was she robbed?' said Ren. 'Had anyone been in her office? Or her home?'

'So far, it looks like a no to all of the above. All her keys were found with her – house, office, car.'

Ren shook her head. 'What do you think the scenario was? Was she taken from her office?'

'Probably in the parking lot, on the way to her car.'

'And where was her car found? It wasn't in the office parking lot.'

'It was by the warehouse.'

'And she was killed outside the warehouse? Inside?'

'Inside.'

'And she was beaten.'

'Very badly. Some kind of blunt instrument was used.'

Ren had nothing to say to that. Nothing that a ripped-apart feeling inside her couldn't express.

'What kind of person was she?' said Glenn.

Shit. She was a therapist: a person you knows you, while you don't know them. 'She was . . . a really good person. Very kind. Intelligent. Witty.' *Got stuff out of me that no one else ever could.* 'She was warm, friendly. A real lady. Dressed conservatively, spoke softly . . .'

'Hardly the type to get involved with a bad crowd,' said Cliff.

'Yes, but don't forget she would have had a few fruitcakes on her books,' said Glenn.

Step away from the patients. 'It's easy to jump on that,' said Ren. 'but it seems a little . . . convenient.'

Cliff shifted in his seat. Glenn finished his potato chips

and wrapped up the remains of his lunch. He wiped his mouth, then opened the envelope he had laid on the table.

'Are you sure you want to see these?' he said.

'Yes,' said Ren. *Before your very eyes, watch how I shut myself down.*

The first photo was a long shot across the warehouse parking lot – wet concrete with patches of snow dotted across it, enclosed in meters and meters of grim chain-link fencing.

The second photo was inside – a distant fully-clothed body, garishly flood-lit. Ren held her breath and turned to the next one. The corpse now had a face and a name. Helen Wheeler lay with her head turned toward the wall, her blonde hair obscuring her features, her chest torn apart. *Too much red.* Ren slowly released her breath. She moved through the rest of the photos. Helen had a broken nose. Her eyes were black. An earring had been ripped from her ear. Ren could see the missing fingernails and broken fingers.

What happened to you?

Ren sat back in her chair, staring at the ceiling, letting tears well briefly in her eyes but travel no further.

Focus.

'OK,' said Ren, 'is the warehouse operational?'

Glenn shook his head. 'It hasn't been used since the DNC.'

'What was security like?' said Cliff.

'There's a swipe-card system,' said Glenn.

'And did someone use a swipe card?' said Ren.

'Yup,' said Glenn. 'The former head of security is being called in as we speak.'

'Any cameras?' said Ren.

'Yes,' said Glenn, 'out of commission. The place is empty, they figure who's going to go in there in March, in the snow. It's not like it's particularly convenient—'

'Huge isolated space where no one will hear your

screams or find your body?' said Ren. 'Hey, who did find the body?'

'Our guys,' said Glenn. 'A former client from out of town had showed up at the warehouse early this morning, tried to use his swipe card and it didn't work. He calls an old friend who worked there. The friend tells him the warehouse has been shut down for months. And the out-of-town guy goes, "Well, there's a whole lot of tire tracks here that are telling me otherwise." And that's when we got the call. We had to cut through the fence.'

'Has this out-of-towner been run through the databases?' Ren was leaning forward in her seat. Glenn was slowly leaning back.

'Everyone to do with the place is going to be checked out.'

'I know . . . I know . . .' said Ren. 'Let us know what we can do on that score.'

'So the swipe-card thing,' said Cliff. 'Who's that ruling in or out?'

'All the employees of the company, past and present. I guess certain clients would have them. Security staff. Maintenance staff . . .'

'Did the security system record what time the place was accessed?' said Cliff.

'The security guy will check all that on the system,' said Glenn. 'He's not a happy man. And neither is his boss. If they don't come up with every bit of information we need, they're in the shit. And if it turns out they didn't carry out adequate background checks on their staff . . .'

'What about the rest of the streets nearby?' said Ren. 'Any TV from anywhere else?'

'We'll wait and see,' said Glenn. He glanced at his watch.

'I need to head back. I've got a press conference at three.'

'Then you better swap ties with me,' said Cliff.

Glenn glanced down at the grease stain on his. 'Shit. Thanks.'

'I'll leave you guys to it,' said Ren.

'Hey,' said Cliff. 'Did Wheeler have a . . . significant other?'

I hate that expression. And I should know the answer.

'Yes,' said Glenn. 'She did. Peter Everett.'

'Who's he?' said Ren.

'The former husband of Lucinda Kerr . . .' said Cliff.

'And who is she?' said Ren.

'Socialite – comes from one of Denver's wealthiest families. The Kerrs own half the city.'

'How do I not know that?' said Ren.

'Probably because you're not the person who owns the other half,' said Glenn.

I'm not sure I get that.

'The Kerrs are low and high profile at the same time,' said Cliff. 'People know the name, but don't know much about them.'

'And . . . do we know what kind of guy this Peter Everett is?' said Ren.

'Rich in his own right, well respected. Humanitarian type.' Cliff shrugged. 'That's all I know. Oh, and they weren't together long – six, maybe seven months.'

'He's at the station right now,' said Glenn. 'Apparently, he's a wreck.'

I know how he feels.

Ren went back into the office. Robbie was sitting with a stack of files in front of him.

'It's probably a bad time,' he said, patting them. 'These

are the files from Summit County on the Gavino Val Pando bar raid.

'No – go ahead,' said Ren.

'OK, I had a look through them. There were four girls in the bar the night of the raid – two were seventeen years old, two were nineteen. They're all from Denver. They were on vacation in Breckenridge and took a bus to the Brockton Filly. I spoke to them, got them to take a look at a photo of Gavino – nothing. They didn't even remember him. But I figured, teenage girls . . . who knows what they'll lie about. And right now, who wants to tell Daddy she's been with a guy whose mom's on the Most Wanted List. So . . . I called the Brockton Filly and spoke with Billy Waites.'

You what? Billy Waites, bar owner, confidential informant, former lover . . . who will now think I was too chickenshit to get in touch with him myself? I told you to contact Sheriff Bob Gage. No one else. Sweet Jesus, Robbie.

Ren's face kept its composure, but the rest of her was gone.

'Turns out Mr Waites still has the security tape,' said Robbie. 'Because of the raid on his bar that night, he held on to it. And . . . well, he doesn't exactly trust the police, so I think he keeps his cameras rolling all the time.'

Hopefully not after hours . . .

'Excellent.' *Absolutely fucking fantastic.* 'Do you have the tape?'

'It should arrive tomorrow,' said Robbie. 'Do you want me to go through it?'

'Yes, I will too.' *Let's just layer on the emotional trauma.*

17

Ren was late into work the next morning. She'd managed three hours of sleep, broken twice by nightmares.

'Gary wants you,' said Colin, as soon as she walked in.

'Now?' *Screw that.*

'He said when you came in,' said Robbie.

'Not before my coffee.'

'He's not that dumb.'

Ren went into Gary's office with her mug and regretted not having asked if anyone else wanted one. It might have helped their moods. Gary was at his desk. Glenn Buddy turned around from the visitor's chair.

'Take a seat,' said Gary. 'Glenn stopped by to let us know that your details have come up in connection with the Helen Wheeler investigation.'

Glenn looked surprised that Gary went so quickly to the point. Ren was not.

'Well, obviously your number came up when we did the phone dumps,' said Glenn. 'We know you called her once a week or so and tried her again during the time she was missing. So that's all fine.'

Of course that's all fine. Ren glanced at Gary.

'But that's not why I'm here,' said Glenn.

'OK,' said Ren. *What's with the strange atmosphere?*

'We called in the head of security at the warehouse,' said Glenn. 'He accessed the swipe-card system to see who had gotten in the gate the night the body was dumped and . . . your details came up – your name, and the address here.'

'What? Mine? That's impossible. How would that happen?'

'I'm asking you,' said Glenn.

'You were at the building during the DNC, Ren, right?' said Gary.

'Yes.' She turned to Glenn. 'I had to go talk to a few protestors that had been taken in for bad behavior. Anyone coming in and out of that location got swipe cards. That's standard procedure, but that was a year ago,' said Ren. 'The card would have been stripped of all access privileges right after the DNC. You said so yourself – the warehouse isn't even operational.'

Glenn nodded.

'So maybe if they knew they were closing up right after the convention,' said Ren, 'they wouldn't have bothered purging the database.'

'That's correct – they didn't,' said Glenn. 'Your access privileges were still there.'

'Well, weren't everyone's?' She looked at them.

'Yes,' said Glenn, 'but yours was the only swipe card to be used to access the property in the past nine months.'

'But that's bizarre,' said Ren. 'I wouldn't need to access it. There's nothing there.'

'Apart from your friend's dead body,' said Glenn.

'Are you actually serious?'

'Ren, where were you on March eleventh?' said Gary.

Please tell me you are doing this for show. 'I was . . .' Ren paused. 'The night before the body was found? Let me think.' She raised her eyes to the ceiling. 'I was home.'

'Can you prove that?' said Glenn.

'Should I have to?' Ren looked between both of them. 'Are you really serious?'

'I'm not trying to . . .' said Glenn. 'I'm just doing a job, OK? You just need to prove where you were and I can check that box.'

'But I can't prove it,' said Ren. 'Come on. I was home . . . alone. That was the night of the break-in. I mean, obviously I was out when that happened, but you're asking about the night-time, which—'

Glenn gave her a patient look.

'What I'm saying is, I was out for a while in the evening after work. I had dinner at the Hickory Prime Steakhouse. So I can prove that part. And then . . . I swung by Helen's office. Just to see if I could think of anything. Or see if something would hit me.' *Or if the light would be on and she would be at her desk.*

'And then I was back in Annie's surveying the damage . . . Tell me, what was the security guy at this warehouse like, anyway?' said Ren. 'Did he seem like the type who had a clue? Couldn't it just be that he forgot to hit delete or whatever he needed to do? Could my code have been assigned to someone else somewhere along the way?'

'If the system is run well, no one is ever deleted from the database,' said Glenn. 'Anyone who has ever had access to a building remains on the database.'

Ren nodded. 'I know . . . ' She let out a breath. 'I'm sorry, gentlemen, but for now, no, I cannot prove where I was.' She stood up. 'But I can sure as hell tell you where I wasn't.'

Glenn stood up. 'I'm sorry about this, guys. I have to do what I have to do.' He nodded and left.

'What the fuck was that all about?' said Ren.

'All I know,' said Gary, 'is that I feel like my office is your time-out space.'

'Hey, you can't blame me for this,' said Ren, sitting down. 'But when I came in, I thought he was talking about my details in the psych files. Phew.'

'No, Ren . . . nothing as serious as that – just the details of you accessing a murder scene around the time a body was dumped . . .'

'But I know I didn't do that.'

'With that rationale, you shouldn't be worried about anyone knowing the contents of your psych file.'

'My mind, you mean,' said Ren. '"Denver PD – come on into my mind, you're very welcome. Keep your hands inside the . . . " whatever that announcement is at the start of a rollercoaster ride.'

'Beware of flying puke,' said Gary.

'That's the one,' said Ren. 'OK, I'll get back to work.' She stood up. 'That was all a little creepy . . .'

'I would imagine it's just one of those strange computer glitches. I'm sure Glenn Buddy feels the same way.'

Not from where I was sitting.

Colin was the only person in the office when Ren walked back in.

'Here's a weird one,' said Ren. 'Glenn Buddy just stopped by. My security pass was used to access the warehouse where Helen's body was found.'

Colin looked up. 'When?'

'The night she disappeared.'

'Since when do you have a security pass for there?' said Colin.

'Since the DNC,' said Ren. 'I had to go question some

banjo players about "not wantin' no black man in the White House".' *Ugh.*

Colin paused. 'So . . . a year ago? And what's been going on with the place since then?'

'Nothing,' said Ren. 'It was closed up. In nine months, only one card has been used to access the property: mine.'

'What?'

'Gary thinks it's probably just some computer glitch.'

'You reckon?' said Colin. 'Do you not think it's strange that it was *your* card used to access a crime scene. And that the victim was *your* friend?' He went back to his computer.

Thanks for that. Ren felt a flash of fear. 'But how would that work?'

'Any number of ways,' said Colin. 'Someone literally has your card. Someone went in and accessed the computer at the warehouse . . . which, in fact, they couldn't have done if your entry was the only one in nine months. So, the alternative is that someone hacked the system . . .'

But why?

Ren's cell phone rang and her mother's number flashed on the screen. She picked up.

Her mother was sobbing. 'Oh, Ren . . .'

'What? What is it?' Ren stood up and ran to the conference room.

'They came back and searched again,' her mother said between sobs. 'The police. And they found something. They found a T-shirt belonging to Louis Parry.'

'Whoa,' said Ren 'What?' She sat down at the table.

'Yes!'

'Where?'

'In Beau's room!'

'What?' said Ren. 'When?'

'They came back this morning. After I had just tidied everything back up from the last time.'

'But I don't get it,' said Ren. 'Where did they find it?'

'In some hole he had cut into the headboard of his bed. It was under the covering of the headboard.' Her mother cried harder. She was gasping for breath and when she finally caught it, she said. 'What if . . . what if . . . ?'

'Mom, listen to me. I don't know what the hell is going on there, but I am going to find out. You stay put, don't do anything. Leave this with me. Where's Dad?'

'At tennis.'

'Are you serious?'

'There's no need for him to be here, Ren. I'm fine. I can handle these things. Your father is not as strong. Tennis helps him unwind.'

'For God's sake, Mom, there is nothing wrong with needing emotional support. Why don't you get Matt or Lauren to drive up there?'

'I can't ask Lauren to . . . with the pregnancy . . . and . . .'

'Mom, she's not ill,' said Ren. 'You know she'll be wonderful. Just call her. She'll be happy to drive up if Matt can't.'

'OK, OK.'

'But don't do anything else.'

'I feel like marching right over there to the Parrys. If Rita Parry wasn't so sick—'

'Mom, stay where you are,' said Ren. 'When will Dad be back?'

'In about an hour. I'm glad he wasn't here to see all this . . .'

'It's not like it would hit him any harder than you.'

'Can't you come to Catskill or . . . or . . . something?'

'I can't right now,' said Ren. 'But I will try and get to you as soon as I can. I promise.'

'Thank you, Ren. This is . . . I thought losing Beau was the worst thing that could happen to us.'

'No, having me was the worst thing that happened to us.'

Her mom laughed. 'Thank you. Oh, Ren. My heart . . .'

'Mine too. Look after yourself. Sit tight.'

18

Ren dialed Daryl Stroud's direct line at Catskill PD. It took a while for someone to pick up.

'Daryl?'

'This is Detective Reed. Lieutenant Stroud is not in his office right now.'

When Caller ID attacks . . . 'My name is Ren Bryce. I believe some of your detectives searched my parents' home this morning? I just got off the phone to my devastated mother and she told me that you had found a T-shirt belonging to Louis Parry in my brother's room.'

'That's correct, ma'am.'

'And were you one of the detectives there at the time?'

'Yes, ma'am.'

'Well, you have made a huge mistake.'

'I'm afraid not, ma'am,' said Reed. 'The T-shirt was where we were told it would be.'

'By *whom?*' Ren's volume shot up.

'A person who called in the tip.'

'So this T-shirt,' said Ren. 'Would that be the one Louis Parry was wearing the day he went missing . . .'

Silence.

'Yeah, I thought not.'

'It was not that exact T-shirt,' said Reed, 'but it did belong to Louis Parry. We have photos of him wearing it. His family also identified it.'

'Think about that for a second,' said Ren. 'What's the scenario? My brother gives Louis a piano lesson, takes off his T-shirt and sends him home bare-chested? Or he asks Louis to ask his mom could he bring an extra T-shirt to piano class? Or, let me see, he jumps over seven garden fences and takes it from Louis Parry's washing line . . .'

Silence.

'What do *you* think, Detective?' said Ren. 'Seriously. Let me help you out, here: someone is setting my brother up. That cold-case deck hit Rikers with major publicity. So I'm guessing you have a sheriff, a mayor, up for re-election? You have a new cold-case department that needs a collar? Or someone somewhere has a personal vendetta against my family. Or maybe some sick fuck in your department did it—'

'Or maybe your brother was a—'

'Don't you fucking dare,' said Ren. 'You are either ignorant enough not to notice that you are being played by one of your colleagues. Or you are ignorant enough to think you have the right man for this crime. Either way, you are a fool.'

She hung up. She stretched out her arms and laid her head down on the cool glass of the table. The door opened behind her.

'Ren, I got that tape in from Billy Waites . . .' said Robbie. 'Do you want to watch it? It's all set up.'

Ren's voice echoed off the glass. 'I like the way you just ignore that I'm splayed out on the table here.'

He paused. 'Yes. Is everything OK?'

She pulled herself up. 'Look at that—' She pointed to a smear on the table. 'That is my makeup. Gross.' She wiped her sleeve across it.

'Your makeup isn't greasy.'

'Hmm,' said Ren. 'Maybe only when its mixed with the venom seeping out of my pores.' She stood up. 'Give me a hug.'

'Sure.' Robbie put his arms limply around her and gave a quick squeeze.

'Just what I needed,' said Ren. *An antiseptic embrace to counter the venom.*

She went into the AV room with Robbie and sat down in front of the video player. Ren took the remote control and pressed Play. There were a lot of shots of Billy Waites from behind. And out of the crowd, eventually, came the handsome face of Gavino Val Pando. The bar was busy, people pushed in front of him, he was not very tall, so it was difficult for him to get served. When he did, he held the drinks above his head and retreated to the booths opposite the bar.

'There,' said Robbie, sitting forward. He pointed to two booths further down and a table with the two teenage girls.

Ren and Robbie watched as more time elapsed, people came and went. And before long, one of the girls was sitting next to Gavino.

'Well, they look like they're having a good time,' said Ren. She pointed to other parts of the room. 'Look at these little tramps. Gavino and his girl look quite sweet.'

Ren hit Pause. 'I presume this is one of those "and the cock crowed three times" things . . .'

Robbie glanced at her. 'If you're asking me is she one of

the ones who denied his existence, yes, ma'am. Her name is Jessica Ellerbee.'

Ren leaned closer to the screen. She pressed Play. Jessica Ellerbee stood up. 'Well, she looks totally wasted,' said Ren. 'Maybe she really didn't remember him. But . . . I doubt it. I don't think a teenage girl is going to forget a cute guy like that. A night in the sheriff's office is a different matter. But, all I will say is: tough. I'll go talk to her.'

'OK.'

'And look,' said Ren. 'Here she is, back from the ladies' room. And who's helping her on with her jacket? Gavino. And they're walking to the door holding hands. What a little gentleman.'

'Do you think this Jessica would have any information that's going to help us?'

'I think there's a possibility the two may have dated,' said Ren. 'Even for a little while. So she could know where he is. What we just saw didn't look like a sleazy encounter that was going to end up in a one-night stand. Or am I being naïve?'

'Actually, that encounter ended with them both being taken into the sheriff's office.'

'Oh yes. I forgot that part.' *Because watching Billy Waites on screen completely threw me.*

'If we show Ms Jessica that tape, she'll talk.' Ren pushed back her chair and stood. 'And we can find out if she's had any contact with Gavino Val Pando any time recently.'

'Great,' said Robbie. He got up and left.

Ren rewound the tape and paused it at the clearest shot of Billy Waites: the broad shoulders, the toned arms, the Diesel ass.

I miss Billy Waites. Even the back view. Or . . . especially the back view.

Ren popped the tape out and stood, holding it, her mind drifting.

Who am I kidding? She turned off the light and walked into the hallway. *I miss Billy Waites: the inside view.*

19

Cliff called to Ren when she walked in. 'Hey, your brother Matt on two.'

Ren got to her desk and picked up.

'Hey,' said Matt. 'I heard about the T-shirt. What the hell's going on?'

'That's what I'm trying to find out, Matt. I can't understand all this. It's insane. Did you call Jay?'

'Yes.'

'What did he say?'

'He's just like us – devastated.'

'In his little emotional HazMat suit.' *Emotions: hazardous materials Jay Bryce.*

'I'm staying out of it,' said Matt. 'Do you have any idea how that T-shirt wound up in the headboard?'

'Not a clue. Did you know that the hole was even there?'

'No.'

'Who goes into Beau's room?' said Ren.

'Just Mom.'

'Do people ever stay over?'

'Riiight. Look, let's face it, Ren – this is all bullshit. It's not like one of Mom and Dad's friends is randomly going to wander into Beau's room, discover a hole in a headboard and put a T-shirt belonging to Louis Parry inside.'

'I know, I know.'

'We're kind of talking a whole lot of nothing here.'

'That about covers it,' said Ren. 'How are you doing?'

'Crap.'

'Is there anything we're not factoring in? Like, has someone got it in for us?'

'What?' said Matt. 'Are you serious?'

'Well, Beau didn't have anything to do with Louis going missing, so *someone* is obviously trying to frame him.'

'No, I get that. But I don't think that means they want to hurt *us*, like, deliberately.'

'Oh, please Like this would have no impact on the rest of us?'

'Maybe whoever it is just does not care,' said Matt. 'Do you think it could be the person who took Louis?'

'No,' said Ren. 'That would be way too risky. You'd sit it out. Especially if you'd gotten away with it for this long.'

'True.'

'Imagine if no one took Louis,' said Ren. 'Like he had an accident, wandered off somewhere, fell down a hole or something.'

There was silence at the other end.

'OK,' said Ren. 'I know.'

'And just one small thing – I do know where you were coming from, because my angel wife has that healing presence, but she is not the one to be helping Mom right now. Basically she is having a "How can we bring a child into this horrible world?" moment and the closer she is to anything like a child going missing or a dead brother or a traumatized mother, the more freaked out she'll get . . .'

'Oh my God, I am so sorry,' said Ren. 'I didn't think of it that way at all. How didn't I, more to the point? I just thought, Who always knows the right thing to do in times like this? And then I thought of you guys. And I figured you would be working.'

'Hey, don't worry about it . . . but if you so much as suggest that again? Bitch, I will cut you . . .'

Ren laughed. 'I feel really dumb. I just . . . Mom adores Lauren. She's the daughter she never had . . .'

Matt laughed. 'Anyway, don't worry about it. It's not a big deal.'

'Please tell Lauren I'm sorry.'

'Oh, Lauren has no idea I'm calling you. I'm her emotional spokesperson at the moment. She didn't say a thing. She was almost on her way to Mom's. I just knew that, when she came back, she'd be haunted in the eye.'

'Nice save, then.'

'I'm sure I won't give a crap about her for the second child.'

'Thanks for making me laugh.'

'Hey, how are you doing . . . about Helen?'

'Awful. The irony is that she spent almost two years trying to squeeze an emotion out of me. She finally achieves that. Then she's gone.'

'That kind of progress can't be reversed that quickly,' said Matt. 'You'll find another therapist. It will be like the movie *Always*. Helen will be watching over you while you find someone to take her place.'

'Oh, God, that movie . . .' said Ren.

'Step away from the video store.'

Glenn Buddy knocked on the open office door and stuck his head in as Ren was hanging up.

'Hello, there,' she said.

'Hey,' said Glenn. 'I spoke with Colin Grabien.'

Am I supposed to know why?

'And he was right about the transaction database.'

What?

'So, yes,' said Glenn, 'the security guy hadn't looked at it.'

The security guy at the warehouse! 'OK,' said Ren. 'That's great.'

'Someone did hack the system – that's how your name showed up as having accessed the premises.'

'OK . . . so . . . someone was deliberately trying to place me at a crime scene?'

Glenn shrugged. 'Do you know why anyone would do that?'

'I have absolutely no idea.'

'Whoever it was, they did a very good job. Colin was able to see that they had been there, but after that, they left not a trace.'

'That's all very odd,' said Ren.

'Anyway, I'm sorry for having to ask you about all that.'

'No problem, Glenn. What else could you do?'

'Thank you.'

'So,' said Ren. 'How's it all going?'

'Well one development,' said Glenn. 'When we looked at Wheeler's office the day the body was found, there were notes on her desk. They looked like they were notes for a book.'

'What?'

Glenn nodded. 'It had "Untitled" on the top, but it was obviously a collection of case studies from her practice.'

'On what subject?'

'The notes were rough. Patient A this, that . . .' He looked at Ren. 'You didn't know anything about it?'

'No. She didn't mention anything.'

'Well, it's good news for us, because it means we can access the patient files.'

Whoa. 'I can't imagine it will be that easy. Even if the notes were in plain view. You'd have a hard time convincing the DA . . .'

'It's done and dusted,' said Glenn. 'It's a very real possibility that Helen was killed by a patient.'

'But is there anything that made you think there was a killer in those notes?' She gestured for him to sit down.

Glenn shrugged. 'Who knows?' He sat down.

'Well, what did they say?'

'Patient A: male, thirty-one—'

'Loner, gun fanatic?'

'I wish,' said Glenn. 'No – male, thirty-one, married, electronic engineer, schizophrenic, aural delusions, substance abuse problems, failed rehab times three . . . Patient B: female, thirty-seven, single, psychotic episodes—'

'There's our killer,' said Ren. 'Crazy woman.'

Glenn shrugged. 'Psychotic episodes, bipolar, leo, Rx Zyprexa . . .' He scanned down the page. 'Patient C: male, forty-two, married, undertaker, history of depression, alcoholic, physically/verbally abusive to spouse—'

Ren pointed to the page he had in front of him. 'What's that leo thing in patient B? I doubt Helen was doing star signs . . .'

'I said LEO. Law Enforcement Officer.'

Thirty-seven, single, psychotic episodes, bipolar, law-enforcement officer, Rx Zyprexa . . .

Ren's stomach turned.

Glenn was still smiling at her, but Ren could barely respond.

'So,' said Glenn. 'There you have it.'

'How will it work from here?'

'A taint team will access the files—'

'A what?'

'A taint team – there's a lot of crap in those files no one needs to see. I might need to know that Patient A's giant white rabbit friend was telling him to kill all medical professionals, but I don't need to know he wore his great aunt's yellow drawers to his sixteenth birthday party.'

'Right.'

'So this taint team goes in, reads the psych files, tries to match them to these Patients A, B and C, and hands only what they see as the relevant parts of these files over to the judge.'

Ren paused. 'And this is so that a defendant – if you find one – can't file a motion to suppress all the information in the files on the grounds that it could taint the investigators and prosecutors?'

Glenn paused. 'I believe that is correct.'

'And these are the only three files you can access? Just because they were in plain view?'

'That's the law.' Glenn shrugged.

'Do you know who's on this taint team?'

'Three prosecutors from the DA's office that aren't involved in the case.'

'For objectivity.'

'Yes.'

'And who's the judge?'

'Douglas Hammond.'

'And . . . how will it all work?' said Ren. 'I mean, the fact that a patient is a patient is privileged information in itself.'

Glenn nodded. 'I guess they feel that the taint team addresses that. It goes no further than those three people.'

'That doesn't sound strong enough to hold up.'

'Douglas Hammond seems to think so.'

'What did Helen Wheeler's assistant say about the book?'

'She said she didn't know anything about it.'

'And you don't find that strange?' said Ren. 'Her own assistant doesn't know?'

'Not really. Wheeler could have just wanted to keep it on the down low before she told anyone what she was doing. The assistant didn't seem very helpful,' said Glenn. 'Wouldn't you think she would want us to find her boss's killer?'

'Yes, but not to destroy all her patients' mental health in the process,' said Ren. 'I doubt Helen Wheeler would want that either. Also, I'm sure if her assistant really thought one of the patients was a threat, she would have let you know.' *I am talking about this too much.*

'Sure,' said Glenn. 'But it's not like the assistant's a trained psychiatrist.'

'True. Right, well, keep me posted,' said Ren. 'Hopefully something will come up.'

And please God let it not be Patient B's deep dark secrets.

20

Gary was the only person in Safe Streets who knew about Ren's condition. She rushed to his office.

'Gary, I was talking to Glenn Buddy and they're going to try and access Helen's patient files.'

'I wish them well.'

'No – it looks like they're able to do it,' said Ren. 'Apparently Helen was writing a book and her notes were in plain view when they went to check out her office. They were like Patient A, male, thirty-one, whatever. Patient B, Patient C. And I'm Patient B.'

'Whoa. What?'

'I am Patient B. No names, obviously, but it is me. Female, my age, law-enforcement officer, bipolar . . .'

'But they're privileged files—'

'These notes were right there on top of her desk,' said Ren. 'Denver PD's got nothing to go on so far, so they're looking at the patient-gone-nuts angle. The closest they can get to a patient at this stage is these notes.'

'You had no idea she was writing a book?'

'No,' said Ren. 'And I would, let's face it, be the last person to give Helen permission to use me as a case study if she had been. I mean, it's not like I'm relatable to in the grand scheme of things. My case study is too unusual. She was probably writing notes first, then going after permission.'

'Has this been confirmed – was she definitely writing a book?'

'I didn't ask, I was too thrown. Glenn didn't seem to be questioning it.'

'Did she have a publisher?' said Gary. 'Is there anything else to back this up?'

'There might be something in her email. But according to Glenn, her assistant knew nothing about it.'

'That just doesn't add up.'

'What can we do?' said Ren.

'I'll talk to Glenn Buddy and tell him not to go after Patient B's files.'

'Can you do that?'

'If he knows I can vouch for Patient B, he'll take my word. He would know that I wouldn't go out on a limb for that. The judge isn't going to have a problem with it – the less he has to wade through, the better.'

'I hope you're right.'

'You don't need to hope.' Gary paused. 'OK, if I'm going to get Denver PD to bury this, you need to tell me what you were seeing Helen about . . .'

'Everything, really,' said Ren.

'Relationships? Your family? Work?'

'Yes.'

'Ren,' said Gary, leaning forward, 'for now, you are one of three patients Denver PD are interested in. I need to be absolutely sure that your file is not going to hold the key to this entire investigation or even be twenty steps behind the key to this investigation. I need to know that we're not all going to spend weeks or months or years looking for a killer who is named on page one of your patient file.'

'No, not a chance.'

'You're off medication at the moment, right? That's according to my last time checking in with Helen.'

'Yes.'

'Were you discussing the work stuff in detail with Helen?'

'Not major details, no. And I doubt she would have taken them down if I was.'

'Different psychiatrists take different kinds of notes. It's their call. Did you notice – did Helen have separate psychiatry/psychotherapy files? Did she have the meds in one file and notes on the talk therapy in another?'

'I don't know,' said Ren. 'Most psychiatrists do nowadays. Or do they? I mean, if you thought someone other than your therapist would be able to access the inner workings of your mind, you wouldn't tell them everything. And if you don't, then your treatment is a total waste. I would have said that Helen was a "one file for Medicaid, one file for me," kind of person. But then again, I wouldn't have had her down as a secret author . . .'

'Do you think there's something up with that?'

'I don't know,' said Ren. 'I mean, why would she tell me about a book if it was early days? Maybe it was just a confidence thing.' She shrugged. 'I really don't know.' *But I'm a little rattled.*

Gary nodded. 'The other thing is – and I'm asking because I have to – was there any tension between you and Helen?'

I must meet all these devils that my family and friends are being advocates for. 'No, no tension at all. We had an excellent relationship. We were like . . .' Ren's eyes filled up with tears. ' . . . friends. It was a professional relationship, but she was like a friend. She was . . . just . . . always . . . there for me.'

Gary reached out for the phone.

'OK,' said Ren, standing up. 'Thank you.' She turned back as she reached the door. 'Do you think Glenn Buddy is going to guess that it's me?'

'Does that matter? The point is you're being eliminated from his investigation. I know a lot of agents, I've moved around a lot. I could be vouching for anyone. And Helen's worked as a shrink for over thirty years in different places, with different law-enforcement agencies and in psychiatric units . . . this could be anyone.'

'OK . . .'

'Don't worry.'

'Thank you,' said Ren. 'I'm heading out now. I've got to speak with a possible girlfriend of Gavino Val Pando . . . Oh and I almost forgot: I need to fly to El Paso Monday . . . please . . .'

21

Jessica Ellerbee lived with her parents in a well-tended middle-class suburb of Denver. She was dressed in an oversized white bathrobe when she opened the door to Ren. Her blonde hair was wet and combed back with a side parting. There were traces of mascara under her eyes. She was wearing glasses with brown rectangular frames. There was an intelligent prettiness about her.

'Hello, Jessica. My name is Ren Bryce. I'm with the FBI.' She held up her badge.

Barely a flicker.

'Can I come in?' said Ren.

'Sure,' said Jessica. 'I'm sorry, I'm just out of the shower.'

'That's OK.'

She brought Ren into the living room and curled up on the sofa, pulling her legs under her and making sure her bathrobe was tucked in everywhere.

'I'll have to sit beside you to show you something.'

'Oh . . .' Jessica sat up and put her feet on the floor, elaborately fixing the bathrobe again.

'Jessica, I'm with The Rocky Mountain Safe Streets Task Force and we're trying to find Gavino Val Pando.'

'Uh . . . who . . . ?'

Bless your heart. 'This guy,' said Ren. She took out her laptop and opened it on the table in front of them. It was already on and the DVD was ready to play.

'We have a great audio-video department at the office,' said Ren. 'They can take video and turn it into DVD so quick, it saved me having to drag you all the way in to the office to have your memory jogged.' She surprised Jessica when she turned to look at her. Neither of them had realized how close they were sitting. Ren shifted back a little. *Away from the startled teen.*

Ren hit the space bar. The screen went from black to snowy to the inside of the Brockton Filly. Jessica went very still.

'I'm sorry,' said Ren, hitting pause. 'But I'm under a little time pressure with these cases and I want to stop you from having to lie when I know you don't really want to. I also understand that this video is probably a reminder of a night at the sheriff's office that you'd rather forget.'

Jessica let out a breath, but said nothing. Ren let the footage play a little longer and paused again. 'This looks like you and Gavino are punching each other's numbers into your cell phones . . .' she said.

'We were playing a computer game,' said Jessica. There was sweetness in her delivery. *But none in the lying.*

'OK . . .' Ren played the tape. 'Wow – a thirty-second computer game? Who won?'

Jessica shifted again in her seat.

'And this is you leaving,' said Ren, pointing to the screen. 'And being ushered back in by the sheriff's department and taken in for under-age drinking.'

'I'm sorry, I can't really remember,' said Jessica.

'That's understandable,' said Ren. 'It looks as though you'd had a lot to drink.' *I had the same problem myself in that bar. And screwed up on a grander scale. But there you go. I'm twenty years older than you. And I have a badge.*

'OK – I met him once,' said Jessica, pointing at Gavino. 'It's all there on the tape. We got separated at the sheriff's office. And I never saw the guy again.'

Ren put a photo of Gavino on the table. 'He's not just "that guy", though, is he?'

Jessica looked at the floor.

'I think I can understand your position,' said Ren. 'You were in trouble last year and I'm sure your parents were mad at you and you swore you'd never give them any trouble again? And now your boyfriend's connected to Denver's Most Wanted list . . .'

'My parents don't even know that he—'

Bingo.

Jessica started to cry when she realized what she had said. She took off her glasses and wiped her tears with the sleeve of the bathrobe.

'Are you and Gavino together?'

Jessica shook her head. 'He . . . we weren't . . . I didn't sleep with him.'

'That doesn't concern me.' *So there's no need to lie about that either.*

'I really didn't,' said Jessica. 'He's . . . so sweet. Was.'

'So, you're not together? I'm a little confused.'

Jessica shook her head, tears streaming down her face. 'No. He left Denver when you guys brought out that list. He left because of me. He knew that my parents would kill me if they found out I was with him . . . if they found out anything about his family.'

'I can understand that.' Ren nodded. 'It must be very difficult for you.'

Jessica glanced at her to check for sincerity.

'Hey,' said Ren. 'I may be over twice your age, but—'

'You're over twice my age?'

Ren nodded. 'But I do know what it's like to break up with a boyfriend. It's the worst feeling in the world. And with you and Gavino . . . well, things are even more complicated.'

Jessica nodded. 'He's not a bad guy. I don't know why you guys are looking for him.'

'Gavino is not safe,' said Ren. 'That is why we really need to find him. He's eighteen years old, Jessica. That's not as old as it sounds. He's vulnerable.'

'Why?'

'For reasons I can't get into. But if you could help me at all, I would be very grateful. When was the last time you were in touch?'

'Two weeks ago.'

Ren let out a breath. 'I really wish you hadn't said that.'

Jessica stared at her. *Nervous eyes.*

Ren slid a list of phone records from a file. 'These are phone records.' *Not yours, but hey.*

'OK, OK . . .' said Jessica. 'So you know we talked this week. But we don't want to break up. We love each other. We don't know what to do . . .' She cried harder.

'Where is Gavino now?'

'He's gone,' said Jessica. 'I don't know where. I promise.'

'Are you sure you don't know where?' said Ren. 'This is really important for him. To make sure he is safe.'

'The worst part is, I really don't know,' said Jessica. 'He wouldn't tell me where he was going.'

'When was the last time you saw him?'

Jessica dropped eye contact. 'Just before you came. He . . . saw you coming up the path. He said he knew you.'

Shit. Shit. Shit.

Jessica looked up. 'He went out the back door.'

22

Ren clung to the steering wheel on the drive to the airport the next morning. Her eyes had started to close within minutes of leaving the house. She had gone back to the office the previous evening and told everyone about Gavino Val Pando. Then she'd endured another night of worry and anxiety. She had cried for Beau and for her parents, for herself, and for Helen. It was all too much. It had been eight a.m. when she finally made a call to her mom.

'Hey, Mom, it's Ren. How are you doing?'

'I'm a wreck. Have you heard anything?'

'No,' said Ren.

'They won't tell us anything. What can we do? There must be something—'

'Mom, I'm afraid that the best thing we can all do is just to wait. I've done everything I can. I called the station and Daryl Stroud is obviously not taking my calls. And at this stage, going near the Parrys is not a good idea.'

'There has to be something you can do.'

'No, Mom. If I go in pushing my weight around, it will just look like I think I'm better than them because I'm an agent and then, on principle, I won't be listened to. Daryl sounds like he has a chip on his shoulder. I don't think I'm better at doing my job than they are. I just think that I'm better at knowing Beau.'

'They don't care about us knowing Beau, do they?'

'No. Every killer has a family somewhere. All the police care about are the facts. And the problem here is that this T-shirt, to them, is a fact.'

'What are they going to do with it?'

'They'll test it for DNA . . . see if they can find any of Beau's DNA on it . . .'

'From where?'

'Hair, sweat, skin cells . . .' *Et cetera.*

'But . . . I remembered that T-shirt. Louis definitely wore it here to lessons. They could very easily find Beau's DNA on it.'

'Even if they did, it wouldn't prove anything, Mom. That can all clearly be explained. And no matter what they find on it, it's not the T-shirt Louis was wearing when he disappeared. Obviously.'

Her mother started crying. 'Why is someone doing this to us?'

'I don't know, Mom. Please don't be upset. It's terrible, I know. But the facts will come out and then we can put all this behind us.'

'Do you know what else the police are doing? They're tracking down all the other kids who Beau taught and asking them did he ever . . .'

'Oh, Mom.' Tears welled in Ren's eyes.

'It's so terrible.'

'At least none of those kids will have anything bad to say . . .' said Ren.

She could hear her mother, sobbing louder now.

'Mom, please, I know it's not easy. But you need to relax. You'll make yourself sick. All we can do is hope that they'll do the right thing.'

'Yes.' Her mother was still sobbing.

'Is Dad there? Can you put him on to me?'

'Sure.' Ren could hear the phone rattle on the table.

'Ren?' said her Dad.

'Hey, Dad. How are you holding up?'

'The whole thing is a nightmare. Your mother is a wreck.'

'Is she listening right now?'

'No. She's gone into the living room.'

'Dad, this did not come from me, but you need to go into Catskill PD and rip Daryl Stroud a new asshole . . . intellectually.'

'What? How do you intellectually rip an asshole?'

'Do it, Dad. Go in, start by playing the frail seventy-seven-year-old and—'

'I just won the Seniors Tennis League last month . . .'

'Oh, for Christ's sake, go in and be Rocky, then. Whatever . . . what I'm saying is, just use that sharp brain of yours to let them know that you and Mom are not two old fools who they can just dismiss.'

'Damn right, we're not,' said her father. 'Your mother and I will go down there—'

'No, no, no,' said Ren. 'Don't take Mom. She'll fall apart. Go alone. And only tell her after the fact.'

'OK. OK.' He sounded unsure. 'Do you think it's really a good idea?'

'Yes. You won't be doing any harm as long as you keep it even-tempered and dignified, which I know you will.'

'All right. I'll keep it real.'

Keep it real. 'Do it for all of us,' said Ren.

He paused. 'I'll give it my best shot.'

'Thanks,' said Ren. 'I've got to catch a flight to El Paso—'

'El Paso?'

'Oh, it's work. A woman down there came across our Fifty Most Wanted on line . . . has some information on one of them.'

'Well, I hope she's all right.'

Aww. 'Love you, Dad.'

'Love you, sweetheart.'

Ren spent the two-hour flight reading through the file on the Sarvas murder/disappearances. Detectives had gone to the Sarvas boys' high school at the time and interviewed all their classmates. Including the boys Ren was flying in to talk to: Luke's friends, John Reiff, Ben Racono, and Mark Bayne. No, they had said, there was nothing unusual in the months leading up to Luke's disappearance. No, there was nothing unusual that day. No, there was no sense that he had family problems. No, he did not do drugs. No, he did not express concerns about anyone following him.

Oh, but there were a few more questions you should have been asked. Or if you had been asked them, they were questions you should have answered truthfully.

The three boys had been placed in separate rooms in El Paso police HQ. They were already rattled that detectives had brought them in to meet with an FBI agent from Denver. And each time Ren opened the door to one of the rooms, each boy looked rattled to see a woman walk in. Ren's script didn't vary and after the question none of them was expecting to hear, the first two boys responded: 'I want a lawyer.'

Ren's last hope was John Reiff. When she walked into the interview room, she was more surprised by him than he was by her. Unlike his dude friends, Reiff was pale-skinned with mousey, shoulder-length hair. *A Twi-hard's dream.* He was dressed in beige linen trousers and wore a light sports coat over a pale pink shirt. His legs were crossed and Ren could see one foot – in green-and-purple retro Nikes – stretching out from under the table. Like the others, he was tall and loose-limbed, making the same effort to appear relaxed.

'John Reiff? My name is Special Agent Ren Bryce.' She threw a small plastic evidence bag on to the table in front of him. He looked up at her, not sure whether he could touch it.

'Go ahead,' said Ren.

Reiff picked it up, but quickly dropped it on the table.

Inside were broken fragments of ceramic. There were two pieces that stood out. One was no bigger than a quarter – a white skull with a black hood. The other piece was a tiny gold crown. They were both spattered with blood.

Ren stared John Reiff down. 'So,' said Ren. 'What happened over spring break?'

Reiff's pallor dropped a few shades on the color chart. He frowned. 'I . . . ' He stared down at the table.

'Do you know where I found this?'

'No,' said Reiff. 'But . . . that's blood.'

'Yes, it is blood,' said Ren. 'It was found in the SUV. Michael Sarvas . . .' Ren paused. 'Did you meet Michael when you used to stay over in the Sarvas house? He was fifteen. Do you remember him?' Ren held his photo in front of Reiff's face until he turned away. 'Michael liked skulls. He had skull T-shirts, a skull keychain . . .'

Reiff's eyes returned to the bag. He looked ill.

'But this is not Michael's,' said Ren. 'This is something a little more sinister, isn't it?'

She studied Reiff. 'You have to suppress your intelligence

too much in this new, dumbed-down teenage world, don't you, John? Well, now is your chance to be smart. Tell me what you know. Take the opportunity.'

Reiff nodded. He stared at the bag. 'It looks like . . . Santa Muerte.'

'Yes,' said Ren. 'Santa Muerte. Saint Death. Patron Saint of drug traffickers and prostitutes and murderers . . . Patron Saint of the dark side . . .'

Reiff held the back of his hand to his mouth. He swallowed hard.

'This tiny figure was found on the floor of the Sarvas' SUV,' said Ren. 'That's Gregory Sarvas' blood, by the way. Do you remember him from when you used to stay over in the Sarvas' house?'

Tears welled in Reiff's eyes.

'Michael was not a drug user,' said Ren. 'I would venture that he was too busy focusing on his studies, had never even traveled anywhere without his parents. I'm guessing that Gregory Sarvas, lawyer, and father of three, was not heavily into blow or meth. So, the question remains: what happened on spring break?'

23

The Sarvas house was in an upscale El Paso neighborhood on a half-acre lot. Access to the property was through a security gate with a keypad.

Ren got out of the car and pushed the call button. Catherine Sarvas buzzed her in. The gates swung slowly open and Ren drove through into a cobbled courtyard and a stunning two-story stucco house.

Catherine Sarvas was suddenly face-to-face with the woman whom she had been happy to talk to only because she was hundreds of miles away at the other end of a phone line. Her hands were shaking.

Ren smiled. 'Thank you so much for seeing me. Sorry I couldn't give you more notice.' She shook Catherine's hand and held it briefly.

Catherine's shoulders relaxed a little. 'Thank you,' she said. She led Ren into the kitchen and poured her water from a jug that had lemons and tiny white flowers floating in it. They sat on high stools across the counter from each other.

Catherine's fine, glossy blonde hair was tied in a pony-tail.

Her freckled skin was tinted with light moisturizer, a little blusher. She was a natural beauty. But her ordeal had clearly taken a toll on her.

'How was your trip?' she asked.

'The trip was fine,' said Ren. 'Catherine . . . I spent this morning at the El Paso police HQ interviewing Luke's friends.'

'Oh.' Catherine looked taken aback.

Ren nodded. 'I had some questions that I needed answers to.' She paused. 'How much do you know about what's happening along the Mexican border?'

Catherine frowned. 'I read the newspapers . . . but what has that got to do with anything?'

'OK, I'm going to have to tell you a few things about Luke that may be difficult to hear.'

'Oh, God . . .' Catherine held a hand to her chest.

'In April last year, Luke told you that he spent spring break with his friends in San Diego, is that right?'

Catherine nodded. 'Yes.'

'He did spend two days there,' said Ren. 'But the boys crossed the border into Tijuana for the rest of the vacation.'

'Tijuana?'

Ren nodded.

'Why would he go to Tijuana? Tijuana is—'

'While they were there,' said Ren, 'they . . . partied hard.'

'Meaning . . . ?' Catherine waited for Ren to answer.

Ren nodded. 'Yes – drugs.'

'But . . . there is no way Luke would touch drugs. Maybe some of his friends, but still . . . we made it very clear to Luke what the dangers of drugs were and what the consequences would be if he went down that route.'

'I spoke with his friends,' said Ren. 'And I'm afraid they confirmed that he had been doing drugs.'

'Did they say that they had too?'

Ren nodded.

'I . . . I . . . just can't believe this.'

'Also,' said Ren, 'there were girls . . .'

'With them?' said Catherine. 'From school?'

'No.'

Catherine stared at her. 'What kind of girls?'

'Prostitutes.'

Catherine looked ill. 'Prostitutes.'

'A couple of the boys, yes,' said Ren. 'But we're not sure exactly what Luke did. They were very drunk, they had been taking cocaine. The boys' memories are hazy. But enough of them have backed up the story.'

'Luke wouldn't need a prostitute,' said Catherine. 'That's ridiculous. He's a very handsome boy . . . Girls lined up for him.'

'Boys get swept up in this kind of environment,' said Ren. 'They were at one of the table-top bars—'

'What's a table-top bar?'

'Like a strip club. Full contact. You can touch the girls. It was that kind of atmosphere. Apparently Luke went outside at one point – halfway through the night. The guys didn't know where he went, but they say he was gone for at least an hour, maybe more.'

'I'm a little lost,' said Catherine. 'What has Luke's trip to Tijuana got to do with what happened to my family?'

'We're not sure yet,' said Ren. 'But what I do know is that the Mexican cartels are recruiting American teenagers to take drugs across the border. There is so much traffic going through every day, Border Patrol just can't check every vehicle and every person in it. A lot of these kids are strapping packages to their bodies—'

'Hold on a second.' Catherine shook her head. 'This sounds

ridiculous. There is no way that Luke would carry drugs across the border for anyone.'

'He may have had no choice,' said Ren. 'Based on something that happened during his trip to Tijuana. It could have been anything. He could have hit on the wrong girl in one of those bars and had to trade his way out of the situation. He could have been forced to do it. Maybe he tried to get out of having to do it and what happened to you . . . and your family was the result of that.'

'Me? But . . . there's no way. Would these . . . drug dealers . . . come all the way up here to do that?'

'Look at Erubiel Diaz,' said Ren. 'And not long ago, San Diego State arrested a lot of middle-class students who were dealing on campus and had direct links with Mexican cartels. We're looking into it. There is also a possibility that Luke willingly agreed to take drugs across the border for money and may have made a mistake that led to something else—'

'Luke did not need money,' said Catherine. 'Once our boys got good grades at school, we were very generous with them. Greg wanted to show them that hard work pays off – he wouldn't give them money for nothing. They valued it. And they valued earning it honestly. In fact, Greg had given Luke a thousand dollars for spring break. Along with what Luke had saved up already, he wasn't in a vulnerable position financially.'

'Mrs Sarvas, I'm trying to help you find out what happened to your family,' said Ren. 'I'm not judging Luke or you or your husband. Luke is young. Kids his age do that separation thing – in his head, he could have been just "driving". These kids can get four or five thousand to "take a drive". If they make it through in one piece, depending on the kid involved, the rush can get a lot of them hooked on doing it, which could account for the several months between the trip to Tijuana and the events last July. He could have been doing this for several months.'

'This is insane.'

'That hour that Luke disappeared when he was in Tijuana?' said Ren. 'That was a crucial gap. And it will be extremely difficult for us to fill in what happened during that missing time. But, I think that whatever happened in Tijuana may be linked to what happened here.'

'But, how?' said Catherine. 'This is all crazy. Luke involved with drugs and prostitutes—'

'Please don't look at it that way,' said Ren. 'He had – from what we can gather – one blowout vacation where he behaved, yes, out-of-character or irresponsibly, but he would not be the first.'

'He was going to study law . . .'

'He might have been overwhelmed,' said Ren. 'Scared he couldn't live up to the behavior expected of a lawyer.'

'But . . . drugs? Sex?'

Ren shrugged. 'Sounds to me like Luke was a good guy who spent one weekend living a very different life—'

'That ruined his whole family's lives, if what you're saying is true.' Catherine started to sob, sucking in huge breaths that after a while, she was starting to lose control of.

Ren poured her some water and handed her the glass.

'I am so sorry. I . . . What about Michael?' Catherine wiped her nose with a Kleenex.

'We don't know,' said Ren. 'I'm sorry. Right now, we're going to presume they're both together.'

'Dead . . .'

'No. We have no reason to believe that.' *Apart from precedent.*

'I know they are alive,' said Catherine. 'I just know they

are. No one believes me. Not even my Church any more. They think I've lost my mind.'

'It's hard for other people to watch the kind of pain you're going through,' said Ren. 'They feel helpless and they just want it all to go away. It's more about them than you. I'm sure no one thinks that you're crazy. They just don't know how to handle your grief. They want you to have hope, but they don't want to be the people to give it to you, because they don't want to be to blame if that hope is shattered. They see how devastated you are now, they can't imagine how bad it would be if you got worse news.'

'This is a nightmare,' said Catherine. 'My worst nightmare.'

'I know,' said Ren. 'But we're going to do everything we can to find your sons. And to find out the truth. Are you OK here? Is there anyone you'd like me to call?'

'No, thank you. I'm fine.'

'I'm sorry I'm going to have to leave this for now.' Ren began gathering her things. 'I don't have much time. I have a flight to catch.'

'That's OK.'

Ren reached out, lay a hand on Catherine's arm and looked her in the eye. 'Don't try to do this by yourself. Please leave this in our hands. You know the situation along the border. You've seen the news reports.'

Catherine nodded.

'These people are animals,' said Ren. 'They are conscience-less.'

'I feel so helpless.'

'You would not be safe down there,' said Ren. 'Which means that you would be no use to your sons . . .' Ren left the sentence open. *I am not the person to give you hope.*

24

The flight to Denver was grounded on the runway for an hour and the air conditioning had died. Ren was trying to read her way out of the panic of being in a small stranger-filled space, breathing in stranger germs. Her eyes started to close. The heat was overwhelming. She flashed back eleven years to Domenica Val Pando's compound in New Mexico – waking up in the mornings, the darkness of the room. The sense of a searing sun behind the shutters.

Don't go there.

Ren picked up her book and started to read again. She could feel a rising tension in her chest. It was the claustrophobia of the airplane, the oppression of being surrounded by people you didn't know.

I am trapped.

Ren was back to the compound again, remembering the tension of the noise – the raised voices of the men, the trucks pulling in and out, the screeching of the birds. And then there was Domenica Val Pando's voice, the type of screaming that would make you rigid.

The first time Ren had awakened, rigid, it was six a.m.

and down the corridor she could hear the stamp of Domenica's foot.

'*¿Qué chingados es esto? No. No. Malo. Malo. Malo. ¿Qué tu madre ni tu abuela te enseñaron nada? Deshaz eso. Vuelve a empezar. Mírame a los ojos, pendeja. Si quieres hacerla en este país cada cosa la tienes que hacer perfectamente. Yo no estaría aquí si no fuera por eso.*'

What the hell is this? No, no, no. Wrong. Wrong Wrong. Did your mother, did your grandmother teach you anything? It looks like this! This! Take that off. Start over! This is how it should be! Do not insult me! Do not insult me! If you want to succeed in this country, you do every job to the best of your ability. Look at me! I wouldn't have got where I am today if it wasn't for that!

Ren had gotten up and tip-toed toward the room. Domenica was making a bed, working the sheets into perfect hospital corners. A trembling sixteen-year-old maid stood watching her.

Domenica was teaching her how to make *Una cama bien echecita! Una cama bien echecita!*

The same type of 'well-made bed' with the constricting sheets that Ren had pulled loose every night before she got in.

Army corners/hospital corners – why would anyone want to recreate those conditions?

Ren was about to go back to her book, but she had set off on a course of pressing down on emotional bruises. Her next one was Ricky Parry. Even his name was trapped in time: Ricky. Ren remembered how hard he tried to be cool. When he was fourteen, he had started wearing tight black jeans, a black leather biker jacket and some sort of metal chain hanging from his belt. He had blond spiked hair, but a chubby, red-cheeked face and two middle teeth that were slightly longer than the rest. A chipmunk in chains.

Ren had liked Ricky Parry. After Beau's suicide, they had come together as friends with a connection they never spoke about – they were the kids who wondered if there was anything they could have done to prevent what happened to the brothers they adored. So they swapped all that wondering time for talking and laughing and watching the same movies and reading the same books. The pretty little dark-haired girl and the sullen blond death-metal dope-head, taking the bus to Albany to shoot pool.

Before Ren realized it, she was replaying the scene in Beau's bedroom, but instead of her mom yelling 'He's dead, he's dead', she was yelling, 'Oh thank God, he's alive, he's alive.'

And they would all rush off in an ambulance and down the hallway at the hospital holding on to the side of the gurney, surrounded by doctors who were doing all the right things. And Beau would be lying in the bed, young and handsome and happy to be alive. And the whole family would collapse with relief and cry and laugh and Beau would promise never to worry anyone like that again. And he would be waiting for her at the airport to tell her that every-thing was going to be all right.

Glenn Buddy was in the office talking to Cliff when Ren got back.

Please don't want to talk to me.

'Hey,' said Glenn. 'Were you out of town?'

'I was in Texas,' said Ren. 'And just off a flight that spent an hour on the runway with no air conditioning.'

'Ooh,' said Cliff. 'Did they not know you were on board?'

'How's everything going with the investigation, Glenn?'

'The taint team was about to go through the files, trying to match A, B and C to their real files, but I got a call to lay off Patient B.'

'Oh,' said Ren. 'Why is that?'

'Beats me,' said Glenn. 'But I have the word of a high-ranking honorable man, so I'm happy with that.'

'Who?' said Ren.

'I can't reveal that part. But . . . I went to Judge Hammond with that request. He says sure, no problem. I'm the investigator, he trusts me and it's one less file for him to go through.'

Ren nodded.

'But here's the weird part,' said Glenn. 'Hammond comes back to me a few hours later and says, actually, the taint team *does* need to look at Patient B.'

What? 'What?' said Ren.

'Hammond said that it was important to know the nature of the psychotic episodes at least. And that if the person was law enforcement, it could give them access to firearms, they could manipulate their position of trust, they could snap under the pressure of the job . . . blah, blah. He said as long as the taint team was looking through the files, pulling Patient B would not amount to too much extra work. Which I guess makes sense.'

No it does not. No. No. No. 'All right,' said Ren. 'Well, there could well be something in there.'

'Maybe, maybe not, who knows?' Glenn shrugged. 'I'm just glad I'm not the one who has to trawl through the crazy talk.'

Ren's mind started to race. The thought of anyone other than Helen looking through her file was nauseating. But why were 'psychotic episodes' so prominent in Patient B's notes? They weren't Ren's most prominent symptom. Now, if paranoia had been mentioned, that would make more sense.

It must be to create drama in the book I'm unconvinced Helen was writing. Everyone loves a psycho. And if it's linked to someone on the right side of the law, it sounds more glamorous to the less clued-in.

Ren took some deep breaths. *It's OK. It will all work out.* The worst-case scenario was that several attorneys she did not know would read her file. They wouldn't find anything to make her look suspicious. She had problems, but she wasn't unhinged. *Yet.* Her 'psychotic episodes' weren't violent. She didn't suffer from aural delusions.

Sometimes, I just believe things that aren't real. Like all of the above.

Gary told Ren she could come in to his office, but he sounded tired. *Weary.*

'I'm sorry, Gary, I know I'm bothering you a lot, but you have got to call Glenn Buddy again. For some reason, Hammond didn't buy eliminating me from the taint team's hit list. They absolutely cannot get access to my file.'

'Calm down, calm down,' said Gary. 'What did Hammond say?'

Ren filled him in.

'OK, I'll call Glenn again. I'll get him to go back to Hammond. How long's the taint team going to be working on this?'

'Max another twenty-four hours.'

'I'm on it,' said Gary. 'But, Ren – what's the worst that can happen? Even if they do read your file, they won't find anything incriminating. I understand the violation. But . . . from what you've said, you have nothing to worry about. If Hammond is sitting with your file in front of him in the morning, I don't think the world is going to end.'

I do.

25

Ren was running an hour late for work the next morning. She had decided to attribute half an hour of it to a fake traffic jam caused by an imaginary truck skidding on dramatized ice. It would take less energy than having to talk about waking up and being hit with a deadening sense of loss.

She called Matt.

'Matt, remember when I moved and I had to send you some of my stuff to store?'

'You mean, do I remember the half of my garage that I have to look at daily, but can never make use of?'

'That would be it,' said Ren. 'Would you mind trawling through that to find something for me?'

'Oh, God. Yes, I do mind. Big time.'

'Please?' said Ren. 'Ugly please?'

'Ugly please. I haven't heard that in years.'

'I haven't said it in years.'

'Were we vile children?' said Matt.

'No. We had this conversation with Mom at the time. The girl who inspired the phrase may not have been the purtiest

142

horse on the carousel, but it's not about what's on the outside. It's what's on the inside. And her inside was uhg-ly.'

'OK, I feel better,' said Matt. 'Because my answer really will depend on whether it's worth the trouble to look for it.'

'It's a little notebook—'

'Right,' said Matt. 'So, not only is it the one thing you have millions of, it is also one that could be naked to the human eye.'

'It's not that little. You're such a drama queen. And it's not in one of the notebook boxes. It's in with the teddy bears.'

Silence.

'Oh, for Christ's sake,' said Ren. 'There are only three boxes of them. The notebook will be the object that is hard to the touch.'

'What does it look like?'

'It is covered in scratch'n'sniff stickers.'

'Ooh. Do you think they still smell?'

'I hope so.'

'What's in the notebook?' said Matt.

'Stuff.'

Matt let out a breath. 'Is this about Louis Parry?'

'How did you know that?'

'Well, Nancy Drew, let me think . . .'

'Ha-dee-ha.'

'But, wow, your Nancy Drew phase lasted way longer than most girls.'

'All or nothing, Matt. All or nothing. Born to sleuth.'

'But ugly please don't tell me you are expecting to find something through the eyes of a nine-year-old.'

Maybe. 'No . . . Just – who knows?'

'Bless your heart. OK. I'll find it,' said Matt. 'Am I allowed to read it?'

'Lord, no! I have no idea what I may have written about you.'

'With the passing of the years and all that, I might be OK with reading "Matt is a jerk".'

'I was nine, not three,' said Ren. 'I'm sure it was like "Matt is inconsequential" or—'

'The fat cat sat on the Matt . . .'

'B'bye.'

'B'bye Nancy—'

'Dwew.'

Gary's office door was open when Ren tried to walk past. She was dressed in a black parka that went down to her ankles . . . and made a lot of noise when she moved.

'Get in here,' said Gary.

Shit.

'Where were you last night?'

Ren frowned. 'Why . . . ?'

'Come here—'

He turned his monitor so she could see. The *Denver Post*'s lead story filled the screen: *Top Judge Dies in Horror Fire*. Under the headline was a photo of Douglas Hammond. Beneath that was a burnt-out car and the caption: *The devastating crash in Genesee where Douglas Hammond died late last night.*

Oh. My. God. Ren leaned on the desk for support. 'Oh my God . . .'

'Yup,' said Gary. He was about to click off the story.

'Wait! Let me read it. What happened?'

'He went off the road, crashed into a tree on his way back from the city. Instant fireball.'

'That is so awful . . .' Ren scanned through the article. 'I . . . it's so hard to believe.' *Holy shit.*

'Yes,' said Gary. 'But it solves your psych-file problem . . .'

Ren looked at him. 'You are sick.'

'Well, it is a temporary solution, you've got to admit . . .'

Ren went to her desk and saw an email from John Reiff via the El Paso PD. She had asked him to send the photos from the spring-break trip to Tijuana.

Ren pulled up the photos of Luke Sarvas and his friends. The first was a close shot, four teenage boys sitting by a pool in T-shirts and shorts, eating burgers, probably drinking the first beer of the day. The next shot was a wide one of a beautiful, sprawling, white stucco multi-story building. Ren paused.

Where the hell were you staying?

It was like something out of Condé Nast Traveler. It wasn't a hotel, it wasn't even like those nice bungalows in the grounds of hotels. It was a stunning luxury house, high over the sea with a spectacular view. Even if Gregory Sarvas had left $20,000 on the hall table for his son, he wouldn't have been able to afford this.

Weren't teenagers supposed to stay in shitholes?

Maybe they were just visiting someone. But as Ren continued through the photos as they moved from afternoon through to evening and into the night, from inside the house and out again, it was clear that this was where the boys were staying. The more empty beer bottles, the more girls and the less clothes and, by the end of the photos, there was a pool full of the happy and the naked.

Catskill '89, red bikini bottoms, legs wrapped around Daryl Stroud.

Ren went through the photos again.

Where did this house come from?

Ren picked up the phone and called John Reiff. He didn't

know anything about the house. He couldn't remember the address. There was no connection to anyone who was at any of the parties. There was no connection to relatives, girlfriends, work prospects, nothing. The accommodation was free. Yes, they all thought that was weird . . . and awesome. And they were all so grateful to Luke Sarvas for hooking them up.

Why can't I go on holiday to a place like that? Or would it mean selling my soul to the devil?

'Are rich people more unhappy than poor people?' said Ren when she put down the phone.

'Shitty things happen to everyone,' said Colin.

'It's just that I seem to be on a run of visiting well-off people in shitty circumstances,' said Ren. 'I'm seeing beautiful houses bearing not-so-beautiful lives.'

'Did you see the photo of Peter Everett's house in the newspaper?' said Cliff. 'Helen Wheeler's guy.'

'No,' said Ren. 'What's it like?'

'Stately.'

'What is Peter Everett's story?' said Ren.

'My wife bored me with this at breakfast the other day. She used to watch *Dynasty* – she can keep track of family sagas. Everett married Lucinda Kerr when they were in their mid-twenties. He was a bright guy, lots of ambition, no money. Daddy Kerr set him up in business in Lupero Technologies. The marriage went down the toilet about ten years ago.'

'Not so happily Everett after . . .' said Ren.

'Despite the money, it was amicable, apparently. Are you looking for something sinister in Peter Everett?'

'No, by all accounts, he is devastated.'

'And apparently he has a multi-confirmed alibi,' said Cliff. 'According to the detectives who notified him, Everett was as shocked as anyone they'd ever seen. He fell apart before their eyes.'

'Wow,' said Ren. 'Sounds as though he was very serious about her.'

Cliff shrugged. 'I guess so.'

'It must have been quite whirlwind.' Ren paused. 'What about his ex-wife? Could that have bothered her? If they were still friends, maybe she might have wanted a reconciliation . . .'

'Well,' said Cliff, 'switching from my wife as source, to some of the Denver PD guys who worked security for the family, Lucinda left Everett.'

'Ah,' said Ren.

'But apparently, she's a very nice woman. She dated one of her security guys. It wasn't common knowledge. He wasn't going around bragging about it.'

'Ah, a love affair.'

'There you go again, Ren,' said Colin from his desk. 'Looking for love in all the wrong places.'

'God, you are painful,' said Ren. 'What happened to you? Who abandoned you as a child?'

'I don't know,' said Colin, 'but do you think you could abandon me as an adult?'

'This cynical bullshit sucks the lifeblood out of me.'

'Everything sucks the lifeblood out of you,' said Colin. 'I'm surprised you have any lifeblood left.'

Ren let out a breath. 'Borrriiiiing.' She turned to Cliff. 'Stand between us. Break up the current.'

26

Ren turned back to her computer and opened a celebrity gossip website.

'Why do people take those kind of photos with their cell phones?' said Robbie, leaning in.

'I know,' said Ren. 'And why is it never the ugly, overweight ones that do it?'

'Is that what you want to see?' said Robbie.

'Maybe . . .' Ren paused.

She could see Robbie's reflection nodding in the screen.

'I mean, the thought of taking a photo of myself in my bathroom mirror . . .' said Ren. 'And is today my day for seeing photos of naked people?'

'Guess who wants to hear the real story of the demise of Douglas Hammond?' said Cliff, putting down the phone.

'What real story?' said Ren.

'It was homicide,' said Cliff.

'No way,' said Robbie.

Ren said nothing.

'What happened?' said Robbie.

'Something was dicked with in the car,' said Cliff. 'And there was an accelerant used . . .'

'By someone clearly not interested in hiding the fact that it was a murder,' said Colin.

'Something is rotten in the state of Denver,' said Ren.

'Colorado,' said Robbie.

Sweet Jesus.

'Glenn Buddy is sure earning his money right now,' said Cliff.

'Does he think Hammond's death is linked to Helen Wheeler's?' said Ren.

'I don't know,' said Cliff. 'We didn't get into it. Give him a call.'

'No, no,' said Ren. 'I'll leave him to it. He's got a lot on.'

Her phone rang. It was Glenn. 'Hey, Ren. I'm sure Cliff filled you in about Hammond. I just wanted to let you know that it's obviously stalled things for a little while on Helen Wheeler's case. A new judge will have to be drafted in. But I'm sure once that happens, it'll speed on up.'

Why would that speed things up? 'Why?' said Ren.

'Well, isn't it a little unusual that the judge who was about to access patient files is killed the day before they're due to land on his desk?'

'I think it was unusual that patients were being looked at in the first place,' said Ren. 'There was no indication that this was linked to a patient. And none of those patients knew that their files were going to be accessed, right?'

Glenn let out a breath. 'None of this looks good. I just need to work out how the hell it all fits together.'

'I wanted to talk to you about something else,' said Ren. 'You guys went through Helen's computer I presume.'

'Yes.'

'Just – was there any trace of her searching any book-related stuff?' said Ren. 'Like had she researched publishers of non-fiction or what length a book like hers should be, et cetera, et cetera.'

'No,' said Glenn. 'But . . . it was early days.'

'Even so, a doctor of sixty-two years of age is not going to even jot notes down without checking first if there's a market for what she's about to do.'

'Maybe she didn't care,' said Glenn.

'Yes,' said Ren, 'but it makes no sense for her to write a book about psychiatry if she didn't plan to share it with people. It's not like there would be a burning urge in her to commit something to paper. I mean, she had already done that by writing patient notes in the first place.'

'But she had to have been writing a book – we found the notes on her desk. And Peter Everett confirmed that she was.

'Well, I just don't get it,' said Ren.

But if it weren't for the notes, no one would be able to access those files. They were the only thing on plain view on that desk. The book notes were the only route to the patient files.

Later that night, Ren sat on the sofa in her pajamas, surrounded by food wrappers. She changed channels, skipping past soap operas, reality television, pausing on true movies and ending up on a nature channel. Ren didn't do nature. *But what the hell is this?*

A crocodile was lying in the sun watching a tiny bird flying in front of him. The crocodile opened its jaws wide. Ren sat up.

'No, little bird, get away from him. Nooo!'

Ren closed her eyes and sucked in a breath. But there was no sound of flapping wings or piercing screams. Ren slowly opened her eyes. The bird was inside the crocodile's open jaws.

What?

Ren turned up the volume and heard the deep voice narrate: *'So can we call the plover bird brave?'*

'Yes, we can,' said Ren.

The narrator continued: *'No, because the plover bird knows that he is safe, because one of nature's unspoken barters was in place before this tiny bird was ever born. This "crocodile bird" feeds on the scraps lodged between the crocodile's teeth. And in return for sparing the bird's life, the crocodile has house calls from a tiny winged dentist. Truly an extraordinary relationship.'*

Ren turned off the television. *And I thought* I *was nuts.*

She went upstairs and started brushing her teeth. *This is the way to do it.* She thought of the strange dynamic between the bird and the reptile. Nature doesn't always play fair. Some day, that crocodile would snap its jaws shut. Ren thought of Domenica Val Pando and the minions who did her dirty work. Some of them flew in, blindly trusting. Some of them flapped about, high on danger. And then there was Ren, always aware that those jaws were programmed to snap shut.

Domenica Val Pando worked by exploiting weakness. And once she had leverage, she could get people to do whatever she wanted. She had top accountants, legal experts, ex-military. She had links to border patrol agents, police and Mexican government officials. Domenica bartered. And the deal was always in her favor. She used illegal immigrants who needed money for medical bills or to pay 'coyotes' – the guides who would bring their families across the border. Ren knew she had given shelter to a businessman on the run from fraud charges.

At some point in her life, Domenica Val Pando had learned the value of leverage. And from then on, that was her personal drug of choice. Not heroin, not coke, not meth.

Leverage.

27

Robbie Truax was sitting at his desk with a giant green hat on. Ren paused in the middle of the floor.

This is familiar . . .

Robbie raised his hands. 'Happy Ren Bryce Day!'

'Oh my God, it is March seventeenth,' said Ren. 'This is officially the first year I have not known about it until the actual day. I am losing my touch.'

'Do you want a Leprechaun hat?'

Not on any level. 'Aw, thank you so much.' She put it on her desk.

'We're all hitting Gaffney's later.'

'Gaffney's is going to be mobbed.'

'That's never stopped you before,' said Robbie.

Ugh. 'True,' said Ren. 'I guess I could use a night of alcohol consumption. I might even wear my hat.' She sat down at her desk. 'I was watching this nature show last night, about the plover bird and the crocodile. Did you see it?' Robbie shook his head, making the green hat wobble. 'They have this weird symbiosis. The crocodile opens its jaws and lets the plover bird fly in. The plover bird pecks at the food caught in the crocodile's teeth. It's like a fly-thru takeaway dentistry thing . . . that could be fatal.'

'Only if you're the bird,' said Robbie.

'What is it with you and crocodiles?' said Colin, looking up. 'Last time it was pedophiles are like crocodiles because they haven't changed since the dawn of time . . .'

Ren turned on him. 'Listen, you – you're either in a conversation or you're not. Just keep your eyes on your frickin' screen. You can't just listen in, then look up every now and then like some little old lady from her knitting.' She addressed Robbie, but spoke a little louder. 'So there's symbiosis,' she said, 'and *anti*biosis. Where two things in close proximity – work colleagues for example – have a relationship where one of them does not benefit at all.'

'Yeah?' said Colin. 'I know which is which.'

'Does the plover bird not get nervous?' said Robbie.

'I can think of easier ways of getting food without picking it out of a crocodile's teeth,' said Ren. 'Think about it – every meal would be stressful. It would be like a first date every time.' She paused. 'But I guess if you're already in his mouth, that would take some of the pressure off later . . .'

Colin looked up.

'All right, all right,' said Ren. 'What's with you giving me the skank eye? Since when did you get all Holy Mary?' She paused. She smiled slowly. 'Oh. My. God. Robbie – Colin Grabien has a lady friend.'

Colin went red.

'Look at you,' said Ren.

Colin smiled despite himself.

'Wow,' said Ren.

'That's great,' said Robbie.

'Yes,' said Ren. 'I must pick her brain. What *is* the best way to go from a standing position to upside-down on the pole without losing any of the money stuffed into your g-string?'

'Yeah? You can ask her tonight,' said Colin.

'Ooh,' said Ren. 'She's coming out? I can't wait. What's her name? Kitty Miaow-Miaow? SINderella?'

'Naomi,' said Colin.

'Nice,' said Ren.

'Now, shut the hell up,' said Colin.

He has it bad. Ren adjusted her screen and dragged her keyboard closer. 'No work-out bag!' she said, turning to Colin. 'That's why you haven't had your work-out bag every morning. You've been staying in bed a little longer . . .'

Colin completely ignored her. She opened Google and typed in Douglas Hammond. She scanned down the news reports. They all seemed to be repeating the same story.

The ninth hit was from a blog and had the headline *Second Tragedy Hits Hammond Family*.

What? What was the first tragedy?

The main article was on Douglas Hammond's car accident. The fact that it was a homicide still hadn't been released. Tragedy number one was detailed underneath in an image of a newspaper article from 1983.

Shock as Woman's Body Found in Everdale Home

Tragedy struck the small community of Everdale yesterday morning when the body of Mrs Trudie Hammond, 26, was discovered by her husband, Douglas Hammond, 28. Mr Hammond, a lawyer, had left the family home at 8 a.m. but returned later that morning to find his wife brutally slain. Their two-year-old daughter, Mia, was found, unharmed, in her crib. Neighbors expressed shock and sadness at the death of the young mother.

There were two black-and-white photos – one of a perfect street marred by squad cars and crime-scene tape. The other was a head and shoulders shot of Trudie Hammond. She had shoulder-length feathery hair, over-plucked eyebrows and thick mascara on long lashes. She had thin but pretty lips and a warm, friendly smile.

Ren scanned through the piece again. It was a preliminary news report; light on details, simplified, tired phrases.

What was the full story?

Ren read through the later articles, they had only a little more information. Hammond had been a lawyer, so if anyone was able to keep the details out of the press, it would have been him. And if they were particularly gruesome, he would want to save that little two-year-old girl from any future pain.

Trudie Hammond's killer had never been found.

Ren dialed Glenn Buddy.

'Hey, Glenn. It's Ren. A propos nothing, did you find any prior connection between Helen Wheeler and Douglas Hammond?'

'No,' said Glenn. 'Nothing.'

'She wasn't an expert witness in his courtroom or anything?'

'No.'

'Under a maiden name?'

'We've gone through all her last names,' said Glenn.

'All?'

'Three.'

'Wow,' said Ren. 'Divorced?'

'Widowed,' said Glenn. 'Divorced by two.'

'She doesn't seem the type.' *I should know this information if she's my 'friend'.* 'She didn't talk about it much.'

'Why would she?'

'How come the three husbands didn't make it into the papers?'

'Well, not in the news reports,' said Glenn. 'But probably in some future special double-page feature on the attractive murdered psychiatrist from next-door-to-the wrong side of town.'

'Could Helen have just walked in on a deal in that parking lot behind her office?' *You're grasping.*

'Anyone dealing by her office would know her,' said Glenn. 'And know to avoid her. She obviously turned a blind eye.'

'I doubt she'd turn a blind eye,' said Ren. 'It was probably that they just did their business when she had closed up for the evening. Did anyone round up some of these dirtbags to "axe" them some questions?'

'Easier said than done.'

She paused. 'What about Helen's two ex-husbands? Not that dumping a body in a warehouse is particularly husband-like . . . but could one of them have hired someone to kill her? Would they have any reason to? I don't know . . . none of this sounds like Helen should be involved in it. I can't get that out of my head. This is Helen Wheeler . . .' She let out a breath. 'It's all so screwed up.'

28

Gaffney's was Irish, loud, friendly and hopping. There was poetry etched into the wood paneling, pictures of Joyce and Beckett, the framed words of the national anthem and photos on the wall of sunburnt Irish bar staff through decades of hot Denver summers.

Colin Grabien stood by the bar with his hand resting on the lower back of a much shorter woman. She was a smiling, low-key blonde. She was understated. She was in her thirties. No glitter, no tits out. Ann Taylor Loft meets Aerosoles meets Seventh Heaven.

Quite the turnaround, Mr Grabien.

Ren walked over to them. 'Hi,' she said. 'You must be Naomi. I'm Ren. I work with Colin. It's lovely to meet you.' *It really is. But calm down, Ren.*

'You too,' said Naomi. 'I've heard a lot about you.'

'And it was going so well,' said Ren.

Naomi laughed. 'It was all good. I promise.' She smiled up at Colin.

'Well, thank you.' *Your new boyfriend is soo full of shit.*

Robbie came in after Ren.

'Hello,' said Naomi. She shook hands with him. 'Nice to meet you, Robbie.'

'You too,' said Robbie. 'Colin talks about you a lot.'

Robbie, you brat. Ren smiled at him, then at Colin. *And in two seconds, Colin will buy drinks for everyone.*

'What are you having to drink, guys?' said Colin.

'Coors Light, please,' said Ren. 'Thank you.' He walked up to the bar to order. Ren turned to Naomi. 'So how long have you guys been dating?' *Because Colin will never tell.*

'Five months now,' said Naomi.

'That's great,' said Ren. She paused. 'Colin's got a huge brain.' *Hello? Why did I say that?* Ren was reminded of her friend looking at a newborn in a baby carriage and saying to the mother, 'What a beautiful . . . blanket!'

'It's going great,' said Naomi.

'I've never seen him like this,' said Ren. *I really haven't. Now, how many other things can I say to fuck him up before he comes back with the drinks?*

Colin had to pry Naomi away from Ren to take her to dinner. Naomi announced that they were meeting Colin's parents. Colin's smile was fixed.

'They are so getting married,' said Ren when they left. 'I love her.'

'She's seems like a really nice lady,' said Robbie.

'Yes,' said Ren. 'For a woman who is obviously on her way in or out of a mental health facility.'

'Just be happy for them,' said Robbie.

Ren paused. 'OK – I'll split the difference. Can I be happy for him? And saddened for her?'

Robbie smiled. 'Look – booth.'

'Grab it.'

People around them were dropping off like flies. Most of them had been there since lunch-time. Robbie was on caffeine-free Coke number three, Ren was on Coors Light number four.

'Oh, what the—' said Robbie. He grabbed Ren's beer. 'It's St Patrick's Day . . .'

'Hey,' said Ren, trying to take it back from him. 'What are you doing? Mormons don't drink.'

'Yes,' said Robbie. 'And we have the highest rate of porn addiction in the US.'

'Are the two connected?'

'I'm just saying,' said Robbie.

'Look who's all disillusioned with the Latter Day Saints . . .'

'No,' said Robbie. 'I just want to have fun.'

'I can't believe I'm about to say this,' said Ren, 'but there are other ways of having fun.'

'I guess alcohol isn't always the answer.'

'Unless the question is "What is Ren Bryce's favorite thing in the whole wide world?"'

Robbie laughed. 'Look, just go with me on this. If there was any person to have my first beer with, it's you.'

'That's grim,' said Ren. 'Like, come here, little boy, have some Jesus juice.' She hung her head.

Robbie ordered his first beer.

Troubling.

When it arrived, he clinked bottles with her and she saw a teenage twinkle of rebellion.

Oh. Dear.

Three hours and four Coors later, Ren was merry and staring across the table at a man she had never met before – Hammered Robbie.

'Ren, you are amazing,' said Hammered Robbie. 'You're,

like . . . amazing.' He pulled her hand in between both of his.

'Ding ding,' said Ren. 'Official confirmation that you are very . . . very drunk.'

'But you *are* amazing,' said Robbie.

'But you *are* drunk.'

'I always think you're amazing,' said Robbie. 'You just . . . are. You come in to the office and it's, like, fun.'

'That's because of Colin,' said Ren.

'He's such a jerk to you.'

'I love it.'

'You're so beautiful.'

Sweet Jesus.

Robbie reached a hand up towards Ren's cheek. She stopped him gently. 'I am taking you home.'

Something flashed in his eyes.

'Nooo,' said Ren. 'I mean you need to get some rest.' *You are not losing both virginities in one night.*

'Come on,' said Robbie. 'How can you be with every other guy and not me?'

'Ouuuch.' Ren pulled on his wrists. 'Come on, mister, get up.'

'I'm better than any of those other guys.'

'OK, Robbie? Listen to me,' said Ren. 'You're like a little brother to me, OK? That's how I see you.'

'What? That is so creepy.'

Maybe from where you're half-sitting half-standing. 'No, it's not,' said Ren. 'Now, move your butt.'

Ren helped Robbie up the path to Annie's and managed to drag him over the threshold.

'Hmm, which room to choose?' said Ren.

'Yours,' said Robbie.

161

'Hey, I thought you were asleep down there,' said Ren, giving him a light kick on the leg. 'That question was for me. Based on what is the easiest room to secure you in.'

'I'm just drunk, I'm not, like prone to violent outbursts. Why did you kick me?'

Ren let out a breath.

'Are you like this when you're drunk?'

No, I would be having sex with someone by now . . .

Ren dragged him up by the arm. 'You've seen me drunk a million times.'

'Oh yeah,' said Robbie. 'Why aren't you drunk tonight? Am I not fun to drink with? Am I a bad drunk?'

'You're a sixteen-year-old drunk,' said Ren. 'Which is adorable. But ultimately making me feel dirty. And not in a good way.'

'You hate me now.'

'Yes, you're right – our prom date is off. I'm going with Biff.'

'Who?'

'Doesn't matter,' said Ren. 'Right – I have chosen your room. It's up one flight of stairs. That's all I'm asking.'

'Where's *your* room?'

'On the eleventy-sixth floor. Come on. Move it. We have work in . . . you don't want to know.'

Four hours later, Ren arrived, showered and dressed, into the guest room. Robbie was on his side, staring her way, gray- and shame-faced.

'Oh, Lawsy.' He groaned and tried to sit up. 'Ohhh.'

Ren sat on the edge of the bed.

'Lay back down,' she said. 'Trust me.' She stroked his forehead with the back of her cold hand.

'Thanks,' said Robbie. 'I am so sorry. And I don't even know for what. I'm an idiot.'

Ren looked at the floor. 'Ah. There's the water I couldn't get you to drink.' She picked up the empty glass and put it on the nightstand. 'You don't need to be sorry, OK? You didn't do anything.'

'I feel like I did,' said Robbie.

'Sweetheart, anyone who says "Oh lawsy" instead of "Oh Lord" or "ye gads" instead of "Oh God" can't be all bad,' said Ren. 'In fact, I'm the one who should be apologizing.'

'Why?' said Robbie.

'I really am every mother's worst nightmare. Even at thirty-seven years old.' She smiled at him. 'You have nothing to worry about, OK?'

'You're just being nice.'

'Like all women who get thirty-year-old beer-virgins drunk.'

'Oh – laughing is not good.'

'Don't puke in Annie's bed.'

'Then get out of my way.'

29

Robbie Truax did not speak to Ren until lunch-time. His gaze moved between his computer screen, the floor and the television.

When everyone else had left the office for lunch, Ren stood up at her desk and held a bottle of water in her hand like an Oscar. 'I'd like to thank my colleague, Robbie Truax, for casting me in the role of the Sensible and the Sober in the movie of the same name. I'd like to thank the Academy . . . at Quantico. I'd like to thank the basement karaoke bar you dragged us into – you don't remember that do you? – where we brought to life that great American country classic "Long-Neck Bottle, Let Go of My Hand". Thank You.'

Robbie smiled at her and relaxed back in his chair. 'Ren, you are—'

'Amazing, I know. I get it . . .'

Robbie blushed.

Ren laughed. 'Dude, you are not used to what is known in Irish circles as "the drink talking". Drink makes you think people are more fabulous than they are and goes on to make you say this out loud to them. That's all it is. So it's your first time: that always hurts a little.'

Robbie looked up. 'You are obsessed with sex.'

'Me? You should have heard you last night.'

'Aw, Ren . . .'

'Aw, I'm sorry,' said Ren. 'I'm only teasing.'

'Why would anyone want to do this to themselves all the time?'

'Those long-neck bottles hold hands real well. And as soon as you let go of one of them, you discover that shot glasses are verrry sticky,' said Ren.

Robbie's face was desolate. 'We were in a karaoke bar.'

'Come on, baby,' said Ren. 'Do that little dance for me again. Shake it, baby! Shake it!'

Douglas Hammond's funeral was covered in a short report on 9 News late that afternoon. According to the newscaster, his daughter Mia was the woman standing at the front door of the church behind her father's coffin, her face pressed against the chest of a man believed to be her fiancé.

Colin stopped what he was doing and watched the screen. 'I didn't know you could be cremated and then buried in a coffin,' he said.

'You're sick.' Ren looked at him. 'I really liked Naomi. She's very warm. She's got a very pretty face.'

Colin took up his new sport of blushing. 'Uh . . . I know. Thank you.'

'She's a keeper,' said Ren. 'So keep her, for Christ's sake. The best advice ever is "be yourself" . . . but that advice is just for other people.' Ren paused. 'In your case? Please don't. For the love of God, don't be yourself.'

Colin smiled.

'Check the Hammond daughter out,' said Ren, pointing to the screen. 'She's a carbon copy of her mother.'

'I've never seen her mother,' said Colin.

'Google Image her,' said Ren.

'I don't care that much.'

'She's like a modern version of her mom.' Ren leaned in a little closer. 'But with her father's eyes.' She glanced at Colin. 'Don't worry, I don't expect you to respond, I'm just entertaining myself.'

Cliff got up from the file cabinet he had been fighting with. 'Da-da! Fixed.' He stood beside Ren and watched the television with her.

'That poor girl,' said Ren. 'I hope I die before everyone in my family. And before all my friends.'

'Look who we have here,' said Cliff, pointing at an attractive, well-dressed woman in the crowd, wearing a beige coat and fur hat. 'That is the famous Lucinda Kerr.'

'Peter Everett's ex-wife?' said Ren.

'Yup.'

'I wonder how she knows Douglas Hammond.'

'Same circles, probably,' said Cliff.

'Just because they're rich?' said Ren.

'It could be anything – legal stuff, charity work, whatever . . .' Cliff shrugged. 'She was at Helen Wheeler's memorial too.'

'Was she?'

'Yup, Glenn mentioned it. Why didn't you go?'

Because I couldn't bear it and conveniently arranged a flight to El Paso the same day. 'Unfortunate timing,' said Ren.

'I guess Lucinda Kerr was there to support her ex-husband.' Cliff gave a shrug. 'Like I said, they were still friends.'

'Maybe she's one of those professional mourners,' said Ren. 'Maybe she's so rich, she has to find new things to amuse herself, and showing up at funerals is her thing.'

There was more footage of the crowd and then it was back to the regular news.

'Did you see Lucinda Kerr's father there?' said Ren, gesturing toward the television. 'Old Mr Kerr?'

'No,' said Cliff.

'She looked like she was on her own.' Ren frowned. 'Wouldn't she have been with her father if it was a business connection? Or a charity thing? Maybe she plays golf with Douglas Hammond. Or . . .'

Cliff looked at her. 'Sometimes your mind moves at such a speed, I feel like I'm on a car chase and you're all over the road, taking all these side streets and I keep losing you . . .'

Mortifying.

'Ren Bryce, you are actually blushing,' said Cliff. 'I meant it as a compliment. It's like you have these bursts of thoughts and—'

'Maybe I shouldn't say them all out loud?'

'Exactly,' said Colin.

Cliff put his arm around Ren and squeezed her shoulder. 'There are always a few gems in there.'

'Your screwdriver is sticking into me,' said Ren.

'Nah,' said Cliff. 'I'm just happy to see you.'

Ren arrived home late that evening. As she walked up the path, she could see a yellow envelope lying on the wet tiles of the front porch. She picked it up and brought it inside. She dropped her bag and slid out the thin document. The title page was on Helen Wheeler's headed notepaper with *Patient: Ren Bryce* written underneath.

Ren's heart started to pound.

What the fuck is this?

She started to read it. *Oh no.* These were Helen's notes. And they were not in shorthand.

167

Ren's stomach turned. Her legs were weak, her hands shaking.

What is *this? Who left this here?*

She grabbed the envelope and flipped it over as if there would be a sender's address. Anything to delay reading what was in front of her. She eventually put the title page to one side and started to read:

Patient B, Special Agent Ren Bryce, first presented to me in 2007, having spent the previous nine years under the care of three different psychiatrists for bipolar disorder. During that time, she spent periods on and off medication, but declined psychotherapy until a month into her treatment with me.

OK . . . that's OK.

Ren continued to read.

Ren Bryce has expressed overpowering feelings of guilt following a serious transgression during her time as an undercover agent with the Val Pando crime organization in 1998/9. Agent Bryce concealed vital information from her contact agent and still appears to be distressed by this. This was a period of high stress in Agent Bryce's career and leaves me with concerns as to her capacity, then and now, to perform as an agent.

In 2008, Agent Bryce carried on a sexual relationship with a confidential informant during a homicide investigation in which he was a suspect. In the course of this, she experienced delusional thoughts and repeatedly engaged in risky behavior.

During this time, Agent Bryce has consistently refused medication and after a recent period of psychosis, failed to fill her prescription for the anti-psychotic drug Zyprexa.

Following a careful analysis of Agent Bryce's mental state, my recommendation is that she should be withdrawn from service as an FBI agent, pending further notice.

It is my considered opinion that Agent Bryce is a danger both to herself and to her colleagues.

Ren sat motionless on the stairs. She stared at Helen's signature at the bottom of the page. And she knew one thing: this could not have been written by Helen Wheeler.

Could it?

30

Billy Waites was sitting at a table in the corner of the Hotel Teatro bar, where he and Ren had once spent the night. He had traveled from Breckenridge and had made it in the hour-and-a-half he had promised when she made the emergency call.

When she saw him, something shot through Ren that she couldn't file; love, lust, sadness, pain. Billy looked up – nothing else moved, just those pale eyes.

Lust, sadness and pain. Love? There were too many months of burying the break-up to work that out.

Billy Waites had that tattooed thing. Ren hated the idea of tattoos, had talked friends out of getting tattoos, had talked herself out of getting a tattoo. But the right kind of man with a tattoo? It was a beautiful kind of dirty. And to contrast with the worked-out body and the ink, Billy Waites had a smile like a child on his birthday. *Heart-melting.* Ren smiled back.

Here we are again.

Billy pushed his big parka up along the leather seat to make room, but Ren sat opposite him.

'Hello, mister,' she said.

'Hello,' said Billy. 'Not even a peck?'

'I'm too nervous. Look at my hands. What's wrong with me?'

'Aw,' said Billy, and squeezed them between his.

'Thanks. You look . . .' *amazing* ' . . . great.'

'So do you.'

'Ugh,' said Ren. 'I can not thank you enough for meeting me. I'm a mess.'

'How are you doing?' said Billy. 'What's up?'

'Oh, Billy. Lots of things.'

'Well, it is *you*, after all.'

'I know.' Ren paused. 'It's so great to see you.' *And already it's killing me.*

Billy was two feet away, across the table. How strange life is. A body you knew so well, but you no longer had the right to touch the same way. That strange physical space between two people that they spend their first encounters trying to close. Then, bam, it's over and you bounce back to where you were in the first place as if it had never happened.

The arms. 'I'm sorry,' said Ren. 'I don't know what it is about your arms.' *They fuck with my head.*

Billy glanced down at them. 'And I'm not even flexing.' He flexed.

'Don't do that,' said Ren. 'I'm not in this for your personality.'

He laughed. 'In what?'

'Ooh,' she said, 'you're quick.' *Quicker than me, clearly.* She let her head fall to the table. He rubbed it gently. She looked up at him. 'You're like a bottle of champagne that I don't want to pop the cork on.'

'So you're saying I don't exist?'

Ren laughed. 'Just – if I open the bottle . . .'

'It'll spray everywhere?' said Billy. He raised his eyebrows.

'Why did I say champagne?' said Ren. 'In fact, why did I come out with a Danielle Steele-style analogy in the first place?'

'Yes. I think your relationship with champagne is more clear-cut than ours ever was . . .'

'That's kind of mean,' said Ren. 'And true.'

'At least champagne never makes you feel bad.'

'Hey, neither do you.'

'But caring about me did.'

'Big fat no to the therapy,' said Ren. 'I'm currently of the opinion that dwelling on my problems is making me feel worse.'

'So, what's up?'

Ren looked around. 'Maybe we should go somewhere quieter. I'm not comfortable talking here. Why don't you come to the house I'm sitting? It's not far.'

'Sure.'

He locked eyes with Ren; beautiful nervous eyes. A muscle on his bicep twitched. Ren's gaze was drawn towards it.

She looked at him again. Billy Waites smiled.

No. More. Men: Rewind. Pause.

Ren and Billy sat side by side on Annie's deeply uncomfortable sofa.

'OK. Billy, I'm in trouble.'

His eyes immediately filled with concern. 'What is it?'

'I'm not sure.' She looked around. 'OK . . . a file arrived on my doorstep tonight – a file whose contents I was familiar with. I'm talking about a personal file that no one should have had access to, but they did. Someone has doctored the file. Very well. Elements of truth and then total bullshit. But

I'm the only one who can tell the difference. The person who was supposed to have written the file is dead. And I have no idea if anyone else has read it. But, if a particular person has read it – as may be the case – I'm screwed. Because that person is also dead. So . . .' She shrugged.

'You're shaking.' He took her hands again. 'You need a drink or something. You're in shock.'

'I . . . Billy . . . I'm looking at . . . it's all over for me. I'm . . .'

'Do you want to tell me what this file is, Ren? And who these people are?'

Oh, God. If I say them out loud, then those names are out there. And what if I can't even trust you?

They sat in silence until Ren finally started to talk. 'My psychiatrist, Helen Wheeler, disappeared the night of my last appointment with her. My swipe card was used to gain access to the crime scene the night before the body was found. The judge, Douglas Hammond, who wanted to access Helen's patient files was murdered. And my doctored psych file is like one big finger pointed in my direction. And . . . there's other stuff. None of it looks good.'

'Who do you think is doing this?'

'I don't want to say. Until I have at least some proof.'

'There is a way out of this, Ren. I know there is. We will work something out here. I'll do what I can to help you.'

'I'm worried that there'll be more,' said Ren. 'I need to get a few steps ahead of everyone, so I can find out what the hell's going on.'

'It sounds like the first thing to do is to stop anyone getting access to these files.'

'Which has been made very hard by the judge dying . . . And that's not the only thing . . .'

She told him about Beau. Billy wrapped his arms around

173

her and held her until she fell asleep. He carried her upstairs, put her to bed, kissed her forehead and slept in the bed beside hers.

31

Ren woke up, momentarily confused by the rumpled bed beside hers. She got dressed in jeans that hung from her hips, a gray sweater and pink socks and went downstairs. As she reached the hallway, she could hear Billy opening the refrigerator, then opening and shutting cupboards.

'Unless you're planning to bake a cake, I'd venture you'll come up empty in this kitchen,' said Ren.

'But you cook,' said Billy, turning around.

'Not when (a) I'm too busy and (b) I'm falling apart. My appetite is gone.'

'If I get supplies, will you eat something?' said Billy. 'Pancakes?'

'Ooh. I don't think I've ever said no to pancakes.'

'OK.' He went to walk past her.

'Can I have a hug?' said Ren.

He stopped. 'Sure you can.' He wrapped his arms around her and squeezed her tight.

'Thanks,' said Ren, stepping back. She sat against the kitchen table. 'Oh, Billy. I feel paralyzed by all this.'

'Don't worry. It will all work out.'

'God, I really want it to. I want to be fast-forwarded to a time when this is all over. But you know when you try to fast-forward a DVD, only you hit the next episode button instead and suddenly you're past the end and the screen is black . . . And there's no more story?'

'And then you hit the menu button and the little circle that says it's not allowed. Or you end up in the extras, finding out more of the plot than you need to before you've seen it and then—'

Ren's eyes narrowed.

'Hey, I love how you explain things to me using everyday technological devices,' said Billy.

'Do I do that a lot?'

He nodded. 'But don't stop. Remember you described your reaction to something as "like the noise that Skype makes when it opens"? I loved that.' He caught her expression. 'OK, back to the DVD. Can you see the theme in all this?'

'Yes,' said Ren, eventually. 'A loss of control. Being at the mercy of something else.'

Billy nodded.

'But that's just who I am,' said Ren.

'Which is fine. But . . . workable on . . .'

Ren said nothing.

'I mean this in the nicest possible way, Ren, but you're a little spoilt with the control thing. You have that power automatically with your job. And, let's face it, you call the shots in relationships a lot.'

'That sounds terrible.'

'I don't mean it to.'

'And it's not true.'

Billy paused. 'OK . . .'

'I don't like that. I don't want to be that way. Anyway,

we're getting sidetracked. None of this is about relationships. Someone is trying to fuck me up. And I'm here having distracting conversations with you. I am a pro at that, Billy. I am all-singing, all-dancing, all-dying inside. And I am close to losing my mind.'

'You're not going to lose your mind, Ren.'

'Do you know something?' she said. 'Mazes freak me out. They always have. There was a maze near my home when I was a kid and in summer, lots of the other kids had their birthday parties at the park where it was at. And I would play sick. Every time. I would even play sick in the middle of the parties. Well, after the cake, at least . . .'

Billy smiled.

'Mazes terrify me,' said Ren. 'And however many years on, they still do. And right now, I feel like I'm in one. Dropped right into the middle. Everywhere I turn, I'm hitting a wall and the walls are moving towards me and the ground is shifting under me and the sky is slowly coming down and the oxygen is being sucked out of the air.'

'Well, you're safe here. It's a big house, but it's fairly easy to navigate.'

Ren looked at him. 'Can I ask you a question?'

'Don't tell me – you want me to pick you up a compass at the store.'

'Nope,' said Ren. 'I would like to know . . . why did you sleep in the other bed last night? I'm not saying I wanted anything to happen . . .'

He smiled. 'I wasn't going to take advantage of a woman in distress.'

'Aw.'

'But also . . . I'm seeing someone.'

Something sank inside Ren. *Nooooo*. 'Oh. Wow. Since when?'

'Not long. Just two, three months. I'm not sure if it's going anywhere, but she's a very nice lady and I wouldn't want to hurt her like that. Or you. Or me, for that matter.'

'Well, she's a very lucky lady.'

Is she prettier/thinner/funnier/taller/smarter/sexier/more emotionally stable than me? Does she have better skin/hair/teeth/clothes/shoes/body? 'What's her name?'

'Edith.'

Oh. Dear. 'That's . . .'

'Beyond your powers of laughter suppression clearly.' Billy smiled.

'You have to admit, it's a bummer of a name.' Ren paused. 'Like I can talk.'

'Well, she doesn't look like an Edith.'

Which means she is prettier/thinner/funnier/taller/smarter/sexier/more emotionally stable than me with better skin/hair/teeth/clothes/shoes and body.

Billy went to the store, came back and made breakfast. Ren managed to eat. They sat, talking, in the living room.

'Hey, look at you,' said Billy, pointing to the Bryce family photo. He walked over. 'What a cutie.'

'Mom made that suit, before you ask.'

'Who's this dude?' said Billy, smiling back at her.

Ren leaned over to see where he was pointing. 'That would be my eldest brother, Jay.'

'You've never mentioned him. So tell me – did he run away and join the circus in those pants and you've never seen him again?'

Ren laughed.

Billy sat down beside her. Ren slid back into the corner of the sofa and turned to face him. 'Jay and I . . . don't really get along.'

'Ah,' said Billy. 'Why?'

'Well, he broke my cardinal rule. He betrayed my confidence a few times too many. And I . . . don't trust him. We just clash. Much like our outfits in that picture. I never realized that. There it is, preserved in a photo – Jay and I clashed from very early on.'

'Go on,' said Billy.

'OK, this sounds petty, but it sums him up . . . when he was fifteen, he started drinking, just a little, because our parents were so strict. But then he was like all his friends and he'd go out and get wasted every weekend. He drafted me in to lie for him, hide empty bottles, distract my parents when he was climbing in or out his window. I defended him if they asked too many questions. I hated it. I'm a bad liar and I used to be so stressed out because of it. Like, physically sick with worry. Then, when I was sixteen, I went to my friend's house and we had two beers from her parents' liquor cabinet. Two beers. On the way back to my house, I met Jay. The following day, I had to sit in my living room with my parents, my best friend and her parents to listen to this lecture on the dangers of alcohol and the disappointment they all felt in knowing that their daughters had been stealing. I found out later from Matt that Jay had gone to my parents and said "I think Ren has been drinking." Can you believe that?'

'That's pretty shitty. But it can't have been the only reason you're not close.'

'It just shows the type of person he was,' said Ren. 'And still is. He over-rides everyone. He decides what is right. So if you tell him not to tell someone something, he will say "sure" and then you'll find out he has told them, because *he* believes they should know. I tell him almost nothing any more.'

'That's a shame.'

'I know. I've tried to reach out. He's . . . he's just in his own world.'

'Right.'

'I just think you have to accept what's important to other people and respect it, whether you understand it or not. Trust and confidence are important to me, so Jay should respect that. Even if I tell him something and he is thinking "Wow, why would Ren not want to tell X about her promotion in work?" He should just know by me telling him to keep something quiet, that I have a reason for that. And it's a reason I don't have to tell anyone if I don't want to.'

'Do you two talk much?'

'We talk when people die.'

'Any people?'

Ren smiled. 'I know it sounds terrible, but even when Jay asks me how I am, it just seems weighted with . . . I don't know . . . judgment.' She shrugged.

Billy said nothing.

'Maybe he needs to get to know you a little better,' he said.

'But if he did, he'd walk away thinking he knew more about me than I did. I swear to God.'

'Aren't you being a little hard on him?'

'Aren't you being a little annoyingly on-his-side about him? I don't want to talk about Jay any more, because I don't want to get mad at you.'

'OK. I'm just trying to show you his side.'

'Why?'

'I don't know. I don't have brothers and sisters, so I guess—'

'You romanticize them. I love Jay dearly. I wish we got along, I wish it more than you do.'

'OK.'

'He's teetotal too.'

Billy laughed loud. 'And so we come to the real problem. He makes you feel bad for drinking.'

'Very funny.' Ren let out a breath. 'His last hurrah was at Beau's funeral. In spectacular fashion. Enough to make him never want to drink again.' She paused. 'I'm surprised anyone who witnessed it ever wanted to drink again.'

'Ooh,' said Billy.

'I have to say – I can't blame him. Beau's funeral was so weird.'

'How?'

'It kind of drew some people to it and repelled others. And there was this strange sense of shame hanging over the whole thing. I remember sitting in the church and wanting to get up on the altar and just shout at everyone, "What is wrong with you all? This is not shameful. It's tragic, it's devastating, it should not be how anyone's life ends, but it's a fact. And Beau is not the only depressed person in the world and there are probably people sitting here today who have thought about committing suicide. Yup, he committed suicide. Everyone – after me – Beau committed suicide. You can say it. No one's going to die."'

Ren glanced at Billy. 'You know what I mean. And the worst part was the people who didn't show. I mean, sure, they may have seen this big black sinful cloud hanging over our family, but what happened to compassion and kindness? These were some of the people that Mom had been so good to. Or Jay had mowed their lawn or Beau had taught their grandchildren . . .'

Ren sat in silence. Her mind wandered to another funeral – Douglas Hammond's – and the shame-free sorrow that everyone was free to feel because his death wasn't 'at his own hand'. People had no problem showing up at that funeral.

Ren paused.

But still, why was Lucinda Kerr there? Lucinda Kerr who had been married to Peter Everett who had been dating Helen Wheeler who had been murdered and whose files had been due to go to Douglas Hammond who was murdered and whose wife had been murdered almost thirty years previously.

WTF?

32

Mia Hammond was a twenty-nine-year-old orphan. There was something so poignant about it. Ren didn't want to intrude on her grief, but if she ever let that feeling stop her, she would get nowhere. Sifting through wreckage was all part of the job.

When Ren introduced herself, Mia Hammond looked like she could have laid on the ground right there and curled up into a ball.

'I'd just like to speak with you about your father's funeral, please,' said Ren. 'It won't take long.'

Mia looked surprised. 'His funeral?'

Ren nodded. 'I saw that Lucinda Kerr was there. Can I ask how you know her?'

'I don't, actually,' said Mia. 'I recognized her, obviously, because of who she is. I just thought that maybe she knew my father through work. But she came up to me afterwards and said that she remembered me from when I was a child. She and her husband used to live on our street. I had no idea.'

The Everetts lived on the same street as Douglas Hammond?

'Did she say when this was?'

'She said I was a toddler. So that would have to have been around 1983, because we moved shortly after mom died. Obviously, my father didn't want to stay in the house.'

'That's understandable,' said Ren.

'Sorry, but what has Lucinda Kerr got to do with anything?'

'I'm information-gathering at this point,' said Ren.

'For what?'

'I can't say.' *I'm not sure myself* . . .

Peter Everett's house was another in Ren's straight run of beautiful homes with not-so-beautiful stories to tell. He invited Ren in and led her to his study, a room with a glass wall that overlooked a softly lit pool area surrounded by pale granite flagstones, dotted with patches of snow. The house was tastefully designed and decorated, but the sadness was overwhelming.

Or maybe that's because I know what he has lost.

Everett's face betrayed it all – he was a very attractive man being seen at his worst – exhausted, puffy-eyed, hollowed out. He was tall and slim with dark hair in an old-fashioned side parting. He was dressed in a pink V-neck cashmere sweater with a white T-shirt underneath, a pair of dark blue jeans and brown loafers. Despite the preppy look, Ren imagined he drew all kinds of women to him without even trying and without even realizing it.

'I'd like to talk to you about Helen,' said Ren.

Everett nodded, but looked as though it was the last thing he wanted to do.

'She was a wonderful person,' said Ren. 'You must be devastated.'

He seemed thrown. 'Yes. I . . . you knew her?'

'I always had a lot of time for Helen.' *Scheduled time.*

He rubbed his face with his hands. 'Everyone did.' His voice cracked.

Ren could barely hold it together herself. 'Mr Everett, I wanted to talk to you about the book you said Helen was writing?'

'It was in its very early stages.'

'Did Helen say what the book was about?'

'It was about her practice, about the treatment of a broad spectrum of mental illnesses, about medication versus talk therapy, et cetera.'

'And when did she start writing it?'

'I don't know,' said Peter. 'I wouldn't say she had particularly started writing it. It was more at the thinking stage. Maybe for the past few months.'

'Did she have a publisher?'

'No. But I don't think that would have been a concern at that stage. What she'd really been working up to was putting together a synopsis and a pitch.'

'And had she requested permission from any of her patients for their details to be included?'

'As far as I know, not yet,' said Peter. 'It wasn't going to be public knowledge any time soon. Helen wouldn't have dreamed of releasing anything without a patient's permission. And a publisher would certainly never publish without it. She was even careful about the initial notes she was making.'

Not careful enough. 'Are you saying that no part of the book was actually written?'

'The only thing she had done were the notes that you have. She and I were the only ones who knew that that was what she was doing.'

'Yes, we have the notes, but there's not a lot of information in them.'

'That doesn't surprise me. Helen was discreet . . . obviously.'

Ren nodded. She stood up. 'Thank you for your time.'

'May I ask how the book is relevant to the investigation?'

'I'm afraid I can't disclose that information,' said Ren. 'Oh, by the way, I was just speaking with Mia Hammond – Douglas Hammond's daughter . . .'

'The judge?'

'Yes,' said Ren. 'She told me you used to be neighbors.'

'A long time ago.'

'You weren't at the funeral.'

'No.'

'Your ex-wife, Lucinda was there. She went up to Mia Hammond and introduced herself.'

'Ah,' said Peter. 'That's the type of thing Lucinda would do. Yes. We lived in Everdale on the same street as the Hammonds. It wasn't for long. I guess it was just a year or so.'

'Were you living there when Trudie Hammond was murdered?'

'Sadly, yes,' said Peter. 'It was a terrible time.'

'Were you in Everdale for long after that?'

'No – Lucinda was pregnant with our daughter. Everdale was only meant to be a temporary home, while our new house was being built.'

'Ah,' said Ren. 'Did you know the Hammonds well?'

'No. They were across the street and down a few houses. But they seemed like a nice family.'

'OK,' said Ren. 'Well, thank you for your time.'

'That's no problem,' said Peter. 'If there's anything else I can do . . .'

Ren shook his hand and left.

* * *

Gary called Ren into his office when she arrived back.

'Good news,' said Gary. 'Looks like your files are going to remain secret for a long time. One of Helen's patients got wind of the cops wanting to access privileged files, the word spread and a whole bunch of patients' lawyers waded in.'

'Thank God,' said Ren. 'Thank God. I wonder how it got out.'

'Could've come from anywhere. Helen's secretary would be a strong candidate . . .'

'Yes.' *Go, Sandy, go.*

'So there you have it.' Gary nodded. His we're-done-here nod.

Ren stood up. 'You are . . .' *So clinical. And impassive.*

Gary looked up at her. 'What?'

'You are . . .' Ren paused. 'Do you play poker?'

Gary laid his pen down. 'Yes. As a matter of fact.'

'Do you win a lot?'

'Yes. But I don't play for real money.'

'Isn't that part of the fun?'

'Maybe to some people.'

'And when you say "people", you mean "losers"?'

Gary was back writing. He didn't look up. 'Every opponent of mine is a loser by definition.'

Men are simple folk. Compete. Win. Repeat. Apply liberally to all areas.

33

Ren went to her desk and sat very still, her hands in her lap, her eyes straight ahead, staring at nothing.

My file is safe.

She couldn't quite believe it would stay that way. She pulled her keyboard toward her and typed Trudie Hammond's name into Google. Almost a decade ago, Trudie Hammond's murder file had become the responsibility of the Jefferson County Cold Case Unit – a one-person unit run by a detective Janine Hooks. Ren went to the website and scrolled through the forty cases posted on it – missing persons, homicides, unidentified remains – the text broken up with images of the victims or their possessions or their reconstructed clay faces. She scanned through the reports. Trudie Hammond's case was the twelfth one in and read like the news report. There were three other cold cases listed whose victims had last names beginning with H. Ren picked one at random and studied it. Then she grabbed her jacket and purse and headed for the door.

The Jefferson County Cold Case Unit was housed in a government complex off Main Street in Golden. Ren had been there before – to Dr Barry Tolman's office, the pathologist to sixteen counties, including Jefferson. Ren went to reception and asked for Janine Hooks.

There was a temp on reception who looked as though she had never used a phone, a piece of paper or a pen before. She managed to get through to Hooks on the third attempt. She turned to Ren. 'She'll be free in about ten minutes. Are you OK to wait, ma'am?'

Ma'am. 'Yes, thank you,' said Ren. 'I'm going to go outside for a cigarette.'

'They're not too keen on smoking out front,' said the receptionist, as if she was delivering a death notification.

'OK,' said Ren.

She went out the front door and took a cigarette from the pack she kept in her purse for use whenever she needed it. Real cigarettes, fake uses. She headed round to the back of the building where two PAs stood smoking and bitching. They gave Ren a light and, in pushing a few buttons on a keypad on their way back in, provided some helpful information she didn't even have to ask for. She stubbed out the cigarette, popped two sticks of cinnamon gum in her mouth, and strolled around to the front entrance and up the stairs to the second floor.

Janine Hooks worked in a blow-your-brains-out office: small, brown, beige, seventies. Hooks was sitting in the visitor's chair, facing her own empty chair. From the back, she looked like a teenage boy, her neck skinny and sinewy, her head small with short, wispy dark brown hair. She turned at the sound of Ren's footsteps. She had huge brown eyes, faintly shadowed, sharp cheekbones and a large, wide mouth with prominent teeth and full, angular lips. Individually, it was a strange collection of features, but it came together to create a pretty vulnerability. If dogs could look like their owners,

Janine Hooks could look like her job – there was something lost in there, waiting to be saved. She was a living cold case.

'Hello,' said Hooks, standing up, trying to repackage a sandwich with her left hand while holding out the right one.

Ren was thrown by Hooks' body. She wondered if Hooks was used to people having a delayed reaction to her – she was remarkably thin. *Probably anorexic.* Her shirt was tucked in as far as it could go, her pants tied with a belt that she probably had to cut in half to fit. She was immaculately dressed. She offered Ren coffee and revealed a warm smile. There was something likeable about Janine Hooks.

'Hi,' said Ren, carefully shaking Hooks' tiny hand. 'Ren Bryce from Safe Streets in Denver.'

'Yes, sit down, sit down.'

'I'm sorry to arrive unannounced, but I read that you are investigating the . . . Hopkins murder from 1989 and I was wondering if I could ask you a few questions about it.'

'Why?' said Hooks. She didn't take her eyes off Ren.

Shit. 'I read online that Hopkins was shot and his body was dumped in the Golden River. I was wondering if you could give me any further details on that. Last year, I worked a case where the victim was dumped in the Clear Creek River. Dr Tolman performed the autopsy, in fact, if you'd like to check with him.'

'So, what . . . you're looking at body dumps in rivers as being connected?'

'Yes, actually,' said Ren. 'Why not?'

'Sure, but . . . ' Hooks shrugged, got up and walked over to a cabinet and pulled the file. Hopkins, filed under H. Hooks' files were organized by the victim's last name, not the year of the crime, not type of crime, not in a file cabinet hidden away in a back office – just right here in this grim little space.

She opened the folder. Her tiny hands had long, delicate fingers. 'OK, let me see . . . here it is. GSW—'

'My guy was shot close range, back of the head with a .22,' said Ren.

'Nope,' said Hooks. 'Hopkins was a chest wound, 45 caliber.'

I could care less. 'Ah. OK. Well, thank you for that.' Ren stood up and said her goodbyes before Janine Hooks had the chance to ask her why the hell she didn't just call.

Ren was drawn to cold cases, but to investigate them every day would have driven her crazy. Knowing that, before you even started investigating, many people – experts with the same information at their disposal – had tried and failed, had a certain predestination about it. The older the case, the more likely it was that the evidence had been compromised, the original investigators were retired or dead or the witnesses were dead. If anyone was still alive, their memories had most likely faded.

What lay in Trudie Hammond's file could be something or nothing. What it could not be was 'asked for'. If she'd walked into Janine Hooks' office with a request for Trudie Hammond's file right before the story broke that Judge Hammond had also been murdered, Ren might as well have walked into Denver PD and held out her hands for the cuffs to be slapped on. There was no official reason for her to be there.

Billy Waites got out of his car when he saw Ren pull up outside Annie's. He jogged up to her.

'Hey,' he said. 'Why the mystery?'

'Not so much mystery,' said Ren, 'as . . . well, yes, mystery, I suppose. In many ways.'

'How does Misty feel about it?'

Ren smiled. She put the key in the door and they went into the living room.

'Take a seat.' Ren sat beside him on the sofa. 'OK . . . I wouldn't ask this if I wasn't – as the song goes – Desperado.'

'In the land of Ren, desperado could mean so much,' said Billy.

'You know what?' said Ren. 'You are correct. But take it as a compliment. I am asking you because (a) I think you are up to it and (b) I will watch your back for the entire process.'

'OK – what is it?'

'It's . . . well, it is a biggie. I need you to break in . . . somewhere.'

'Whoa, I did not see that coming,' said Billy. 'Are you for real?' He looked at her. 'Oh. You are.'

'I am,' said Ren. 'And obviously I'll understand you saying no . . . actually, more than I understand you saying yes.' *But please say yes.*

'Hmm. There is steel in your eyes,' said Billy. 'Which I respond to better than that puppy-dog crap.'

'Not quite steel,' said Ren. 'What you see in my eyes is a substance one hundred times stronger than steel, a material incapable of destruction.'

'Right. Jesus, Ren, I'm not sure about this.'

'I have a watertight plan—'

'What, water with the power to tighten my ass muscles one hundred times more than regular plans?'

'There's a reason why I'll be watching your . . . back.'

Billy shook his head. 'Tell me your plan.'

'I need you to break into the office of Detective—'

'Oh no, no detectivey things, no law-enforcementy things.'

'Hear me out,' said Ren. 'It's a low-security office. It belongs to Detective Janine Hooks of the Jefferson County

Cold Case Unit. I need a file from a cabinet that I will mark clearly on a room plan. It's under H for Hammond. Trudie Hammond.'

'As in Judge Hammond Hammond? Hey, why don't you throw a few congressmen's offices into the mix, maybe the DA?'

'It's the file of his wife's homicide in 1983,' said Ren.

'And then what do I do?'

'I'm trying to think of the best thing to do . . .' Ren paused. 'Use your digital camera.'

'I don't have one.'

'Use mine, then.'

'And how will you be watching my back while this is going on?'

'I'll be in my car in the complex. I've already been in Janine Hooks' office, so it is not beyond the beyond the bounds of possibility that I could be there again. Anyway, the JeffCo pathologist is there too. I have a few options.'

'And . . . ?'

'And I can make a big show of arresting you if anyone stumbles across you. Which they won't, because you are so good.'

Billy rolled his eyes. 'What about the security guard?'

'There's no one at the back door,' said Ren. 'It's punch-code access. And I have the number.'

'Cameras?'

'May have been tampered with,' said Ren. She handed Billy the map she had drawn.

'What is it with you and Douglas Hammond?' he said, studying the map. 'Why does it matter?'

'Because,' said Ren.

'You child,' said Billy. 'You will tell me at some stage.'

'I will. I promise.'

Billy stood up. 'OK, let's do it,' he said.

'Now?'

Billy nodded. 'Billy Waites: Photo-copying While-U-Wait.'

34

Ren sat alone at Annie's kitchen table with print-outs of the photos Billy had taken of Trudie Hammond's file. Having pushed away her guilt at lying to Janine Hooks and at roping Billy into her mess, she was struggling to bury the fear of getting caught. She needed a sharp mind to put together the pieces of something she was not even quite sure of. It was like the ingredients of a cake laid out on a table without the recipe – you had to start baking it, but you had no real idea what cake you were making. A lot of it came down to guess-work, and the end result could be a disaster. With a cold-case file, you were dealing with out-of-date technology and the inexperience and limited resources of an older police force. Re-investigating it could make you the person who turns up decades later at a forgotten mine and strikes gold. Or the person who shows up and confirms that there was nothing new to be uncovered.

In Trudie Hammond's case, there was a twenty-seven-year gap and a file that was disappointingly slim. Ren ran through the details, starting with a series of shots of the blood-soaked crime scene.

Trudie Hammond, housewife and mother of one was found dead by her husband at 11 a.m. on August 16, 1983. He had left for work at 8 a.m., returned unexpectedly to pick up a work file and found his wife lying dead on the living-room floor. She had been struck several times on the head with a glass vase and had crashed through a glass coffee table.

The couple's two-year-old daughter had been asleep in her crib and was awakened by a female police officer and brought to a family member's home. There were no signs of sexual assault. Mrs Hammond had had sex that morning with her husband before he left for work.

In evidence: one nightgown, fragments of broken glass from the vase, one piece of carpet.

All twenty houses on the street had been canvassed. The only name Ren recognized was Lucinda Kerr, who had been home sick from work, but was sleeping and had not seen or heard a thing. Her husband, Peter Everett, had been out jogging and had also not seen or heard anything suspicious. He had returned to find police cars on the street. Most of the residents discovered the tragedy when they came home at the end of the working day.

Ren studied the photos. Trudie Hammond was dressed in a white nightgown with a halo of blonde hair spread out above her head. It was the same nightgown that she had been wearing when her husband had left her that morning. She was heavily made up, but tears had clearly washed her mascara down her cheeks. Her bright pink lipstick was gone, leaving behind a faint stain.

Why did she have full makeup on when she was killed if she had not showered since her husband left? Would a woman shower, apply makeup and put on the nightgown from the previous night? Little things, maybe, but odd.

And how had little Mia Hammond slept through all this? An

intruder entering the house. Shattering glass. Her mother's crying and probable screaming. Her father's car pulling up. His arrival into the house.

Ren felt a surge of frustration at not being able to walk through the rooms of the Hammond house, of not being able to question the non-witnesses, at not being able to talk to Douglas Hammond or any of the detectives on the case or . . . There was one name she recognized, signed at the bottom of the autopsy report under the pathologist's name: Dr Barry Tolman.

Ren liked Barry Tolman. He had a nice manner, was efficient and easy to deal with. Could she trust him to give her details on the case without blabbing to Janine Hooks?

Hmm.

Ren closed the file, shoved it under the sofa and went to bed.

Few wise decisions can be made at four a.m.

At eight the following morning Ren was standing in front of the kitchen cabinet reaching for a box of peppermint tea, wishing there would come a day when four hours' sleep would not leave her feeling nauseous. As she reached for the kettle, the house phone startled her. One day, four hours' sleep would not make her jumpy.

Few people had Annie's home number. Or would expect Ren to ever be home, no matter what was going on in her life.

'Hello?' she said.

'Did you know Beau had been doing drugs?' Her mother's voice was painfully shrill – the voice that heralded a conversation riddled with ridiculous statements.

Ren looked at her watch again. 'What? It's eight a.m., Mom. Jesus.'

'Jesus doesn't care what time it is,' said her mom. *Ridiculous statement #1.*

'Hello?' said Ren. 'It's early, you know I have to go to work in a little while. So, tell me, calmly, what is going on.'

'Don't tell me to be calm,' she said. 'Would you be calm if the whole world said your son was a drug user?' *Statement #2.*

The whole world. Ren took a deep breath. 'Why did you call me? To take out your anger at the police? Or for . . . what exactly?'

'I want to know if you knew that Beau was doing drugs.'

'I want to know what makes you think that he was.'

'For Christ's sake, Ren, drop the lawyer/therapist act.' *Statement #3.* 'Was Beau doing drugs?'

'No,' said Ren. 'And if he was, would it matter now? And would it matter if I knew or "the whole world" knew?'

'Well, according to Daryl Stroud, when his detectives spoke with Beau's friends, they said that he had been doing drugs. The detectives asked them had they been to his room, did they know of this hole he had in the bed—'

'Does it matter? Seriously?'

'Of course it matters,' said her mother. 'He suffered from depression. He was not supposed to be doing drugs. Drugs would make everything worse for someone like Beau. And how did your father and I not notice? I can't believe he was doing drugs under our noses and none of us noticed.'

'Mom . . . can we believe whoever said this?' *And can anybody let Beau rest in peace?*

'It changes everything,' said her mother.

'What do you mean?'

'There *was* something we could have done. If I had noticed, I could have put a stop to it. God knows how they were affecting his brain. He could still be here today if I had been paying more attention. I'm his mother.'

'Mom, you and Dad could not have paid more attention to us if you tried – short of following us all around every day.'

'Obviously, that wasn't enough.'

No – it was too much. 'Whatever you'd like to think about this revelation, it doesn't change a—'

'Of course it does, Ren. I have spent how many years being told by people "There was nothing you could do", and finally I had started to believe it. I allowed myself to be convinced that I had done everything I could for Beau. But now it's obvious that was not the case. I failed my son.'

'I know you're not going to hear this right now,' said Ren, 'but I'll say it anyway. You did not fail Beau. Please do not look for an excuse to go back and punish yourself again. You did everything. After that, it was Beau alone with his mind. And his mind was shooting out faulty messages. And at that moment in time, he listened to them. *He* had no control over that. So you definitely couldn't have.'

'How can you be so calm about all this?'

'Years of therapy is how,' said Ren. 'Maybe you should give it a shot.'

'I don't need therapy.' *Statement #4.*

'Everyone needs therapy, if you ask me.'

'It wouldn't do any good at my age . . .'

I give up. 'Well, if you think it will make you feel any worse than the way you do right now, you're absolutely right not to go.'

Silence.

'I've got to get back to work,' said Ren. 'Take care. Hi to Dad. And Beau didn't do drugs.'

35

Ren called Dr Barry Tolman from the Jeep on the drive to work.

'Hey, Barry,' she said. 'It's Ren Bryce from Safe Streets.'

'Hi, Ren,' said Tolman. 'How are you doing?'

'I'm good, thank you. I'm just calling to see if I could talk to you about a case you worked on.'

Tolman paused. 'Sure . . . what case?'

'It was a homicide. Trudie Hammond, 1983,' said Ren.

Tolman was slow to answer. 'I'm sorry, Ren,' he said, 'I can talk to you about any other case – just not that one.'

What? 'Oh,' said Ren. 'OK . . . can I ask why?'

'You can, but I'm under strict orders not to say a word.'

'By whom?'

Tolman sighed. 'Janine Hooks.'

'What?' said Ren.

'Yes,' said Tolman. 'I'd love to help. But for some reason, known only to Janine, I can't. If it's any consolation, I was an assistant on that case, so who knows how helpful I could be to you.'

'Oh, I'm sure you'd be helpful if your hands hadn't been tied,' said Ren.

'You know I'd always be happy to help you,' said Tolman. 'I have no idea what's going on with Janine.'

Ren paused. 'Are you guys friends?'

'Janine's a nice person,' said Tolman. 'But we're not friends. She's a little intense. Like, goes around with this permanent look of concentration on her face. We pass each other in the hallway every now and then, but that's it.'

'How is she work-wise?'

'Does not miss a trick,' said Tolman. 'On a mission. I wouldn't want to mess with Janine Hooks.'

It may be a little late for that.

The only sounds in the Safe Streets office when Ren arrived were tapping keyboards and papers being shuffled. Ren sat quietly at her desk, wondering what to do about Janine Hooks. *What did she know? Was this all a huge coincidence? Should I call her?*

Whatever had happened, Janine Hooks was calling the shots and Ren wasn't about to do anything else until she had more information.

Ren stared at the Fifty Most Wanted list, the place where her attention should have been, instead of on the strange tangle – if there was one – of Helen Wheeler and Douglas and Trudie Hammond. Domenica Val Pando's face stared back at her from the noticeboard.

What are you to me? Ren felt a strange stabbing in her chest as the answer hit her. *The most screwed-up relationship I've ever had. Domenica is like the boyfriend I was cheating on who was cheating on me at the same time and we both found out about it.* No man had ever gotten under her skin the way Domenica Val Pando had. The thought turned her stomach.

'Holy shit,' said Ren, jumping up. 'Domenica is not the crocodile. She's the plover bird.'

The tapping of keyboards stopped. The guys all looked at her.

201

'There is someone bigger than Domenica out there,' said Ren. 'She's not the big boss any more. She can't be. Think about it. She lost power – and face – when the FBI got right inside her world. She screwed up big time, people who worked for her were killed. Back then, she had no idea how the FBI ended up storming her compound. She was raped by two men in front of her child, she was beaten down emotionally, physically and where it hurt her the most – financially.'

'After that, there was no way Domenica could pass herself off as this shrewd "business" woman. She wouldn't be as respected or trusted as much. There's been a massive power shift. And like any relationship with a power shift, it either falls apart or it takes time to get back on track. Domenica realized she could never be the big boss again after that whole mess, but she could still be very useful to the right kind of people, providing many different kinds of services. But . . . only if she could put her trust in something and someone more powerful, which, let's face it, along the border, means something or someone that could be potentially lethal to her – those jaws could snap down on her any time. But what can Domenica do right now, except take the risk?'

The guys nodded.

'All we need to find out now,' said Ren, 'is who is the crocodile?'

'I guess we have two choices with Domenica,' said Colin. 'We find Gavino and work our way up to Domenica, or we find this possible new boss of hers and work our way down.'

'The boss could be the better route,' said Ren. 'I would say he is an angry man now that she's turned high profile again with our list.'

'Well,' said Cliff. 'Her next high-profile moment will be her arrest.'

'You bet,' said Robbie.

'I'm going to get on to Nogales and see what I can find out about some of the big players,' said Ren. 'And while I'm at it, I'll find out the latest on Erubiel Diaz.'

An hour later, Ren got off the phone and called everyone in for a briefing.

'OK,' she said, 'the authorities in Nogales still have Erubiel Diaz down as collateral damage in the Puente cartel's blood-bath. The interesting part is that the original arrest of the Puente second-in-command that set the whole thing off happened because of a tip-off, believed to have come from a man known as "El Coyote Panzón".'

'El Coyote Panzón,' said Colin. 'The fat coyote?'

Ren nodded. 'I'm presuming the coyote in question is one of the guys who helps people cross the border.'

'That's what they're called – coyotes?' said Robbie.

'Yup,' said Ren. 'But . . . it's a little weird. If I were trying to get across the border as fast as my illegal legs could carry me, I wouldn't be putting my hand up for the fat coyote's team.'

'Is El Coyote Panzón with one of the cartels? Is he a boss?' said Cliff.

'No one knows,' said Ren. 'All we know is that he has seriously pissed the Puente cartel off. And somehow Erubiel Diaz was part of the mix.'

'Could Domenica Val Pando be the coyote?' said Robbie.

Ren laughed. 'Domenica would be far too vain to allow herself to be called fat anything.'

'Is there anything more on this coyote?' said Colin.

'I've put the word out with Border Control,' said Ren. 'If there is any more information, they'll be the ones to find it.'

Everyone went back to their desks and continued to work in silence. It was as if they were all suffering the after-effects of a bad night. There was no small talk, no group lunch. When Ren came back into the office at two, Colin looked up from his computer.

'Did you hear about this?' he said. He quoted the headline. 'Trudie Hammond Murder Inquiry Re-opened'.'

What? 'Where did you hear that?'

'The *Post*.' Colin scanned down the screen.

'What are they saying?'

'A lot of nothing.'

'But there's no mention that Hammond's death was homicide,' said Ren.

'No.'

'It won't take a genius to work out that someone is suspicious. After all these years, around the same time as the husband dies in an "accident", his wife's murder inquiry is being looked at again?' *Shit. Shit. Shit.* 'But, why now?' Ren's heart was pounding. 'And who's quoted? Where did this come from?'

She got her answer about who the suspicious party was with the ping of her Inbox. As if by magic. It was an email from Janine Hooks: Subject: Ha/Ho.

This is not good.

Ren opened the email:

'H-A . . . goes before H-O . . .'
Regards,
Janine Hooks

Oh, Billy, you didn't.

36

Billy arrived at Annie's that evening wondering what it was that could be so urgent – again. Ren slumped down on the sofa. 'Billy . . . '

'What happened?' he said, sitting beside her.

'Oh, Billy,' said Ren. 'You put the file back in the wrong place.'

'What?'

'You put the Hammond file behind the "H-O" file.'

He put his head in his hands. Then he looked back up. 'Are you sure?'

'I got an email from Janine Hooks. She's reopening the case.'

'Is that not a good thing?'

'No,' said Ren. 'Not on any level.'

'Shit. I'm . . . so sorry. That is not the kind of mistake I make. Are you screwed?'

'I don't know. But what a fucking mess. There's no telling what she's going to do.'

'Will she talk to Gary Dettling?' said Billy.

'She better not,' said Ren.

'Thank you for not blaming me,' said Billy, taking her hand.

Oh, I am. I am blaming you. But it was an accident. So I can't say it out loud. Or maybe I will. Don't do it. I can't help it . . .

'You have no idea what you've done,' said Ren. The volume was rising. 'My whole career—'

Billy let go of her hand. 'I've heard the "my whole career" line before.'

Ren looked up. 'Well, thanks for ignoring that and screwing up anyway.' Her eyes were lit with anger.

'It was *because* of that line,' said Billy, 'that I helped you out. I'm not expecting a thank you here.' He stood up. 'All I wanted to do was to protect the "whole career" you love. And protect the person who loves it.'

'Sit down,' said Ren. 'Please. I'm sorry.'

He sat down. '*I'm* sorry.'

'I know you are. I know. I just . . . I'm scared.'

'I feel that my very existence jeopardizes your job,' said Billy.

'My job is not your responsibility,' said Ren. Her tone was gentle.

'I guess I felt it was my responsibility before . . . when we got together—'

'Even then, it wasn't . . . I could definitely hold your ass responsible for that, though.'

'We went through a lot,' said Billy '*You* did. You fought hard. So I'm not going to let anyone take that away from you. If I have to take the rap, I will.'

'Don't be ridiculous,' said Ren. She hung her head. 'Billy, what am I going to do with you?'

'Not be mad at me.'

'Jesus, how could I be mad?' said Ren. 'I mean, taking the file for me was amazing. The putting it back part – not so much. Your fuck-up could be the biggest fuck-up I've ever made. But it all started with me. So, it'll all end with me.'

'No one will find out,' said Billy. 'And if they do, no one will find me. Do you have any idea how long you motherfuckers were tracking me back in the day – until you caught up with me?'

Ren laughed.

Billy stood up in front of her and held her head between his hands. He kissed her on the top of the head three times: 'Do. Not. Worry.'

Ren stood up and hugged him tight. 'You crazy, crazy bitch.'

'The world is not closing in on you,' said Billy. 'Look at it like this – there's a way out of every maze—'

'Noo,' said Ren. 'Not mazes. Do not speak of them.'

'Listen to me. Mazes are usually made of hedges, right? So what you're afraid of is some pruned shrubbery. Which doesn't sound too scary, right? In fact, it sounds a little harmless . . . and, if you have the right chainsaw, you can rip right through it.'

'Yes . . .'

'What was the only thing that would have stopped you ripping through that hedge when you were a kid, if you needed to?'

'I left my chainsaw back in my Wendy house?'

'Convention is what stopped you,' said Billy. 'Manners, society expectations, fear of letting down your parents or drawing negative attention to yourself or ruining someone's birthday party . . .'

Ren smiled. 'Ah.'

'Yes,' said Billy. 'There is a way out – you just need to break a few rules.'

'I'm an obeyer of rules . . . mainly.'

'Well, I'm just glad you broke a few last year,' said Billy. 'And remember: if there's something strange . . . in your neighborhood . . . who you gonna call?'

Ren laughed. Billy hugged her again and left.

Annie's phone rang. Ren stared at it. *I'm tired. I'm busy. I'm rushing. I'm under pressure. I'm exhausted. I haven't slept . . .* She felt exhausted even thinking of the effort it took to always be on, to have a few words to throw out to distract someone from guessing that always, there was some other crap going on under the surface. She wondered if she would ever turn to someone else and say, 'I feel very vulnerable right now. I need to be alone.'

She picked up.

'Jay told me that you phoned Ricky Parry,' said her mother.

You have to be kidding me. What is wrong with him?

'Why didn't you tell me?'

'God, Mom, I didn't want you to worry. I didn't know what his reaction would be. I wanted to talk to him, I have – or thought I had – some connection with him. As it transpired, I was wrong. But I wanted to give it a shot.'

'Well, you should have told me, Ren. Your father and I live here, for God's sake. What kind of fool would I have looked if we had run into him on the street and he had mentioned it? Or someone else had?'

'I'm sorry, Mom. I did what I thought was right.'

'I know, sweetheart, but . . . I don't like to be kept in the dark. You don't have to protect me.'

'I'm sorry. I can't help it.'

'And how come I didn't hear about this cowboy boyfriend you had?'

Boyfriend . . . the fling with the extreme rider at the Western Stock Show. You have to be kidding me.

208

'What?' said Ren. 'He wasn't a boyfriend.'

'Well, what was he then?'

Hmm. 'We went on a few . . . dates.'

'Why wouldn't you even tell me that the man exists?'

To limit my official numbers. 'Well, maybe because I didn't think he was special enough to meet my mommy.'

'If you felt he wasn't important enough to mention him to your father and I, then why would you want to date him?'

Sweet Jesus. 'Because not everyone I meet is someone who I will walk up the aisle with. Let's face it. Mom, I'm incredibly busy right now. This conversation is not helpful.'

Ren could sense one of her mother's weighty pauses.

'I just wonder . . .'

Here it comes.

' . . . have you been trying to replace Beau in your life?'

Beau? What? 'Well, please stop wondering,' said Ren. 'About anything. Ever. And stop watching daytime psych shows. You blend the advice from hundreds of different topics.'

'Hundreds? I don't watch hundreds.'

'And I don't try to find guys who remind me of my dead brother,' said Ren. 'That's just creepsville.'

'It's not "creepsville". I'm talking about there being a hole in your life ever since Beau died. I explained myself badly – it's not Beau you're trying to replace – I meant that maybe you are trying to fill the void that he left.'

'Well, that sounds a bit more normal,' said Ren. 'But you're still wrong. I'm fine. I'm not looking for any man.' *A historic moment.*

'Are you . . . sleeping with men?'

'Oh my God,' said Ren.

'I read that people like you sleep with men.'

'Women, you mean?'

'I meant people with your . . . condition.'

'Mom? I've got to go,' said Ren, 'a comfortable conversation has just come up somewhere.'

'Well, just remember that a lot of men just want to sleep with you and once they get what they want, they'll leave.'

And hopefully not let the door hit them on the way out.

Ren sat at Annie's giant mahogany dining-room table with the stolen contents of Trudie Hammond's file. She wondered how she could get Janine Hooks' . . . hooks out of her.

Did she re-open the case to spite me? Or to alert me to the fact that she knew I had stolen the file? Or because Hooks, too, felt that there was a link between the two deaths? Are we going to end up racing each other to a finish line on this?

Ren looked down at the pages and photos she had spread in front of her on the table.

Somewhere in here, there will be something that I will find without having to speak to a single person who was involved in the previous investigation. Because Janine Hooks will kill me. And dump me in a river for effect.

Three letters floated around Ren's head: OPR: the FBI's Office of Professional Responsibility. The people whose heads would spin if they knew about breaking and entering without a warrant . . . carried out by a confidential informant who an FBI agent had a prior relationship with when he was a suspect in the murder of another FBI agent whose death she was investigating.

Ren let out a breath. *Their heads would spin. My head would roll.*

37

Ren spent the weekend going back and forth over what to do about Janine Hooks. It was Monday morning and she was acting on her most recent decision: She didn't think Janine Hooks would accept her visit. But she was invited straight in when she showed up at the depressing brown office.

'Hi,' said Ren. 'Thank you so much for seeing me. I'm mortified. I wanted to apologize for taking the file. But if you could let me explain, you'll see why I did it.'

'Your arrogance was unbeliev—'

'I can see how it came across that way,' said Ren, 'but it really was not arrogance. Please hear me out. My accessing this file *had* to fly under the radar. I couldn't let you know why I needed to look at that case again. I couldn't draw your attention to it, because it is a mess. I don't know how yet, but the Hammonds' murders are—'

'Hammonds? Plural? Murders?' said Hooks.

'Yes,' said Ren. 'Douglas Hammond's death was not an accident. That is something that cannot get out. We know that, so does Denver PD, but we were trying to keep a lid on it. What I was about to say was that I think his murder and his wife's are connected . . . and there are also links to a wider network of ongoing investigations that I need to work out. And I feel that part of working that out is to take another look at Trudie Hammond's case. What I did to you was wrong, but I didn't know anything about you and alerting anyone to my suspicions would have made me and them more vulnerable.'

Hooks sat back in her chair. 'Ah, you did it to protect me . . .' Her voice was flat.

'I didn't mean it that way,' said Ren. 'But I have to tell you, going public with reopening Trudie Hammond's murder was a massive mistake. It was exactly what I was trying to avoid.'

'Oh, I think I'll survive.'

'Maybe you will, but . . .'

'What is the link?' said Janine. 'Why do you think there is one?'

'Before I say anything, I want to ask you: will you work with me on this?'

Hooks looked at Ren like she was nuts.

'I'll be really honest, here,' said Ren. 'I cannot let my superiors know that I'm looking into this because, as you may have noticed, it has nothing to do with Safe Streets – it's *your* cold case, it's nearly thirty years old, and I can't go to my boss for my permission to look at it when we have so much else going on.

'And there are other, private, circumstances in connection with Douglas Hammond that put me in a difficult position. I know that I have done nothing wrong, but me knowing and everyone else knowing is a different story.'

'Why would that concern me?'

'It doesn't,' said Ren. 'But I'm sure your budget does.'

'Excuse me?'

'OK, I would like to help you,' said Ren. 'Genuinely. When I came into your office that first time—'

'The time you weren't actually breaking in.'

Ren paused. 'Look, I knew instantly that I had fucked up. I walked in, I knew that you knew your shit and there was something about you that I liked. But I knew I couldn't back out at that point. And because of everything else that was at stake, I knew I had to keep going with my plan. I am not a person who breaks into places and steals things,' said Ren. 'I would not have jeopardized my position for something that wasn't important.'

'How did you know I wouldn't have gone to the authorities about the break-in?'

'Because I knew you couldn't have proved it was me.'

'I could have innocently called . . .' Hooks glanced at a Post-It on her desk, 'Gary Dettling with "that information you were looking for".'

'And I could have come up with a reason why that information was relevant,' said Ren. 'The point is this. Two things – I know about budget cuts here and I know the cold-case unit is under threat. I also know that you love your job.'

'Blackmail. I love it,' said Hooks.

'It's not blackmail,' said Ren. 'It's for our mutual benefit. I could stand back and let you at this case yourself and I have no doubt you would work it all out. But I've found something in that file that I think is crucial.'

'Oh, me too,' said Hooks, gesturing to a stack of files on the desk beside her. 'That doesn't mean I get to follow through.'

'We have different set-ups,' said Ren.

'Yes,' said Hooks, 'if *you* wanted to go and search, let me see, the four locations I feel could have been used as burial grounds by various killers in these files here, you could just go right ahead.'

'Not necessarily,' said Ren. 'But yes, I obviously have access to a lot more resources, which is exactly how I would like to help, here.'

'Go ahead.'

'I just need you to get me to run some DNA.'

'So,' said Hooks, 'you are going to tell me something, I pretend I came up with it myself and I ask the FBI's help to speed the sample through their lab . . .'

'Yes.'

'Why would I do that?' said Janine.

'Because if I'm right, the case will be closed. And that will help your track record. And support any budget campaigns. I think your track record is excellent, by the way, but a poor economy still screws talented people and the more you can do to promote your cause, the better. I'm not in any way trying to be patronizing. This is actually something practical we can both do.'

'What did you find in the file?' said Hooks.

'I don't know yet, but . . .'

Robbie was smiling at Ren when she walked into the office.

'Good morning, smiley face,' she said.

'I got some good news for you,' said Robbie.

'Shoot.'

'Now I feel bad calling it good news,' said Robbie. 'I mean, it is for you, just not for the other person.'

Ren looked at him patiently.

'I took a call for you while you were out,' said Robbie. 'From Hunt Memorial Hospital in Nogales, Arizona. They've just roused Luke Sarvas from an induced coma. Almost every bone in his body is broken.'

'Wow,' said Ren. 'What happened?'

'He says he fell from the border wall.'

The wall along the Mexican border had been heightened over the years to deter jumpers. The problem was that it didn't. It just meant a longer drop and more serious injuries.

'He was obviously trying to get the hell out of Mexico and couldn't do it the legal way,' said Ren. 'Now, why would that be?'

'Would I be right in saying you're on a flight to Nogales to find out?'

'You sure are . . .' Ren paused. 'What about his brother? Michael Sarvas?'

Robbie shook her head. 'Unfortunately, there's no word of him. Luke was alone.'

Gary stuck his head into the office 'Ren, Glenn Buddy's just shown up. He's in the conference room.'

Please let it be more good news.

Glenn stood up when she walked in. His face was blank. But his eyes were hiding something. And whatever it was was not good.

'You've been to Breckenridge, right?' said Glenn Buddy.

'Yes, last year,' said Ren, sitting down. 'Why do you ask?'

'Why were you there?'

Hello? 'You know why I was there,' said Ren. 'I was on the Jean Transom case.'

'Did you know Douglas Hammond was also in Breckenridge last year?'

'I'm sure a lot of people were,' said Ren.

'Do you know the Friends of Breckenridge?'

'No.' *But I bet a woman in a hand-knit sweater came up with the name.*

'Hammond and his friends set it up. Anyway, they went

215

there every year, some of them twice a year, some just came for ski season. There was always a group of them for summer and winter every year. They celebrated their fortieth anniversary President's Day weekend last year.'

Good for them. 'OK . . .'

'Were you in Breckenridge at that time?'

'I was.' Ren paused. 'Please don't tell me you're exploring some connection here . . .' *What the hell is going on?*

'I'm giving you the benefit of the doubt, so allow me to ask a few questions. I'm just looking at your links to Hammond.'

'What links?' said Ren. 'There are none. It's a coincidence, that's all.'

'Jesus, Ren . . . I'm going to come right out with it. What were you doing with Judge Hammond the night he died?'

38

Glenn Buddy's expression was exhaustion edged with fear.

Ren let out a breath. 'Hammond approached me in Gaffney's one evening. He said he wanted to meet with me.'

Glenn slumped back in his chair. 'Why did you not tell anyone this?'

'I . . . he asked me not to.' *Lame.*

Glenn's look told her that he agreed.

'I didn't know that he was going to die,' said Ren. 'So, in my head, I was having a – yes, secret – meeting with Judge Douglas Hammond, but that was it.'

'Right . . .' said Glenn. 'And where was this meeting to take place?'

'In a rest-stop between Hiwan Country Club and his house.'

'And this seemed totally normal to you?'

'Of course not,' said Ren. 'But I knew it must have been something important.'

'What did you think it was going to be about?' said Glenn.

'I . . . don't know,' said Ren.

'And what did he say?'

'Not a lot. I know none of this sounds good for me. I acknowledge that, but to be honest, I was at a loss as to what his point was. The best way I can put it is it was like he invited me over to tell me something, then changed his mind once I got there.'

'Could there have been something . . . sexual involved?'

'What?' said Ren. 'With me?'

Glenn nodded. 'Yeah: like, was he hitting on you?'

'God, no. No. He seemed afraid. There was something not quite right.'

'Then why didn't you—'

'It wasn't a "you're going to die" bad feeling. Just that something was off.'

'Could he have been drunk?'

'Well, your tox reports will answer that. I smelled alcohol on his breath, but I wouldn't say he was drunk.'

'Had you met Hammond before?'

'No.'

'Had Helen Wheeler?'

'As far as I know, no.'

'Was there another reason for you to meet Douglas Hammond?'

'No,' said Ren. 'And, for the record, I did not kill him.'

'No one's accusing you of being a killer,' said Glenn. He paused. 'Do you know the expression, "the point of no return"? Well, I'm here. And what a great location it is.'

The world was no longer a wonderful, magical place to Glenn Buddy.

'I have allowed you in further to this than I should have,' said Glenn. 'I've made a huge mistake. And you've helped me make it. I was doing you a favor and now I feel manipulated.'

The darkest place is often to be found on the wrong side of the sunniest person. 'What? You think you can't trust me?'

Glenn Buddy's face was all the answer she needed.

'I know,' said Ren. 'I know. But . . . please. From here on, I promise, I will ask you for nothing. And right here, right now, I can promise that there is nothing I have done that you need to—

Ren's cell phone rang. She glanced down. 'I'm sorry, I have to take this. It's my brother. It's a family . . . issue.' *Jay, of all people, to the rescue.*

Glenn gestured that he was going to go out for a cigarette. Ren nodded. She answered the call.

'Hi, Jay.'

'I was talking to Mom,' he said, straight in. *Just like mother.*

'And?'

'She found out that Dad went to see Daryl Stroud.'

'And?' said Ren.

'Well, do you think that was wise?' said Jay.

'If I thought it was unwise, would I have suggested that Dad do it?'

'Well, I think it was unwise.'

'OK.'

'OK, what?'

'You have your opinion and I have mine. Mine happens to be shared by Dad and Matt.'

'You *made* Dad go and talk to Daryl.'

'Are you for real?' said Ren. 'He's a grown man. I suggested it. He was happy to do it.'

'You know he would do anything for you.'

'As he would for any of us. Including Beau,' said Ren. 'So, Dad paid Daryl a visit. It's not like he was going to compromise the entire investigation and Beau's reputation because of something I suggested he do. You are being ridiculous.'

'You can be very reactive, Ren,' said Jay. 'And impulsive.'

'So, if I say "fuck you" right now, will that fall under one of those categories? Will that have no merit either?'

'I don't want to get into anything,' said Jay.

'So calling me was meant to, what . . . ?'

'To let you know to step back,' said Jay. 'And . . . not to make things any worse for Mom and Dad. They're very vulnerable.'

'Jesus Christ,' said Ren, 'you're acting like I'm a door-to-door salesman looking to scam the elderly out of their life savings. Give me a break. And why, in God's name, did you tell them about that fling I had?'

'How do you know I told them?'

'Oh, please. Like Matt would,' said Ren. 'That stuff is my business, Jay. Do you understand that concept?'

'Matt mentioned it to me, that's all,' said Jay.

'To *you*,' said Ren. 'Not to anyone else. And not, I would imagine, in a gossipy way. Why the hell would I tell Mom and Dad that kind of shit?'

'Yeah, well, I don't know why the hell you wouldn't.'

'Jesus Christ!' said Ren. 'That still doesn't make it your call. Will you ever, ever respect someone else's wishes? Ever?'

'Maybe I was just looking out for you,' said Jay.

'How exactly was that looking out for me?'

'Well, maybe these flings aren't good for you.'

Ren exploded. 'How fucking dare you! Where do you get off—'

'Go ahead, Ren, fight with the world.'

'I am not fighting with the world,' said Ren. 'What the hell are you talking about?'

'You're so angry.'

'I am not angry.'

'Yes, you are. It's unbelievable.'

'Did you ever think I'm just angry with you?' said Ren. 'The world is fine from where I'm standing. Maybe I'm just fighting with you.'

'Me?' said Jay.

'Yes.'

'Why?'

'Nothing,' said Ren.

'Oh, grow up,' said Jay. '"Nothing" – you're like a child, Ren.'

'You are the most patronizing . . . fuck you.'

'Do you behave like this at work?'

'Oh my God, what in the hell does that have to do with anything? Work? Is that what's important here? How I am in work? What are you going to do, call my boss? See how I've been doing?'

'What is that supposed to mean?'

'You know nothing about me. You have no clue. And do you know why? Because you don't listen. Because you think you are better than everyone. You judge. You watch and you judge. And it's the Jay filter. Which is a shit filter. And do you want to know why?'

'Sure, Ren, go ahead: why?'

'Because . . . why did you go to Mom and Dad about *me*?'

'Huh?' said Jay. 'What are you—'

'I covered your ass. Why did you go to Mom and Dad about *me* drinking?'

'Are you talking about when you were fifteen?'

'Yes!' said Ren.

'This is ridiculous,' said Jay.

'You told Mom and Dad that I was drinking. Two beers!'

'Are you actually talking about—'

'I'm talking about Beau!' shouted Ren. 'Why wasn't it

Beau that you told on?' She held back tears, but her voice was cracking. 'Why didn't you tell them about Beau? Why didn't you tell them he had been smoking shit every night? Why didn't you say that he had a little bag of pills he carried around with him? You knew. I know you knew. So, fuck you. You didn't over-ride him when he asked you to keep a secret. You over-rode me. And you were wrong. Hasn't that ever entered your head? Ever? You were wrong. You picked the wrong fucking sibling to rat out.'

She slammed the phone down.

Glenn Buddy coughed.

Ren swung around. 'I'm sorry,' she said.

'I just caught from "so, fuck you" onwards.'

'Right . . .' *What did you hear? I can't even remember what I said.*

'Do you always talk to your brother that way?' said Glenn. 'Was that your important call?'

'There are extenuating circumstances.'

Glenn took a seat opposite her again. 'Are you taking any of this seriously? I come here to talk to you about your close connection with a murdered judge and you take a personal call?'

'I am taking everything seriously,' said Ren. 'This is very important. And so was that other call. You'll just have to—'

'Don't tell me – trust you?'

Ren let out a breath.

'I don't have a lot of time, here,' said Glenn. 'I just want to know is there anything else you're not telling me?'

'No.'

'Agent Bryce, you know the position I'm in here. I am investigating the death of a federal judge. You are with the

FBI. And Cliff James was the best man at my wedding. Do you see where I'm at?'

Oh, God, I do. 'I understand, Glenn. I really do. I wouldn't do anything to jeopardize your position.'

My own, however, is a different story . . .

39

One week earlier

By a stand of trees on a quiet Genesee road, Douglas Hammond was parked in his green BMW. Ren jogged up to the passenger door. Hammond unlocked the door and she sat in.

'Thanks for coming,' said Hammond.

Jesus, 'Thanks for coming?'

He looked at her expression. 'Well, you might not have.'

'Do you really think so?'

Their breaths were white in the cold air. Hammond's hairline was dotted with tiny beads of sweat.

'So,' she said. 'Why am I here?'

'I am highly recommending that you give up your psych files,' said Hammond.

Ren stared at him. 'How do you know—'

'Just do it,' said Hammond. 'Just back down.'

'Why would I do that?'

'Because I am meeting you on a dark road in the middle of the night to tell you to.'

224

'You don't even know me,' said Ren.

'I asked around.'

'And?'

'You don't back down,' said Hammond.

'When I have no reason to, no,' said Ren.

'Trust me, you have every reason to.'

'What are you talking about? What could possibly interest you in those files?'

Hammond looked at her. 'You're shivering,' he said. 'Are you cold?'

Ren frowned. 'Yes.'

He glanced at the heating dial, but didn't move. Ren turned on the heating, blasting hot air from a loud fan.

For a moment, they sat in silence.

'I didn't just hear that you wouldn't back down . . . There was a lot more to hear about Agent Ren Bryce.'

Ren's anger was spiking, but she held her hands still and she kept her breathing under control. And it didn't quite work. 'I am sorry,' said Ren, her voice quickly rising, 'but I have no clue what the point of all this is. It is passive/aggressive bullshit. You have power, Your Honor, you don't need to get cryptic with me. You shouldn't need something to get an extra little kick. I've driven all the way out here in the pitch dark.'

Hammond was staring straight ahead.

You smug prick. She turned and grabbed the door handle.

'Agent Bryce, please.'

She looked back at him. *Holy shit.* The fear in his eyes was stunning. Before Ren had time to react, he gripped her forearm and pulled her close. She could feel his hot breath in her ear. 'You,' he said, his voice barely audible, 'you don't know what you're getting involved in.'

'What the hell?' said Ren, pulling her arm from his grip.

Hammond let out a breath. 'I'm getting the sense that within twenty-four hours, your file will be turned over to the taint team.'

'Don't trust your senses.'

'Do it, Agent Bryce. Or maybe I'll get your boss to back off. He might be interested in taking a look at your file.' He was half-turned away from her, as if trying to physically end the conversation. She realized Hammond was shaking, and it had nothing to do with being cold.

'Why didn't you just call me instead of bringing me all the way out here?' said Ren.

Headlights struck up on the road behind them. Hammond jumped. His left arm seemed to spasm. Ren glanced down at it. He was holding his cell phone. He jerked it quickly toward her. There was a text message on the screen:

this is not just about the psych 345

He hit delete. Ren opened her mouth to speak, but when she looked into Hammond's eyes – black with fear – she stopped dead.

This is not just about the psych 345? WTF?

40

Ren sat in a window seat on the flight to Nogales. Ren liked aisle seats, but today she was wedged in by a skinny child with a giant backpack at his feet. He was playing a Nintendo DS with the sound on. Every beep was Chinese water torture. Ren glanced down at him. He gave her an adorable smile and raised the console a little to show he was doing well.

Bless your heart.

A wave of sadness swept over her – the boy was about eight years old, the same age Ren had been when she had the only childhood memory of not feeling quite right. In the middle of a burst of wonderful, uninhibited laughter with Matt, a thought had flashed into Ren's mind: 'But are you *really* laughing?'

At the time, that thought had frightened her. And she buried it away. Every now and then, she would remember it and it still creeped her out. 'But are you *really* laughing?' It was like a voice from the dark side.

Ren felt a tap on her elbow – the little boy beside her reached up to offer her some Skittles.

Redemption.

She almost cried. Sometimes strangers could blindside you with simple kindness. It was lonely being bipolar. And once you knew, you knew. *Once a word leaves your mouth, you cannot chase it back even with the swiftest horse.*

There were times when Ren had expected a call from Helen saying, 'I'm sorry, I made a mistake, you're actually fine.' Or she would come to the end of a session and Helen would rubber-stamp her file in red ink: SANE. And it was embarrassing that, at thirty-seven years of age, Ren still had that fantasy.

Despite any or all signs to the contrary.

She glanced at the screen of the boy's DS. He was playing Mortal Kombat 3. R-rated. Two fighters were kicking the crap out of each other. The screen flashed *Finish Him! Finish Him!* The little kid beside her pummeled buttons until he threw his opponent down ten stories and impaled him on metal railings. Comedy blood spurted into the air, followed by an ultra-deep voiceover: 'Sektor wins. Flawless Victory. Fatality.'

The kid looked up at Ren, beaming.

'Good job,' she said.

'I need to get as many fatalities as I can,' he explained.

'That's cool.' *Some day I might meet you in a professional capacity.*

She lay back against the seat and thought again about how much Helen knew about her. And how she would guard that knowledge to the . . . fatality.

This is not just about the psych 345. Ren had typed it into her own phone after she had met Douglas Hammond, and when she pressed 345, her predictive text gave a first option that was unsurprising under the circumstances: 'fil'.

This is not just about the psych files. What is *it about, then?*

*　　*　　*

Luke Sarvas lay in his hospital bed with the silent television flickering light across him. Ren walked across the room and turned it off. He blinked his eyes with relief. Most of Luke Sarvas' head was heavily bandaged. His face was destroyed. His right eye socket was impacted, his right jaw shattered and wired shut. Any unbandaged surface area was covered in superficial cuts and bruises. His lips were swollen and cracked, covered in a thick layer of Vaseline. There were bruises all over his neck. He kept his head still, but slid his gaze toward Ren. She introduced herself and sat on the chair by his bed.

'Do you know how you got here?'

He nodded.

'What happened?' She almost didn't want him to speak, his lips looked so damaged.

He opened his mouth slowly. The corners were dry and white and took time to break apart. It was hard to look at. 'I . . . fell,' he said.

'From the border wall?'

Luke nodded.

'No, you didn't.'

A fleeting frown crossed Luke's face.

'I spoke with your doctors,' said Ren. 'You have pretty severe crush injuries. Something fell on you.'

Luke closed his eyes slowly. *Bingo.* But he shook his head slightly to disagree.

'It's a medical fact,' said Ren.

He opened his eyes and looked at her.

'What fell on you?' said Ren.

He shook his head again. 'Nothing.'

'OK,' said Ren. 'I'm going to backtrack. What happened in that SUV eight months ago?'

He waited to answer. 'I . . . can't remember.'

'You can't remember anything?' said Ren.

'I can remember up to just before it happened.' Every word came out painfully slowly.

'So you don't know who stopped the vehicle, what the chronology of events were, nothing?'

He shook his head. 'No.'

'OK,' said Ren. 'So your memory was intact right up until that day.'

He nodded.

'In that case, tell me about Tijuana at spring break.'

Luke's eyes flashed, but he caught himself before they shot too wide.

Got you, you little shit. Ren watched as his faux-amnesiac brain flashed through what this FBI lady could possibly know about Tijuana.

'I'm . . . tired.'

Oh, please.

He pressed his thumb down on the red call button. The challenge in his eyes was extraordinary.

I want to put that pillow over your face, you lying little shit.

'OK,' said Ren. 'I'll come visit again. And again. And again.'

He turned his head to the wall. 'Don't bother.'

'Excuse me?' said Ren. 'What did you just say?'

He turned back toward her. 'I said, "Don't bother."' His voice had become very clear.

'OK,' said Ren. 'No problem. It was nice to meet you.' She stood up. 'Oh – wait. I have to show you something. Where is it? Oh, yeah.' She slipped her hand into her brief-case and pulled out a photo. 'Here. Check this out.' She pushed the photo into his face and pulled it back slowly so he could focus on it. 'That's you,' she said. 'And that guy with you? He's your fifteen-year-old brother, Michael, who clearly thinks that the sun shines out of you. But after investigating that possibility, I beg to differ.'

Luke's mouth twitched. He blinked several times.

'I'm going to leave this right here,' said Ren, propping the photo up against his bedside lamp. 'I know you're in physical pain. But you're not the poor little cripple you appear to be. I've seen many people with terrible injuries. And no matter how much training I've been given, I still find it very upsetting. And I would be very upset right now if I thought you were a one hundred per cent innocent victim. What happened to you, your father and your brother was appalling and you have my sympathy for that. But that sympathy waned just a little, right when I heard you try to deny those crush injuries.' She picked up her briefcase. 'I have a job to do.' Ren walked to the door, but turned back as she opened it. 'God help your mother and God help Michael.'

She closed the door gently behind her.

Catherine Sarvas stood nervously in the hallway outside the room.

Nervous because she knew he would tell the FBI agent nothing.

'Luke is saying that he doesn't remember much of his accident,' said Ren.

'No, he didn't,' said Catherine. 'Which is probably a good thing.'

Hello? 'Catherine – Michael is still missing.'

'I know that more than anyone,' said Catherine.

'Luke is back,' said Ren. 'And we need to do everything we can to find out what happened to Michael.'

'Of course you do,' said Catherine. 'So do I.'

'I think Luke knows more than he is letting on,' said Ren. 'I need him to talk to me.'

'Excuse me?' said Catherine, her voice rising. 'Are you

telling me that my son is not telling you something that could help his brother be found?'

'That is a possibility.' *Slash certainty.*

'Maybe in your cynical world it is,' said Catherine. 'I have waited eight months to get my son back. You are insane to think that Luke would withhold any information that could be helpful. He has been through a terrible ordeal. God knows what went on during that time. He is disturbed. Maybe, just maybe he does know something, but bullying him won't get it out of him.'

Bullying? 'Nobody is bullying anyone,' said Ren. 'With the greatest respect, Luke has lied to you before – about spring break. And when I told him just now that I would come back to see him again when he was feeling less tired, he said to me "don't bother". Which I find strange, because his brother is still missing.'

Catherine paused. 'I doubt very much he would say something like that—'

'He did,' said Ren. 'Is it a phrase he uses much?'

Silence. 'If Luke did say "don't bother",' said Catherine, 'all I would hear in that is the response of a distraught teenager who is in physical pain and his been through a terrible emotional ordeal.'

'I understand that,' said Ren. 'I really do. But I think that would be all the more reason why he would not want Michael to have to go through the same. I think that would be the very reason why he would talk to me for hours on end in the hope that even one detail would lead to Michael being found.'

'He can't remember!' said Catherine. The volume was rising, the tone turning shrill.

'Did he even tell you that he had seen Michael?' said Ren. 'Were they taken together?' *Were they taken at all? Did they kill their father and run? Did Luke kill his father and brother?*

'They were taken together,' said Catherine. 'By the man who shot Greg. That's all he can remember.'

'Catherine, I am just trying to help your family,' said Ren. 'And to prevent anyone else from having to go through what you have.'

'It's not helping if you're harassing a seventeen-year-old—'

Oh, sweet Jesus. 'I am reaching out to *you*, Catherine – I am not in there berating Luke. I'm talking to *you* because you're his mother and you're Michael's mother and this is urgent.'

'I am so sorry. It's just . . . I'm afraid. I'm so afraid to hear what happened to him. Or to Michael. I can't bear the thought of what I might find out. And I can't bear the thought of him having to relive any of it—'

'He is not you,' said Ren. 'And this situation is different. Maybe this is the right time for *him* . . .'

'Oh, God,' said Catherine. She gestured toward the room. 'He just looks like a boy who's been in an accident and part of me can wrap my brain around that. And it makes me feel like he could be any other high school student who . . . I don't know if I'm making any sense . . .'

'You are,' said Ren. 'Maybe if you could encourage him to speak with me again . . . if there is anything he remembers . . .'

'He would have told you,' said Catherine. She walked towards Luke's room. As she opened the door, she turned back to Ren. 'Thank you for everything.'

What a total disaster.

41

Ren went straight from Denver airport to Safe Streets. Cliff was the welcome face in the office.

'Help me out here, Cliff,' said Ren, walking in, dropping her bag on her desk. 'As we know, I am without child, so can you explain to me how parents can be so shut down to the possibility that their offspring can do wrong? Or not even that – obviously some parents do acknowledge that. What I want to know is what makes one parent own up to their child's bad behavior and another parent swear blind that they couldn't possibly have done anything wrong? I don't get it. Especially if there is evidence to the contrary.'

'I was in school with this kid,' said Cliff. 'We were seven years old. And he was an arsonist. A full-blown set-a-huge-fire arsonist. Who developed into a set-a-huge-fire-and-jerk-off-while-you're-watching-it arsonist. He *smelled* of fire the whole time. He had burn marks on his hands. The kid *died* in a fire, for Christ's sake. And his parents, one of whom was the school principal, still to this day, talks about his son's "accident". I used to imagine the parents, standing in their garage, shaking a jerrycan and thinking "Oops, we're running low again."'

'It's insane,' said Ren. 'When I misbehaved as a kid – over and over – my mother never once tried to tell anyone I was innocent.'

Cliff said nothing.

'Oh my God,' said Ren. 'That's why I'm fucked up.' She paused. 'Your silence is telling me that that's not normal, my own mother not backing me up.'

'Hold it right there,' said Cliff. 'Mothers have instincts when their kids have done wrong. The crucial thing is – did your mother stand up for you when you were innocent?'

'I never was,' said Ren.

'There you go, then. I'm sure if someone had accused you of something you didn't do, she would have waded right in there.'

'But Luke Sarvas is a liar.'

'He's a seventeen-year-old kid whose mother thought she'd lost him for good.'

'You know in a movie where there's this kid who just has these knowing eyes that slide around the place to flag the fact that there's something weird about them? Luke Sarvas gives me that vibe. It's not that I think he's weird. But he is not some innocent. You can't be innocent if you're doing blow and hanging out in titty bars.' She smiled at Cliff. 'I know I sound like someone's grandma, but I liked it when kids were more innocent. God, if I have kids it's going to be like *The Village*.'

'You'd be surprised at how you adjust,' said Cliff. 'And you'd be surprised at how you can bring up your children a certain way that acknowledges the world we live in and just gives them the coping skills to navigate through it.'

'Wow,' said Ren, 'would you like to be the father of my children?'

'Just up until the point of conception.'

Ren smiled.

'So,' said Cliff, 'about you murdering Douglas Hammond . . .'

Ren shook her head. 'You heard.'

'Of course I heard,' said Cliff. 'Why were you meeting him on a dark night?'

'I can't get into that, Cliff,' said Ren. 'I'm sorry. You know I love you, but . . . I can't.'

'Is it to do with your friend Helen?'

Ren nodded. 'Yes.'

'And while we're at it,' said Cliff. 'Do you know something about Trudie Hammond?'

'Here's the thing,' said Ren. 'I know something about *me*. Like, I did not have a hand in Douglas Hammond's death. I do, however, look as though I did. So . . . if I could, for example, work out whether maybe he was the target of his wife's killer all those years ago, then I could at least have some evidence in my defense.'

'It probably looks like you did because you lied about it.'

'There's more to it than that, Cliff. Which I know is annoying to hear when I'm not revealing what that "more" is. I'm sorry.'

'Don't be, but don't get in trouble because you won't ask for help.'

'OK.'

'So, what is the JeffCo Cold Case Unit looking at in the Hammond case?'

'Running DNA tests – glass fragments, nightgown, carpet.'

'Any theories?'

'Firstly, I think it's weird that Hammond didn't insist on it earlier. And secondly . . . well, let's see what comes up.'

'Was she raped?'

'No signs of rape at the autopsy. She did have consensual sex with her husband that morning.'

'It could just be an intruder expecting to burgle an unoc-cupied house during the morning when people are out at work,' said Cliff. 'They had a nice house, rich pickings . . .'

'But I'm wondering, could someone have been waiting for Hammond to come home?' said Ren. 'Hammond could have been the intended target.'

Cliff nodded. 'Maybe he witnessed something and someone needed to get rid of him. Maybe they felt that his wife's death was warning enough to put him off, but something happened recently that made them think that he could still expose them?'

Ren shrugged. 'Could it have been connected to someone who was part of the original investigation? Like . . . a crooked cop.'

'Doing what?' said Cliff.

'I don't know . . . maybe Hammond came across some-thing recently that led him to believe a cover-up had happened?'

But could Helen Wheeler fit into that scenario? And if so, where?

'If in doubt, coffee,' said Ren.

'Yes, please,' said Cliff.

Ren's phone rang as she was carrying the mugs back in.

'There you go, baby-daddy,' she said, putting one in front of Cliff.

'Thank you, octo-mommy.'

'I have to do it that many times?' said Ren.

'Answer your phone,' said Cliff.

'Barefoot and pregnant, that's all I am to you now.' She looked at the number flashing on the screen. 'It's the lab.' She picked up and listened. 'Wow,' she said. 'OK.'

'What?' Cliff mouthed.

Ren put her hand over the receiver and spoke to Cliff. 'Curiouser and curiouser. DNA on the nightgown. Semen. And not Judge Hammond's.'

She took her hand away and spoke to the lab. 'In that case, could I ask you pretty please to do a cross-match for me?'

42

Ren sat at her desk and rested her hands on her keyboard as if she intended to use it. 'Ooh,' she said, a few moments later. 'Speaking of mothers in denial . . .' She picked up the phone and called Kitty. 'Mom, Cliff and I were talking about moms and kids and denial, etc. I just wanted to know . . .' She got up and walked into the hallway. 'Mom – when was the last time you spoke with Rita Parry?'

'Rita, gosh . . . Well, that is the most upsetting part,' she said. 'It was several months ago, before all this cards business. Ricky called me, he said that his mom wanted to speak with me. So, I dropped everything and went over to her. I was with her for hours, Ren. I even fed her while I was there, I got her out of the bed, I helped bathe her, dress her . . . it was . . . I don't think I'm any saint for doing this, by the way. It just seems such a jump to where we are now.'

'Did she ask Ricky to get you to come look after her?'

'No, no, it wasn't like that. She asked him to get me to come talk to her. The rest was just . . . well, it just seemed like the right thing to do. I wanted to help.'

'What did she want to talk to you about?'

'Death. I mean, the two of us, we're the Catholics on the block, so she thought she could confide in me.'

'About what?'

'She wanted to know my opinion about suicide and sin.'

'The gall of her.'

'No, Ren, it's not what you think. It wasn't about Beau. Well, not strictly speaking. It was more . . . she wanted to know if it was wrong in the eyes of the Church, her wanting to let go. She wanted to know if it was a form of suicide to let yourself slip away, to stop fighting for your life.'

'Euthanasia, you mean?'

'No, no. Just letting go. She knew she was failing and she wanted to give up the fight and let go. Because she wanted to meet Louis again. She told me she was ready to meet Louis again.'

'She thinks Louis is dead.'

'She said that she knows he is dead . . . I think it's possible that she had known it all along. She wanted to know did I feel that way about Beau, did I want to follow him. That was why she asked me over. So, I told her—'

'Mom, I don't need to hear this.'

'You do,' said her mother. 'I told her that I felt that way for quite some time after Beau died. I'm sorry, Ren, but I did. I'm sure that was obvious to all of you, anyway.'

'We tried not to go there.' Tears welled in her eyes.

'Rita said that she had felt that way too. But I told her that many years had passed and that to some degree I had managed to come to terms with the loss and that I loved your father and all of my children so much that I could not bear the thought of being without you. And I told her that if I were in her position right now, I would fight. I would not give up.

'Rita Parry wasn't told she had days to live, Ren. She wasn't given a finite time. I told her that maybe, if I had felt I was hours from slipping away, I would find comfort in knowing that Beau would be there at the other side to meet me, but it wouldn't be a reason for me to *want* to go.'

'Wow.'

'So I told her that, no, she wasn't committing suicide by doing what she was doing, but that I believed she should fight. For Ricky. She could have many more years with Ricky.'

'So, after all that, here we are,' said Ren. 'Mom . . . are you sure her motivation was pure?'

'Pure? What do you mean?'

'Are you sure she didn't believe Beau had something to do with it and was maybe trying to get you to confess to a dying woman?'

'For God's sake, Ren. That didn't enter my head.'

'Did she ask you why you thought Beau killed himself?'

'Quite the opposite. She said that she believed that Louis and Beau were our beautiful boys and that a darker force, stronger than either of them, had taken them from us. Different forces she said, but with the same tragic result.'

'The end is not here yet,' said Ren. 'For either family. Hasn't she even called you?'

'No, . . . No. I heard that she's very, very weak.'

Ren let out a breath. 'My heart goes out to her. I just wish I knew what was going through her head.'

'At this stage, I would say that her only thought is seeing Louis again.'

'How depressing,' said Ren. 'But I guess her whole life has been depressing.'

'Why are you asking about this?'

Ren let out a breath. 'Why do I ever ask?'

'What is that supposed to mean?'

'I have no idea, actually. I'm tired.' Ren wandered back into the office. 'I better get back to work.'

Ren pulled her notebook out of her desk and looked at her notes on the Hammonds. A lot of them had the numbers 345 doodled around them. One page had drawings of files. Another page had fishes in the margin. Ren tried to remember why. *One, two, three, four, five, once I caught a fish alive.*

She sat forward. *Oh. My. God.* She picked up the phone and dialed Glenn Buddy.

'Glenn, it's Ren. Can you do me a big favor?'

'No.'

Silence.

'I'm sorry, Ren. I can't.'

'OK, I understand. But – if I tell you what the favor is, could that make a difference?'

Glenn let out a breath. 'Shoot.'

'Do you have Douglas Hammond's cell phone in evidence?'

'Yes.'

'Could you just check if his texting language is set to predictive text?'

Glenn paused.

'How about we try it this way: I tell you that I think it is not? Could you confirm that his phone is *not* set to predictive text?'

'OK. I guess I could do that. I'll call you back.'

'Thank you, Glenn. I appreciate it. Whenever you get the chance.' *Immediately, please, immediately.*

Glenn called back twenty minutes later. No, Douglas Hammond's phone was not set to predictive text. Ren thanked him, hung up and stared once more at the Fifty Most Wanted faces lined up across the wall. She remembered Douglas Hammond's last-ditch panic when he thought the headlights of a car were bearing down on him and the desperate text message he had punched in. But, she now realized, the quickest shorthand Judge Hammond could find to warn Ren was nothing to do with predictive text. They were what they were: numbers. And they matched the faces that Ren was now looking at.

Three: Domenica Val Pando. Four: Javier Luis. Five: Erubiel Diaz.

43

Ren's heart was pounding. *Douglas Hammond. Helen Wheeler. Domenica Val Pando. Javier Luis. Erubiel Diaz. WTF?*

'What's going on in your tiny mind?' said Cliff.

'Huge thoughts . . .'

'On . . .' said Cliff.

'I'm sorry, I just . . .'

'Have you stopped trusting me?' he said. He meant it.

'I think I have stopped trusting myself.'

'That's very sad.'

'It is,' said Ren.

'Well, if you change your mind . . .'

'Thanks. I feel like my head's about to blow.' She looked again at the photos. 'There's family stuff too.'

'Anything you want to talk about?'

'No, not really. But don't take it personally.'

'I won't, and if you need me, you know where I am.'

'Thanks, Cliff.'

She glanced at the TV to end the awkwardness.

A box on the top right of the screen read: ARRESTS MADE IN DRUGS TUNNEL COLLAPSE.

'Crank it up,' said Ren.

'You have the remote,' said Cliff.

Ren grabbed it and turned up the volume. *When did this happen?*

A photo filled the screen that Ren wished she had seen forty-eight hours earlier. It was of a huge truck beside a gaping hole in a dusty hillside in Nogales, Mexico – the opening to a tunnel under the border that would lead to Nogales, Arizona on the other side. According to the report, it was the fifteenth tunnel found in the area in the previous year and was believed to be linked to the Puente cartel.

The tunnel, which had been under construction for months was detected by Border Control just three days earlier when workers fled from it after a support beam in the ceiling collapsed.

Imagine the crush injuries you'd get from that, Luke Sarvas. You lying son-of-a-bitch.

Ren called Hunt Memorial Hospital and asked to be put through to Luke Sarvas' room.

'Hello?'

'Catherine?' said Ren. 'It's Ren Bryce here. Is Luke there?'

'Yes,' said Catherine. 'But I told you—'

'Catherine, put him on the phone to me right now or within a half-hour that room is going to be swarming with FBI agents who give less of a shit about you and Luke than I do.'

Catherine let out a slow breath. 'He can't hold the phone.'

'Hold it up to his ear! For God's sake, Catherine. This is important.'

Ren heard the phone move and a change of breathing as Luke Sarvas came on the line.

'Luke, it's Ren Bryce. How did the support beam fall?'

Silence.

'Luke, answer me. How did it fall?'

His voice cracked. 'Because I knew exactly how to make it fall.'

Oh my God. 'You did it?'

'Yes . . . we were . . . forced to . . . they told us we would be killed if we didn't do it. I . . . I . . . wanted to get out,' he sobbed. 'I had to get out. I wanted to see my mom.'

Cliff's words rang in Ren's ears: he's a seventeen-year-old kid. Kids seemed so advanced, but really, there was only so far their coping skills could stretch at that age.

'What happened to you?' said Ren. 'What happened to you?'

'I can't . . . I can't . . .' He was sobbing louder.

'Luke, can you tell me – have you heard of the Puentes? Or of a man called El Coyote Panzón? Is that the man who made you do this? El Coyote Panzón.'

There was complete silence at the other end of the phone.

'Luke? Luke?' said Ren. 'You can talk to me. You're safe now.'

Still Luke said nothing.

'You're safe,' said Ren again.

Luke lowered his voice. 'You're not.'

The line went dead.

What the hell? Ren called Catherine Sarvas' cell phone. It was diverted. She tried the hospital again. The line to Luke Sarvas' room was busy.

Why would I not be safe? And how could Luke Sarvas know that? And if he does have that kind of information, he is not safe. Neither is his mother. And neither is Michael. And where is Michael Sarvas?

Ren picked up her office phone and dialed the number for El Paso PD. As she was waiting to be connected, her cell phone rang. Caller ID showed the hospital number. She hung up and took the cell phone call.

It was Catherine Sarvas. 'Ren, I've sneaked into another patient's room. Luke says you've got to back off from all of this. Don't get the police involved. Don't get your bosses involved. And he told me to tell you that El Coyote Panzón is dead.'

She hung up. Ren's heart pounded.

What is going on?

Ren's cell phone rang again. 'This is Mannering Security Systems. Could I speak with Annie Lowell?'

'I'm afraid not,' said Ren. 'My name is Ren Bryce. Is this about Annie's place? I'm the house-sitter.'

'Do you have the code word?' said the man.

'Edward,' said Ren.

'Yes, ma'am. We have a report of an alarm going off—'

Shit. 'Sir, I'm an FBI agent, please do not send any of your men to the property. I will take care of it.'

He paused. 'It's our policy to—'

'Sir, forget your policy. I'm with Rocky Mountain Safe Streets Task Force and I am not in the habit of putting people's lives at risk. So, please, let me take care of the house. And you can keep your employees safe. I'm going to give you my boss's direct line. His name is Gary Dettling. You can call him right away to verify my details. Thank you for the call.'

Ren grabbed her purse and ran. She shouted in to Gary to expect the call and that she would take care of the break-in herself. Or the strong wind. Or the stray cat.

When she pulled up outside Annie's, it looked the same as it had when she left that morning. There were no windows open, the front door was locked. She opened it and walked inside. She called Misty's name. There was no answer. She called again, still no answer. She ran up the stairs to her bedroom. Misty wasn't there. Her heart started pounding. *Why is this house so fucking big?* She ran down the stairs and into the living room, the dining room, the kitchen. She heard a noise out the back. *Oh shit.* It was an enclosed yard. There was only one way in and out. She started to slide her gun from her inside jacket pocket, caught sight of a whirl of black and white through the glass.

Misty! Sweet Jesus. She pushed the gun back into its holster. And pulled the door open. Misty threw herself against her. Ren almost cried.

'If anything ever happened to you, Misty Bryce,' she said. She sat on the step and held Misty to her chest, rubbing her head, tickling her belly.

'Who let you out here?' she said.

Ren brought her back into the house. She went into the living room. A chill swept over her. Someone had been there. And they had left her a gift.

Unlike whoever had broken in the first time.

It was a DVD with a nice neat sticker that had her name on it. She put it into the player.

'Loading' flashed for too long on the top left corner of the screen before it went black. *Stay black. Please stay black. Black has to be better than whatever I'm about to watch.*

Ren had no idea what movie was going to light up her screen, what sound was going to fill the living room. She pulled Misty up beside her on the sofa and wrapped her arms around her. A face she knew filled the screen – an ugly face, an ugly man – number four on Denver's Most Wanted. Javier Luis: a man whose rap sheet included first-degree murder, attempted first-degree murder, aggravated robbery; drugs; rape, assault on a minor . . .

In the mug shot on the wall at Safe Streets, Luis looked

bad. On screen, he looked worse. And the picture was razor-sharp. He looked sixty years old. Meth.

Luis opened his mouth and flashed black and broken teeth. 'From 1996 through 1998, I worked for Augusto Val Pando at his compound in New Mexico.'

So Augusto is being set up to take the fall.

Luis' eyes shifted back and forth. 'Towards the end,' he said, 'I was not happy with my position and I wanted to leave. But I was infectively incarcerated.'

Infectively – I love it. You were all infectively incarcerated, you fuckwit.

'I wanted out,' said Luis, 'but I had no way of escaping.'
No shit.

'What happened was, during this time, a woman who I thought to be a nanny to the Val Pandos' son, her name was Remy Torres—'

Why is he talking about me? What the FUCK?

He continued. 'Well, I was unaware at that time that Remy Torres was, in fact, FBI Special Agent Ren Bryce who currently works with the Rocky Mountain Safe Streets Task Force in Denver.'

What the FUCK IS THIS?

'On the evening of December twenty-eighth, 1998—'

Ren hit Pause. *December 28th?* She stared at the screen. *Oh God, no.* She raised the remote control slowly and hit Play. It was as if she had also hit mute; all sound seemed to be sucked out of the air as the camera panned to the man on his right. Her eyes shot wide.

Oh, no. Oh, no, no, no.

44

Ren dropped the remote control. She ran to the bathroom and threw up. Until there was nothing left in her stomach. As she was walking back to the living room, pale and weak, she heard her cell phone ring. She couldn't remember where she'd left it. It stopped ringing. The sound seemed to have come from the kitchen. The ringing started again, stopped, started again. *Shit.* She went in to get it. It was Colin.

'Ren, where are you?'

'Home. Why?'

'Is everything OK at the house? Gary said you had to go—'

'Oh,' she said. 'Yes. Yes. It must have been a stray cat . . .'

'OK, cool. I'm just pulling up outside. Have you eaten?'

'Whoa, whoa,' said Ren. 'What? I can't go out . . . I . . .'

'Oh, I'm not asking you to dinner,' said Colin. 'I'm taking you to a crime scene. And, apparently, it's not very pretty at all.'

Shit. Shit. Shit. 'Yeah, well don't worry about me throwing up.'

She heard the horn beep outside and down the phone line. 'Give me two minutes,' she said and hung up. *Fuck. Fuck. Fuck. Fuck. Fuck.* She ran into the living room and turned off the TV and DVD player. She ran up the stairs and changed and brushed her teeth. She looked at herself in the mirror. She took a deep breath.

And for my next performance . . .

Colin's car was moving as fast as it could along the icy streets. The wipers were shifting the heavy-falling snow across the windscreen, stopping briefly every couple of minutes, then jerking back to work. *Excruciating.* Ren felt suddenly trapped, walled in by the car, the sound of the wipers, the DVD, the irrational sensation of being taken from her home against her will. She slammed her hand down on the button to open the window. Flakes of snow started drifting into the car. Colin looked her way, but said nothing.

'Sorry,' said Ren. 'I'm . . . hot.'

'Don't worry about it.'

Colin had brought coffee the way she liked it: no additives. *A kind gesture.* She glanced at him. Strangely, alone with Colin Grabien, she was the least likely to fake good humor. He didn't need a performance. She'd work up the energy to do that for the others.

They pulled up at the entrance to a warehouse in downtown Denver. Denver PD cruisers were scattered out front, alongside detectives' and Safe Streets' vehicles. Ren walked toward the building ahead of Colin, flashed her badge and walked into an almost-empty space, flooded with harsh light.

'Take the second last door,' said the uniform.

'Thank you.'

Her heels were louder than she would have liked, echoing

across the bare concrete, drawing attention she did not want. She kept her head down until she got to the door. The smell was already foul and she hadn't even gone down the hallway where she could see the officers silhouetted in the fluorescent light from the crime scene.

'Any ID yet?' she said to the first uniform she met.

'Does faceless dead man count?'

'In some jurisdictions, possibly.' Ren smiled grimly as she stepped past him. She nodded when she saw Gary and Cliff in the far corner. As she walked past more officers, a strange feeling started to crawl over her. To her left, she saw Glenn Buddy directing a group of his colleagues, but the feeling had nothing to do with him. It was an ominous sense of familiarity, something in the walls – a terrible color of watered-down yellow, a huge blank spot of pale green where a bank of cabinets had been ripped from a wall. And it was in the area that held most of the blood and bone and brain matter and scalp and hair and teeth and flesh of the victim.

Gary and Cliff were saying hello, but Ren wasn't registering it. Her head was swimming. She finally reached them and looked down at the leftover face of a man who had obviously been shot at close range with a high-caliber rifle. The leftovers were scraps of scorched skin, a partial jawbone, a creepy skeleton half-smile, made more grotesque by the few ragged teeth.

'No ID,' Cliff was telling her.

'Really?' said Ren. 'How come we're here?'

'The call came into me,' said Gary. 'Anonymous. Just "get to blah warehouse". Nothing more dramatic than that. I called Denver PD when I got here.'

Ren's heart felt like it would explode out of her chest. 'Well, blah warehouse certainly gave up the goods.'

'I was at that concert,' said Gary, pointing down at the blood-soaked AC/DC T-shirt.

I bet the dead guy wasn't.

Ren glanced down again at the body of the man she had just been watching in a different kind of Technicolor.

Denver's Most Wanted number four: Javier Luis, DOB 1973, 5' 2", 160 lbs.

Ren got back to Annie's as quick as she could after the scene was processed. She rushed in the door and grabbed the remote control. She hit Rewind, then Play.

Javier Luis' voice seemed louder. He continued: 'On the evening of December twenty-eighth, 1998 . . .'

As he spoke, Ren could not take her eyes off the man beside him. It was James Laker, Gavino Val Pando's biological father. Laker was blond and rugged, a regular guy in a button-down shirt and jeans. His eyes were warm, clear blue, his eyebrows heavy.

Luis was smiling up at Laker, goading him into the revelation that Ren knew was coming. Her heart pounded.

Ren heard a voice off-camera shout, 'We don't have fucking time for this shit. Laker, tell your fucking story and we're out of here.' Fear flashed in Laker's eyes. He shifted in his chair. When he finally spoke, his voice, the one she remembered, had none of its old warmth. He stared at the floor.

'My name is James Laker. I worked for Augusto Val Pando from 1990 through 1998. Up to that point, I had been a Chief Investment Officer for a proprietary hedge fund—'

'We don't need your fucking resumé,' said Luis.

Laker's eyes flared with anger. He continued. 'Personal problems led me to work for Augusto Val Pando . . .' He stared up at the ceiling. 'My addiction in the late eighties to cocaine, marijuana and methamphetamine. I had defrauded

253

the company I worked for out of millions of dollars, all of which was repaid to them by Augusto Val Pando. In return, I went to work for him. He gave me unlimited access to the drugs I so desperately required. But by October 1998, I wanted out. I befriended Remy Torres, who was, in fact, FBI Special Agent Ren Bryce—'

Oh, James. What are you doing?

'I told FBI Special Agent Ren Bryce of my desire to enter a rehabilitation facility so I could return to regular employment and build a life for myself outside the criminal world. I begged for her help in doing so. The compound was heavily guarded and FBI Special Agent Ren Bryce—'

Stop calling me that. Stop.

'—appeared to be trusted by the Val Pandos.' Laker turned to whoever was behind the camera. 'It's too long, calling her that name. I'm just going to call her Remy – I'll tell the story quicker.' He stared ahead. 'Remy came to me late on Christmas Day and told me that she would find me a way out of the compound, but that it would have to happen within four days. She appeared to be intimately acquainted with the security systems, the staff's shifts and the safest routes to take to avoid detection and to reach the perimeter without difficulty. I can see now that this was due to her own situation, preparation and training as an FBI agent, something of which I was unaware at that time. I believe that because of my sexual relationship with Remy—'

Ren screamed at the screen, 'What are you DOING?'

'—she had developed an attachment to me,' said Laker, 'that led her to defy her superiors and aid my release.'

The camera panned down to the table where a dirty piece of folded paper lay. He held it up to the camera. 'Here you can see the plan drawn up for me by Remy, which includes all the details I mentioned above. Although, for obvious reasons, this plan was not signed, I'm sure a graphologist could confirm the writing as Special Agent Ren Bryce's.'

Yes, they could.

Luis laughed. 'And for how long did you attend rehabilitation when you left Augusto Val Pando's employ?'

'Shut the fuck up,' said Laker.

Luis froze. His face was half-smile, full fear. The camera zoomed suddenly, blurring the picture, then it slowly came into sharp focus, so that all Ren could see was Javier Luis' face. It had a puzzled tilt. Ren would have closed her eyes, but she wanted to watch. She could not take her eyes off him.

It wasn't what she expected. The first bullet was off-target. It grazed the side of Luis' neck, stunning him, but giving him a chance to turn in his chair to get away. So Ren didn't see the next bullet rip through his face. Instead, she saw the back of his skull explode and a flap of scalp and hair shoot up in the air and land back down as Luis hit the floor, spattering the marble tiles with blood and brain.

Two more bullets were fired off-camera and she heard James Laker cry out. But it was the sound of his words that echoed louder.

Sexual relationship? You lying, motherfucking, son-of-a-bitch.
You convincing lying, motherfucking, son-of-a-bitch.

45

There was not one person in the world who could see this DVD. Because her career would be over.

For one year, Ren had lived in a world stripped of humanity. It had been that way long before she ever showed up, it was that way after she left. It wouldn't end with the dismantling of the organization. It would travel with the people who had created it, wherever they went. It would fester in prisons, in homes, it would multiply.

After all, Pando is Latin for 'I spread'.

Mission number one: leave Ren Bryce behind. Mission number two: seduce Domenica Val Pando into believing that there was a woman called Remy Torres, who was twenty-six years old and who had just suffered the harrowing experience of losing her four-month old baby. Mission number three: seduce Domenica Val Pando into trusting Remy Torres. Mission number four: use that trust to find out everything there is to know about Domenica Val Pando.

And, oh, how she trusted.

*   *   *

Part of Ren wanted to stand by what she had done. She understood why she had done it. When she got to know James Laker – she thought he was kind, she thought he saw the world like she did – she latched on to what was the closest thing to normal she had found in the compound. She wanted to help him and she wanted to help his seven-year-old son. Javier Luis had not been part of the bargain. And, until Laker had been forced to do otherwise, Javier Luis had not been part of the bargain in his eyes either.

Whatever Erubiel Diaz did was out of Ren's control. But she felt responsible for Luis. She knew now that in releasing James Laker, she had released Javier Luis to rape and kill.

What she had done then seemed so different to what she would do now. It had gone against all her training. It felt like it was a decision made by a completely different person. Looking back, she felt she had been detached from reality. That ability made more sense when she was diagnosed. Being bipolar, she had a natural tendency to detach. She used it to make her a better agent. But at times like this, another part of her hated it and was afraid of it.

What have I done?

The repercussions of what she had done for James Laker were far-reaching. Just like Beau's suicide. Just like Louis Parry's disappearance.

Guilt. Lying. Guilt. Lying.

Suddenly, all thoughts of the compound were swept away.

Oh my God.

Ren called her mom, 'Mom, it's me. Sorry it's late, early, whatever. Remember when Rita Parry called you over to talk?'

'Yes,' said her mom. Her mom never commented on the strange hours Ren called her.

'How did that make you feel?' It was the first time in Ren's life that she had asked her mother a question about her emotions. Not because she didn't want to hear the answer, but because her mother never discussed emotions – not her own or any of her children's. Another HazMat suit wearer.

'Oh . . . I don't know . . . I suppose I felt bad. Her wanting to die like that. And not having answers to what happened to her son. I felt bad for at least knowing what happened to Beau.'

'You asked Ricky Parry to do some jobs in the house after that, didn't you?'

'Well, yes. The Parry's house was awful, Ren. It was so oppressive. There was no life in it. It was just . . . there. With a sick, depressed woman ready to give up, no matter what he could say or do. It can't have been easy for him.'

'No. I imagine it was the hardest thing he had ever gone through. And he had no idea what to do with the pain.'

Her mother hesitated. 'Yes . . . Ren, what is this about?'

'It's about me taking a day off work,' said Ren.

'Right,' said her mom. 'You do that, Ren. I'm sure you're exhausted with everything. That job of yours—'

'Yup,' said Ren. 'That job of mine. Love to you both, Mom.'

'And to you, too, sweetheart. Go back to bed.'

Ren put the phone down and pulled her wallet from her purse. She took out her credit card and made a phone call. She wrote down the details on a piece of paper. Outgoing flight time: 8 a.m. Return flight: 8 p.m.

The Parry house smelled of sickness and all the chemicals used to treat it. Ricky Parry was skinnier than Ren remembered. It didn't suit him. It made his face appear long and his eyes seem to retreat into their sockets. Maybe they were. Maybe they'd grown tired of looking out at the world.

He tried to smile at her. He gestured her into the room. But instead of walking past him, Ren put her arms around him and drew him into a hug. He froze. She could feel him tremble. She held him a little tighter, then gently released him.

'Can we sit down somewhere?'

Ricky nodded.

'Is your mom here?'

'She's sleeping.' He pointed to a room behind them. 'We converted the games room.'

They went into the living room and sat side-by-side on the sofa. Ricky's head hung. His hair smelled unwashed. His clothes smelled of having been worn too often and left damp for too long. He was oblivious to his right leg bouncing. His fingertips were red raw, the nails bitten halfway down.

The dresser was covered in photos. There were a lot of early ones, before Louis went missing; family vacations, school photos, everything that any other family would have. But at the end were a series of images that made the hairs on the back of Ren's neck stand up. *Oh my God.*

Ricky followed her gaze. The pain in his eyes was heart-breaking.

'I know,' he said.

They were computer-aged photos of Louis, right up until the present. A graphic rendering of what Louis Parry would have looked like at fifteen, twenty-five, all the way up to the present day – a face from a childhood photo, mixed with the filled-out faces and hairlines of older male relations, mixed with the soft jawline he shared with his mother. A cobbled-together photo that had no place in a frame.

'You know why I'm here,' said Ren.

For a while, they stayed in silence. He looked up at her.
'Nancy Drew.' He smiled sadly.

'Oh, Ricky,' said Ren. 'How could you do this to us?'

46

Ricky Parry stared at the floor. Ren could see tears dropping on to the carpet. So many tears. 'I sat on the plane,' said Ren. 'And I thought about you all the way—'

'I couldn't handle it: the playing cards bringing it all back,' said Ricky. 'My mother wanted to be part of that – she heard about it and wanted Louis to feature. And I . . . and there it was all over again. Louis Parry, the media, the neighbors—'

'You couldn't take it.'

He shook his head. 'No.'

'It's dominated your entire life . . .'

He nodded. 'I loved Louis.'

'I know that,' said Ren.

Ricky looked at her with hope in his eyes. 'But I just ended up . . . I was always living in his shadow. Everyone was obsessed. My parents were never there.'

'And when that faded a little when you were a teenager, which was perfectly understandable, the guilt ate you up. I could see that. And through it all, you still missed Louis and you felt for your parents.'

'My father died never knowing what happened to Louis.'

Ren nodded. 'And you didn't want your mother to do the same.'

Ricky shook his head. 'No. I didn't want her to die. I don't want her to die. And I thought, if she knew what happened to Louis, she could focus on that instead of focusing on meeting him in the next life. She kept saying that – about meeting him. I couldn't handle it. It was like she had more to die for than she had to live for. She didn't once talk about leaving me. She just talked about joining him. And I'm here. I'm alive, but why? What's the point?'

'That must have been devastating,' said Ren. 'But then, if it wasn't devastating, you wouldn't have been so desperate to—'

'I'm so sorry, Ren. I had to do something . . .'

'Jesus, Ricky. Beau? I swear to God . . .'

Ricky was crying. 'I know. I'm so sorry. But he's—'

'Yes,' said Ren. 'Dead. Which makes this worse. Did you ever really know how good he was to Louis? Did you have a clue? He was so good to all the kids. He never turned anyone away. He understood them. Did you know he taught Louis for free? Those last few lessons he gave him were for free, because your parents were having a hard time. Beau was—'

'I know all that,' said Ricky. 'God, I know and I'm sorry . . . But it was because of your family and what good people they are that I was able to do this. Your mom gave me these odd jobs to do, because she knew I needed the money. I'm not even any good. But it meant I could get into Beau's room. It was the easiest way to . . .'

Ren shook her head. 'Did your mom really believe that Beau could have done anything to Louis?'

'She's very weak now. She's drifting in and out—'

'So this was all ultimately pointless.'

'How can you be so calm?'

'Calm? On the outside maybe,' said Ren. 'How could you do this, Ricky? How?'

Ricky glanced at the door to his mother's room as Ren's voice started to rise.

'Don't,' she shouted. 'Don't! Right now, I don't care that your mother is sick in there. My brother is dead. And you tried to destroy my family all over again. All we did was try to help you.' She was standing now. She wanted to slap him across the face. 'Look at me,' she shouted. 'Look me in the eye.'

'I'm sorry. I'm so sorry—'

'What were you thinking? Forget about Beau – you almost closed a case that was having its last shot at being solved. Whatever happened to Louis – the person who did it is still out there. The playing card could have worked. Someone could have . . . come forward with new information.' *Ugh.*

'Or someone could not have,' said Ricky. 'It's been nearly thirty years.'

'Did you think this fake truth was going to seep into your consciousness so that, in a few years time, you could believe that it was Beau and you could have some closure?'

'I wasn't hurting anyone who was alive.'

'Oh my God, are you insane? The whole rest of my family is alive! Do you think this doesn't hurt?'

'I . . . I'm sorry.'

'I'm done,' said Ren. 'I have got to get out of here. Daryl Stroud's outside. He'll come talk to you.'

'What's going to happen?'

'I doubt my family will want to press charges, I know I don't, but you can give one more interview to the press. With every detail of what you did – calling Crimestoppers, planting the T-shirt. And all the details that will honor Beau's memory – or, so help me God . . .'

Ren opened the front door. A patrol car was parked at the end of the path. Daryl Stroud got out and nodded as he walked towards Ren. *Pumped muscles, popping neck veins, tan, buzz cut.* He shook her hand.

'Hi, Ren. What's all this about?'

'Ricky is your tipster. He planted the T-shirt.'

'What? No.'

Ren nodded. 'Yes. The world is a fucked-up place.' She started to walk down the path. 'He's inside. Go talk to him. He'll tell you himself.'

'Jesus Christ. I'm—'

She kept walking. 'So, will I see you back at your office?' When he didn't answer, she turned around.

Daryl looked frozen.

'Did you think that was it?' said Ren. 'I was just going to go quietly back to Denver?'

'Does it have to be the office? Can we go to Bob's?'

'Sure,' said Ren. 'What the hell.'

Ren got into her hire car and called her mother's house.

'Ren? Where are you?'

'In Catskill. I'm calling to let you know that everything is OK about Beau.'

'In Catskill? What—'

'I'm not staying for long. I'm exhausted. I'm calling to fill you in. I'm heading back to Denver on the next flight. It was Ricky Parry who—'

'Ricky Parry?'

'Let me finish. It was Ricky Parry who rang in the tip, who put the T-shirt in Beau's room. He made the hole in the headboard when he was doing whatever work he was doing on the house.'

'Ricky Parry? But—'

'I know. It's terrible.'

'But, I always looked out for Ricky. I gave him work, I sent him over meals when his father was ill and his mother . . . I did everything I could for that family . . .'

'He was desperate, Mom. He just wanted to relieve some of his mother's suffering. He couldn't do anything about the physical pain, but he thought this would take away some of the mental pain. It doesn't excuse anything. You can't take this personally. Beau was the easiest person to set up. Ricky had access to the house. And Beau couldn't defend himself.'

'But I don't think Mrs Parry would have been relieved to think that Beau did this. She sent Louis to our house for tuition, she would have blamed herself for—'

'You're just going to have to stop looking for logic in all this,' said Ren. 'There is none.'

'But—'

'Don't torture yourself, Mom. Ricky Parry was just screwed up. That's as much sense as you will make of this. Let it go.'

'I don't know if I can.'

'You have to,' said Ren. 'This is, in its own tragic way, good news. Try it, Mom. Try to feel the good news.'

47

Bob's Diner had been completely transformed since Ren had been home at Christmas.

Nooo. 'What did Bob do?' said Ren, looking around.

'He died,' said Daryl.

'Oops.'

'And his daughter got her hippie hands on it. But she does do great coffee.'

'Thank God.' Ren looked around. 'I'm not good with change.'

'Except in boyfriends.'

Ren smiled.

'I didn't really think it was Beau,' said Daryl. 'I just needed to stay professional. I hope you can appreciate that. I just had to deal with the evidence. The tip came in. The T-shirt was there. Those were facts I had to address, despite my feelings.'

'I understand,' said Ren. 'I would have been the same. But it still would have been hard.'

'Well, don't think it wasn't hard for me.'

'So, where will you go from here?'

'I don't know,' said Daryl. 'I'm sure it's happened to you – you get a tip, you focus on it . . . But it's not like we ignored anything else that came in. All this seemed to do was remind us we had nothing to go on in the first place. Jesus, though. Ricky Parry . . . He's a mess.'

'I know. God help him.'

'And poor your mom. All of you.'

'Do you know the worst part?' said Ren. 'Beau hasn't been vindicated. Still, no one knows what happened to Louis Parry. And the next big event in town was Beau's suicide . . . it just . . . didn't help in that regard. People are so afraid of suicide. They assume that there is some hideous dark secret behind it. Handsome Beau Bryce from that regular family could not possibly have wanted to end his life. He must have been abused as a child, or gay, or a rapist, a pedophile, a murderer. They can't understand depression. Just the despair that someone can go through. You knew Beau, he had a huge brain. It just . . . turned on itself. That's how I see it. It's like your brain just uses its power to convince you of something that is not true: that the world is better off without you or that you are better off without the world . . .'

'I am so sorry,' said Daryl. 'It's still terrible to see you upset.'

'*I'm* sorry,' said Ren. 'I . . . God, it never goes away. I keep hoping that, one day, I'll be able to talk about his suicide, anyone's suicide, and be objective. But . . . my heart is so broken.' She paused. 'Which leads me to . . . Daryl, I need a favor. I was wondering if you could do one thing for me . . .'

Ren stood at the carousel in Denver airport, waiting for her cell phone to kick in. It beeped several times with voicemails. As she was about to check them, the phone rang.

'Hey, Ren. It's Jay.'

'Hey,' said Ren. 'How are you?'

'I just wanted to say well done on Ricky Parry. I never would have guessed.' He paused. 'Not that I'm saying you guessed either. I'm just saying—'

'Thank you.'

'I don't know how you do it.'

'Neither do I.'

'I could barely work out where I was last weekend, and I was *there*.'

'Were you?' said Ren. 'Is there anyone who can confirm that?'

Jay laughed.

'So . . .'

'How's everything else?'

'Good,' said Ren. 'Good.'

'I . . . How are you getting by without your . . . doctor? That must be hard on you.'

'It is,' said Ren. 'I can't even explain how hard.' *Because you probably wouldn't understand.*

'I want you to know that, if you ever need anyone to talk to, I'm here.'

'That's really nice, Jay. Thanks.'

'I mean, it's at the other end of a phone, but . . .'

'Thank you anyway.' *It's the thought that counts, I guess.* 'Jay, Mom's trying to get through, I've got to go.'

'Talk soon.'

'Take care.'

Her mom sounded manic. 'Oh, Ren – Daryl Stroud just called me. The man they interviewed who said Beau had been doing drugs has admitted that he made it up.'

Thank you, Daryl. 'I knew it,' said Ren. 'I told you.'

'I feel terrible now for having believed it.'

Sweet Jesus. 'Mom, stop it. Stop always finding a reason to feel bad about something. You should listen to yourself some time. You have just been told something that made you feel good. And straight away, you went looking for something to make you feel bad. Did you even pause for a minute to feel the good feeling? Or do you think your whole life might implode if you do?'

'What's that supposed to mean?'

'It means: you're only happy when it rains.'

'That's not true.'

'And because you don't believe that's true, it will never change,' said Ren. 'It must be exhausting.'

'I *am* exhausted.'

Ren let out a breath. 'Go, get some rest. Do something nice for yourself. Why don't you and Dad go out for dinner?'

'I'm worried your father might—'

'Might *what*? Steal some of your French fries? Slip on a wet tile in the men's room? Choke to death on a piece of steak? You need to get a swear jar, Mom, but instead of putting a dollar into it when you swear, do it when you start a sentence with "I'm worried . . . " Call it a Worry Jar. And by Christmas, you'll have saved up enough money to go on that cruise around the world that you were worried you would never have enough money to go on. Or would you be too worried that the ship would sink?'

'Sinking is the least of my worries. People are getting murdered on cruise ships these days.'

Ren started laughing. 'Oh, you'll have that money saved up by next week. Anyway, I've got to go. Enjoy your dinner with Dad.'

'What if people in the restaurant are all staring at us?'

'It will only be because they're thinking, "Look at that

handsome couple. Isn't it wonderful that a couple who have been together that long can still be so in love?"'

'Even if your father does drive me crazy sometimes.'

'B'bye, Mom.'

Ren got a cab at the airport and was about to head for Annie's when she remembered her Jeep was at Safe Streets. The taxi dropped her off. There was a light on in the office. She went in and took the stairs to the fourth floor. Gary was in his office with the door closed. Ren carried on walking, into the bullpen. There was an envelope on her desk from the lab. It was the results from the DNA cross-match with the semen on Trudie Hammond's nightgown. She ripped open the envelope and scanned the pages.

I knew it.

Ren looked at her watch. It was 11 p.m.

If I can disturb the dead at this time, I can definitely disturb the living.

48

Peter Everett opened his door slowly and let his arm fall limp at his side. His hair was standing on end, his eyes red, his pupils like pinholes.

'You must have been a very nervous man over the past few weeks,' said Ren.

It threw him. 'Nervous?' He stared at her. 'Why would I be nervous?'

'Can I come in?'

He nodded.

They went into the living room this time. He gave Ren the sofa and stood leaning against the bureau opposite it, his arms and legs crossed.

'Please sit down.' Ren gestured to the seat across from hers. He sat down.

'OK,' said Ren. 'Let's do this.' She slid a photo across the table between them.

Everett's eyes shot wide. He frowned.

'You know who that is,' said Ren.

'Uh . . . yeah. It's . . . Judge Hammond's wife. Trudie.'

Ren nodded. 'It is.' She let the silence between them stretch to minutes. He had stopped looking at the photo after his first quick glance. But Ren could sense, behind his eyes, rapid traveling thoughts.

'I won't show you a crime-scene photo,' said Ren.

Tears welled and disappeared into his eyes. In seconds.

'Tell me,' said Ren. 'I know, but tell me.'

Another long silence.

'I don't know what you mean,' said Everett. 'Tell you what?'

'I'm not playing this game with you,' said Ren. 'This back-and-forth thing. What happened to Trudie Hammond? And do not respond with any variation on "Tell you what?" or "How would I know?" I don't want to hear it. I don't have the time or the patience.'

Everett's hand had a tiny tremor when he lifted it again to rub his forehead.

'Douglas Hammond moved from the area three months after the murder. You and Lucinda moved within two.'

'Wouldn't you have?' said Peter. 'The whole place had changed. We didn't like the idea of bringing up our daughter on a street where someone had been murdered. Especially when the killer hadn't been caught. And as for Douglas Hammond moving, well, he had even more of a reason.'

'Anyway,' said Ren. 'I'm looking through the file and thinking about all of that and how there was something missing. I don't know if you know much about cold-case investigations, but the main bummer is that you're working with, in this case, a twenty-seven-year-old file and the limited homicide experience of the investigators. It was quite a thin file, all things considered.'

Everett had no idea where she was going.

'What we did have, wrapped in a brown paper bag – God

bless Detective Whoever – was Trudie Hammond's night-gown . . .'

Something was slowly dawning on Peter Everett.

Ren kept going. 'So I figured, maybe those blood stains weren't all Trudie Hammond's. There may have been blood stains from the killer; the vase used to beat her to death had shattered, so he may have gotten cut himself. Back then, they didn't have the means to test for DNA and deter-mine who the blood belonged to. So I sent the nightgown to the lab . . . and, no, it was all just Trudie Hammond's blood.'

Everett appeared to be relaxing.

Not so fast. 'But what the lab *did* find was semen stains. On the back of her nightgown. There was so much blood, that no one had paid any attention. And even if they had, Douglas Hammond said he'd had sex with his wife that morning. I might have overlooked that semen stain too, but I believe with a cold-case file you take what's there and do everything you can with it. Especially something that the original investigators didn't. So, what the hell, I ran it anyway. And it turns out, it wasn't Douglas Hammond's semen. But there were no signs of rape, so consensual sex was had.'

'I don't need to hear the details of Trudie Hammond's death,' said Everett. 'Or her file. Or the stains on her night-gown.'

'Oh, you do,' said Ren. 'Back to Helen Wheeler. You're dating her. She is murdered. The judge who is trying to access her patient files is killed. You used to know him.' Ren paused. 'How did you meet Helen Wheeler?'

'At a benefit.'

'When?'

'In September last year.'

'Had you ever been a patient of hers?'

'What? No. Psychiatrists are not allowed to date—'

'Are you for real?' said Ren.

'Look, we met at a benefit. We dated. It went from there
. . .'

'This all seems a little coincidental.'

'Well, it's not. Not to me.'

'So, you didn't come as a patient to Dr Helen Wheeler
and, in therapy, reveal to her that you killed Trudie
Hammond? Something that you were afraid Douglas
Hammond would find if he accessed the files? The newspapers reported that investigators were looking at the possibility that a patient had killed Dr Wheeler, so . . .'

'What are you talking about? This is ridiculous. I did not
kill Trudie Hammond. Nor was I ever Helen's patient. And
I barely knew Douglas Hammond. I swear to God.'

'You may not have known him . . . Most men would
rather not know the husband of the woman they're sleeping
with.'

Everett froze.

'Did you not see that's where I was going with the DNA
thing?' said Ren. 'I had the lab run the semen stain against
the sample you gave for the Helen Wheeler investigation. I
got a match. It's black and white. Either you used Trudie
Hammond's nightgown to—'

I can't stoop that low.

Everett swallowed hard. He said nothing. In the silence,
Ren could not take her eyes off him. She treated times like
these, pauses from the guilty, as a form of meditation, one
of the few times she could be still yet keep her mind on
work. It wasn't healthy meditation, she knew that. It wasn't
as serene as looking at a flickering candle or a statue of
Buddha. She snapped out of it when Everett raised his
head.

'Lucinda and I were married two years. I was . . . young, starting up my business, working out of the house. Douglas Hammond was working as an attorney . . . the whole time. Trudie was . . . home.' He hung his head. 'I guess I can skip the romantic "how-we-got-together" part. But it wasn't just loneliness and it wasn't just sex.'

Here we go . . . 'OK.'

'We would get together during the day in one another's houses, whatever.'

'I'm sorry,' said Ren. 'Where was your wife . . . ?'

'Oh God, my wife,' said Peter. 'She was . . . wonderful. She was . . . most men would give their right arm to be with Lucinda. I tried so hard for her to be all that to me, but—' he shrugged. 'I don't even know why. Lucinda was beautiful, bright, generous, kind – she still is – but you need more than that, don't you? I mean, you could forgo some of those things if you had that special thing with a woman. That indefinable thing that I never believed in until I met Trudie. I loved the ground she walked on.'

'That would be beautiful to hear . . .'

Everett looked up at her, thrown.

' . . . if I didn't know how the fairytale ended,' said Ren.

Everett bowed his head again.

'Let me ask you, were you planning to leave your wife?' He shook his head. 'It was too early for that.'

'Because you had a fledgling business that her family money was paying for?'

Everett blushed.

At the money part.

'Yes,' he said.

'So, you would meet Trudie, how often?'

'Every day.'

'And on one of those days—'

'Douglas came home early and walked in on us.'

Whoa . . . Douglas Hammond came home before *Trudie was killed?*

49

How many dramas have been detonated by people simply coming home early?

'We were . . . Trudie and I had a policy of not doing it in our . . . marital beds.' Everett paused. 'I know,' he said, taking in Ren's look. 'How honorable.'

'Go on,' said Ren.

'Trudie and I were in the kitchen . . . it was all open plan – front door opened into the living room which opened into the kitchen. Douglas walked in. His face . . . we were in the middle of . . . I was behind her at the kitchen counter.'

Oh God, the housewife bent over the kitchen counter. Seventies-porntastic.

Everett went on: 'Douglas had no clue how he had been treating Trudie. No clue. He thought providing for her was enough. He just – he . . . When he saw us, he burst into tears. That's when we realized he was there. We struggled to get dressed and before Trudie had even gotten her nightgown back down, he had rushed over and grabbed her.'

He bowed his head. Ren waited.

'Her arm was kind of half in her nightgown,' said Everett.

'She lost her balance, fell against him . . . he pushed her away and then . . . she fell. Right through the glass coffee table. She landed on her back. There was glass everywhere. It was like shrapnel, like a bomb had gone off.'

Everett rubbed his hair roughly over and over. 'It was so screwed-up. I'm standing there, my underwear half on, and everything's spattered with blood. Douglas is standing with his arm still stretched out, but he's so still, not crying any more, nothing. And I'm there with my dumb tennis shorts around one ankle. We look at each other. Me and Hammond. We lock eyes. And I think what we are both seeing are huge headlines, front-page photos, cops and cuffs and weeping families and jail and . . . we don't even have to say anything. It's like we make this silent decision.'

Jesus Christ.

'We . . . Trudie was still alive at this point,' said Everett. 'She's choking on blood. But not fast enough, God forgive me. And we both love this woman and no one wanted her to suffer.'

Ren opened her mouth to speak, but couldn't think of anything to say that would express how she felt, while leaving her with some form of professional dignity.

Everett started to cry. 'I couldn't watch it any more. I was going to put a pillow over her face. That's what I thought would be the humane thing to do. But Douglas stopped me and said, "An intruder wouldn't do that. An intruder would leave her." I couldn't believe how quickly he said it, how calmly. But the worst part was Trudie heard too. And we both saw that she had heard.'

Jesus Christ.

'I was frozen to the spot,' said Everett. 'I could not look at her. But my life would be over if I were part of all this. Lucinda's life would be over. She was pregnant. Her family . . . who had all been so good to me. And Douglas Hammond had a two-year-old daughter. So I picked up a vase . . . and I . . . I ended it for Trudie.'

'Ended it for Trudie'; the strange language people use to temper the truth. Like veneer on rotting timber.

'Me and the future Judge Douglas Hammond . . .' Everett looked at Ren as if he was talking about someone else.

'What a team,' said Ren.

'We stood there, we were . . . in shock. It was horrific. And next thing you know, I was back in my house, cleaned up like nothing had ever happened.'

'Until – shock horror – you hear that the pretty lawyer's wife who lives down the street was found dead.'

He nodded. 'Yes.'

'Where was your wife at that time?'

'Lucinda was at home on bed rest. She had pre-eclampsia.'

What an absolute shit. If only Helen knew who she had been dating . . .

'Have you ever fallen in love?' said Peter. 'With the right person at the wrong time? The wrong person at the right time? The wrong person at the wrong time?'

'So, this is about love . . .' said Ren. *You have got to be kidding me.*

'I'm not a bad person.'

'If you're not—'

'You surely are not naïve enough to think that there aren't a million other people around the world like me: good people who have done maybe one bad thing and have had no choice but to separate themselves from it.'

'Separate themselves from it? Interesting choice of words.'

Everett looked down.

'Do you think your wife ever suspected?'

Everett's head jerked back up. 'Not for one second. Lucinda just does not see badness anywhere. Or in anyone.'

God help her.

'And so you were able to continue with your life,' said Ren. 'Hold your wife's hand in the delivery room, cry at the birth of your daughter, get that business of yours up off the ground, build it to its current heights and keep it there . . .'

'I was – and am – haunted.'

'Probably by Casper the Friendly Ghost . . .' Ren stared at him. 'I mean, you wouldn't want to upset yourself too much.'

'You have to admit that, if you met me out, in company, in a bar, wherever, you would think I was a nice man,' said Everett. 'We would talk, we'd have things in common. You wouldn't spend the evening with a chill up your spine.'

Ren said nothing.

'Look at Helen . . .' There was pain in his eyes when he mentioned her name. 'She didn't figure me for a killer.'

'You don't figure *yourself* for a killer,' said Ren, 'and you had almost thirty years to make yourself believe that. The human mind is a powerful thing. It also helped you to create that mask of yours and keep on working on it right until . . . well, I suppose the end. Which is round about now. I can't blame Helen for not seeing through you. You're right, I would have met you and not suspected you of anything. But please, don't be foolish enough to take that as a compliment on your acting skills or anything else. Nor is it a sign that, deep down, you really are a good person and that that is what ultimately shone through.' Ren shook her head. 'What you and Douglas Hammond did was possibly the most . . .' She shook her head. 'It's just mind-blowing how you came together in that way. Did you ever cross paths since then?'

Everett shook his head. 'No. I'm sure we both saw each other in the media . . .'

'Deathstyles of the Rich and Famous?' Ren tilted her head. 'What do you know about Douglas Hammond's death?'

'Nothing more than what I read in the paper. A car wreck . . .'

'OK. Well, Denver PD will talk to you about all that when I bring you in.'

'What about it?'

'It wasn't an accident. It was homicide.'

'What . . . why would Denver PD want to talk to me?'

Ren gave him a patient look. She stood up from the sofa. 'Let's go.'

'This is not me,' said Everett. 'None of this. It's just not me. The person who did that to Trudie.'

'If that makes you feel bett—'

Ren broke off as she caught a shadow passing by the glass in the dining room. She took another step, but stopped again. She could hear the faint sound of ceramic rocking on a shelf, as if something had been disturbed.

There is someone in the other room. She looked at Peter Everett. *Did he know? Was someone here all along?*

Keeping him in her sight, Ren slowly reached for her sidearm and began moving toward the door. Suddenly the doors burst open, knocking her gun from her hand and sending her sprawling to the floor. Seeing two masked men, she reached for her ankle holster but a boot slammed down hard on her thin wrist and she lost her grip. She kicked out and caught the intruder in the knee. He buckled. She stood up and moved to punch him in the face, until the hot pain of her wrist shot up through her arm. *Shit.* As she raised her leg to kick again, she caught sight of Peter Everett charging her way. *Oh my God: he's trying to help.* Everett grabbed the man by the shoulders and tried to spin him around. But the room seemed to fill with more people. *Just two more.* But it was enough.

The last thing Ren saw was Peter Everett being dragged, unconscious, from the room.

50

Ren woke up on Peter Everett's sofa. It looked like nothing had happened. *No signs of a struggle.* But two people had struggled . . . against four others. She glanced at her watch. Two hours had gone by . . . and now nothing. The only disturbance was the pounding inside her head. She sat up and slowly brought her feet to the floor. It was dark and clear outside. There was no snow falling. She let her head rest back against the sofa.

Douglas Hammond and Peter Everett killed Trudie Hammond. Now Douglas Hammond was dead. Peter Everett would have been dead, too, if that was what the intruders had wanted.

And so would I.

Ren made a call to Gary Dettling and held the phone an inch from her ear.

There was no evidence of a break-in in Peter Everett's house. The rooms were undisturbed, the intruders had worn gloves, the back door had not been smashed in. There were no foot-prints – no fresh snow to hold them. Everett's car was in the driveway where he had left it. Ren's car was outside on the street.

Gary arrived at the scene with Colin, Cliff and Robbie. Ren went through everything twice. Cliff took her aside gently.

'How are you doing? Are you OK?'

Ren nodded. 'Yes, thanks.'

'Just a heads-up – I called Glenn Buddy myself, to . . . lessen the blow.'

'Oh, God,' said Ren. 'I never even thought of that. He's going to—'

'Hello,' said Cliff loudly. 'Glenn, how are you doing?'

Glenn came up behind Ren and shook Cliff's hand. He reached out for Ren's as an afterthought.

I am the ground zero of all things bad in Denver. 'Hey,' said Ren.

'What happened here?' said Glenn.

'Nothing that you're going to find any evidence of, I'm afraid,' said Ren.

Glenn walked past her. 'Well, we'll see about that. Follow me in here, please.'

Everyone arrived back at Safe Streets at around the same time. Ren made a pot of coffee for ten and drank most of it. The television flickered in the corner. Every media outlet in Denver had heard the news of the missing millionaire . . . minus the detail that he and the dead judge had killed the woman they loved. Ren sat miserably in front of her computer.

The only man who can confirm all that is gone.

She opened a file and began typing in everything Peter Everett had told her. It was seared into her brain.

* * *

It was seven a.m. by the time Ren made it back to Annie's in a hazy painkiller glow. She went into the living room and slumped on to the uncomfortable sofa, dragging a magazine off the table. It fell open at: *How to De-clutter Your Home*. Ren looked around the room and decided to leave the magazine out for when Annie got back.

Just like mom left the 'Telling Your Children the Facts of Life' article from the Times *on the coffee table when I was eleven years old.*

Ren read about de-cluttering and decided to apply some of the tips to her mind. She also read about finding hidden treasures in your home. *Annie, you must have millions.* Ren got up and wandered over to an oak cabinet by the wall. She idly opened the door and made to close it again. But something caught her eye: four boxes marked *The Bryces* were lined across a shelf.

The rest were from another family Annie had been close to. Ren pulled out the Bryce box and opened it. It had photos, letters from her mom to Annie, postcards from vacations. Ren recognized her own writing. She picked up the letter.

June, 1981

Dear Annie

It is SO hot. I am SO happy we're not in school. I've been out on my bike, roller-skating, playing jump-rope. Last night, we went to a concert in the park – in a tent! It was fun!!! Before it, we had hamburgers, fries and milk for supper. Yummy!!! At the concert, we had popcorn and ice-cream. Matt dropped his on his leg and we could not stop laughing. Beau was mad. We were not paying attention.

Mom got mad too. We stayed in the park after. I went on the carousel and the bumper cars. It was fun!!!

Love and hugs,
Orenda XOXOXOXOXO

The innocence. Nine years old with no cell phone, no computer games, no lip gloss, no designer clothes, no staying indoors in the summer. But it was the last summer the kids in the neighborhood had the joy of roaming free. She remembered one little girl saying she hated Louis Parry. Hated, hated, hated him for ruining everything.

Ren put the box away as soon as she saw the corner of a photo with Beau's sneaker in it.

Not tonight. Not alone.

She went up to her room and put on her iPod. Chopin Nocturnes. *This is what my sore head needs.* She fell asleep to it. And two hours later, she jerked awake to it.

Louis Parry. Louis Parry. Louis Parry. The Catskill police had focused on the amusements. *But Louis Parry was into music.* And at the other side of the park, an orchestra was in a tent playing Mozart and Schubert. And Louis Parry had no money . . . so Louis Parry had sneaked in . . . or Louis Parry had stolen the money to get in . . . or someone had given Louis Parry the money to get in . . . or Louis Parry had been promised a free pass in exchange for something else. Ren's stomach lurched.

She grabbed her cell phone and dialed Daryl Stroud.

'Daryl, it's Ren again.'

'Hey, Ren.'

'Sorry for bothering you. I'm . . .' *Wired to the moon.*

'No problem,' said Daryl. 'How are you doing?'

'A little better,' said Ren. 'I think I know what happened to Louis Parry.'

Silence.

'OK,' said Ren, 'But if you could hear me out . . .'

'Sure,' said Daryl. 'Go ahead.'

'Everyone focused on Louis having gone to the amusements that day. Do you remember there was a concert too? I think he went to the concert. Or tried to go and didn't get there.'

'Slow down. I caught "amusements".'

'Sorry, sorry, sorry,' said Ren. She repeated herself.

'Does it matter where he was headed in the park?' said Daryl. 'The park was canvassed. Cops searched the entire area. They spoke to everyone they could who was there.'

'But did they talk to the orchestra?' said Ren.

Daryl paused. 'Uh . . . they left that night. Before it was confirmed that Louis was gone. But . . . I do remember reading in the file that someone called the director of the orchestra and asked him to ask the rest of them. No one saw any kids.'

'So the members of the orchestra weren't individually questioned?'

'No.'

'And obviously there were no background checks done on any of them . . .'

Daryl spoke with the patient tone she would have expected. 'In 1981 in little old Catskill . . . doing background checks on thirty members of a Czech orchestra? No.'

'And what about now?' said Ren. 'Could you do anything about this now? I think it's worth exploring.'

Daryl let out a breath.

'What about this as a scenario?' said Ren. 'Louis went to the park early to get into the concert. That's what he was into – music, not merry-go-rounds. He was not supposed to be there, so he was sneaking around. And what if someone caught him? And felt sorry for him, maybe let him in backstage. Or else . . . something obviously more sinister. Or it just led to something . . . I don't know. I'm not sure.'

'What's this all based on?'

Won't be mentioning my letter to Annie. 'Looking at the dead ends in the investigation, and finding a new way out . . . or in. Louis couldn't go to the concert. We all went. Beau wanted to bring Louis and a few of his other students with us, but they didn't all have the money and Mom and Dad couldn't afford to pay for everyone.'

Daryl's silences were getting noisy. 'Ren, if I go ahead and this is another—'

'I will not keep bothering you about this, Daryl, I promise. Remember, I am desperate. I admit it. More than anything in this world right now, I want Beau to have the untarnished memory he deserves. Sure, who cares what other people think? But this is an exception for me. I do care. He was my wonderful, gorgeous, wouldn't-hurt-a-fly brother. And my parents are devastated.'

'I know,' said Daryl. 'I've seen them. Your father . . . has aged. And your mother is well, trying to put on a brave face. Jay's been checking in with us a lot . . .'

'What?'

'Yes. He's a good guy, Jay. He got very emotional on one particular visit.'

Well, holy shit. 'He . . . visited?'

'Yes. Mainly phone calls, but he visited that one time.'

'Wow . . . you must be having Bryce overload.'

'It's OK,' said Daryl. 'I understand.'

'Thanks. It's just . . . I can't bear to think of the Parrys' agony. I mean, terrible as it was, at least we all know what happened to Beau. To lose a child and not know – I couldn't cope with that. You might as well write off your entire life from that point on.'

'OK . . . let me go check out a few things,' said Daryl. 'I appreciate you calling. You could . . . have taken care of this yourself.' He paused. 'But I'm sure you're very busy with the—'

'It's not that I'm too busy, Daryl. It's your investigation.'

'Thank you.'

'You've nothing to thank me for. Best of luck with it.'

51

There was no point in trying to grab any more sleep. And right now, Ren did not want to sleep. Mania is fuelled by sleep deprivation. And bipolar people like mania. It's the party part.

I get so much more done.

Bipolar self-medication covered anything from coffee to Coors to Coke to coke. Few bipolar people would admit wanting to kick mania into action. No therapist would recommend it. Unless they'd experienced what mania really is – living the best, most productive day of your life on a loop. It's when the world is an incredible place, no matter what shit is going on in your life or in someone else's life, no matter what part you played in any of it. Bipolar people can fiddle while Rome burns.

Until they wake up one morning and wish they had never been born. They've spent a thousand dollars, slept with a string of strangers, alienated everyone who has ever cared about them . . . until the next time. But the low is like the pain of childbirth; by the time mania comes around again, you've forgotten the depth of the low that will follow. You kid yourself – this time, the high won't end; this time will be painless.

Ren drank a pot of coffee and could feel the hyper-alertness kick in.

Bring it on.

She started to think about Mia Hammond and how her world was about to be turned upside down . . . again. Her entire life had been defined by her parents' actions and their consequences. Mia Hammond was like a ball in a pinball machine, an innocent party, still not free from being shunted around, almost thirty years later. And it was about to get worse.

Ren frowned. *Where was Mia Hammond when Peter Everett was screwing her mother? Would Trudie Hammond have just left her asleep with no guarantee that she wouldn't wake up? What did cheating parents do? Would they have sex in the room where their kids slept?*

Peter Everett hadn't mentioned Mia. Was he too ashamed to say that a two-year-old child walked in on them? Or was there all along? Was that what pushed Douglas Hammond over the edge?

Ren dialed Mia Hammond's number.

'Mia, hi, it's Ren Bryce. I need your help. It's about your parents. Can you answer something for me?'

'I guess.'

'You were there the day that your mother . . . died. But you didn't wake up until the police got there.'

'Yes . . .'

'Did your mom look after you full time?'

'I guess so.'

'You don't know for sure?'

'Well, I know I had a nanny for the rest of my childhood. Because Daddy was alone. He worked.'

'Did you have grandparents near by?'

'No. Why?'

I have a hard time believing you slept through everything. 'Just asking,' said Ren. 'I'm sorry for bothering you.'

Ren called Billy on her way to the office and arranged to meet him after work for alcohol and moral support.

When she got to her desk, the phone was ringing.

'Ren, it's Daryl. We looked at the orchestra. There were three other missing children corresponding to towns they were playing over the eight months they were in the country.'

'Holy shit.'

'I know. And here's where you come in – I could try and get in touch with the authorities in the Czech Republic, but I think you'd be able to turn it around quicker.'

'That's no problem,' said Ren. 'I'll get on the phone, right away. Thank you. I'll keep you posted.'

Please let this be it.

The rest of Ren's day passed in a haze of trying to avoid every case she was supposed to be working on. Every time Gary came into the room, her heart started to pound. She expected to be brought into his office and fired because he had just watched a copy of the DVD. Her nerves were jangled, her veins pumping coffee and all the other caffeine-filled liquids she could suck through a straw. She could not get out of work quick enough.

Billy Waites was waiting for her in a bar on Larimer Street. She told him about Ricky Parry. She told him about Peter Everett. But even Billy could not be told about Javier Luis or James Laker. She could not bear to say those giant failures out loud. She looked at him.

You will think you are another mistake I made. And you're not. And the circumstances were different. And I was trying to rescue

*Gavino Val Pando at the time, but it may not look that way. I am
flawed. And I know you know that. But if I say any more out loud,
I will fall apart.*

Billy handed her a box.

'Hello,' said Ren. 'What's this? Can I open it?'

'No.'

Ren smiled and opened it. It was a wooden circle, the size
of a dinner plate, with circular grooves carved into it that
all led to a central point shaped like a flower with six petals.
She frowned. 'It's a labyrinth.'

'Yes,' said Billy. He took a packet of sand out of his pocket
and began filling all the grooves with it. 'It's from Chartres.
In France. It's a replica of a labyrinth that's on the floor of
the cathedral there.'

'So it has no hedges, at least,' said Ren.

'No. What you do is you walk all the way around it and
then you come up the middle—'

'Like Trivial Pursuit . . .'

'Yeah, Ren. Sure. And when you come to the central area,
you go into each of those six little petal things and you pray
about something that you are grateful for.'

Ren smiled. 'That's beautiful.'

'Here,' said Billy. He took her finger and guided it around
the curves through the sand. 'It's like a Zen garden.'

'A Zen labyrinth. I never thought I'd see the day . . .'

'So there you go,' said Billy. 'Everything has another
angle, is my point. One man's scary maze is another man's
labyrinthine path to gratitude and peace.'

Ren kissed him on the cheek. 'I wish I was more like you.
You have such a beautiful way of looking at life. And you
have used the word labyrinthine in a regular conversation.'

Billy laughed. 'Would you expect anything less from a
former crim slash meth addict?'

Ren squeezed his hand. 'I would expect nothing less from a courageous, reformed crim slash meth addict. As if I would have lowered myself to be with you otherwise.'

Billy laughed loud. 'I did the lowering. FBI agent? Jesus.'

Ren hugged him. 'You always make me feel good.'

'You scum of the earth.'

'You drugged-up cartelperson.'

'That's not a word.'

'It's a lifestyle.'

'Shut up.'

'You shut up.'

'Let's get out of here,' said Billy.

'Sounds like a plan.'

Billy drove down Taylor Street. Ren was in the front seat regretting the choice of radio station. Tom Waites was on the radio, hoping that that he wouldn't fall in love again. Since the opening of the song, the silence in the car had almost drowned it out.

'Isn't it amazing how one song can render so many people . . . deeply uncomfortable?' said Billy.

'It's like eating a banana; you never know where to look,' said Ren. 'I think this song actually makes people feel they are in love with whoever's with them.'

Silence.

'Not that I'm saying that . . . *what* am *I not saying?*'

'It *is* a beautiful song,' said Billy.

'Just don't let the next one be "Let's Get It On".'

'It's "Let's Get It Owwwn".'

They pulled up at traffic lights. Billy laid his hand on hers. For a moment, Ren held it. Then she turned to look at him.

'Edith,' she said.

'Is gone,' said Billy.

'What?' said Ren. 'But . . .'

'There was no point,' said Billy. 'It . . . wasn't fair.'

'Why?'

'Don't move your mouth,' he said. 'Don't kiss me back.' He put his hand on her leg, leaned over and pressed his mouth against hers. He held it there as he slid his hand up higher. Then he pushed his tongue inside her mouth.

Whoa.

The lights went green and Billy pulled away from her, hitting the accelerator hard. Ren reached across the seat to him.

'Oh,' said Billy. He took a deep breath. He turned to her. 'I missed that.'

'Me too,' said Ren.

'Do you want to come back—'

Ren smiled.

'Remember the mirrors?' said Billy. 'In the hotel? Wait until you see the one at my place.'

They parked outside Billy's house, but stayed in the car. They kissed, he pulled her towards him, unhooked her bra with one hand and opened her shirt buttons with the other.

'You are good,' said Ren.

'Fluke.' He looked into her eyes as his head went lower. Ren lay back against the passenger door.

Where did he learn this shit? 'OK . . . stop, stop,' she said, sitting up.

Billy's face fell.

'No, seriously,' said Ren. 'If you don't stop . . . I . . .'

'You what?'

'Just, I don't know . . . I'm . . . maybe we shouldn't . . .'

'Ren, shut up,' said Billy.

'But—'

295

'What is wrong with you tonight? Shut up!'

'I'm nervous.'

He stopped and held her cheek. 'You have nothing to be nervous about.'

'You're right,' said Ren. 'Let's go.'

They made it into the dark hallway of the house. Billy pushed her up against the wall and leaned hard against her. Then he pushed her higher until her legs were wrapped around his waist. He carried her into the living room and laid her down on the floor. He knelt between her legs and pulled her toward him.

'Your floor is wet,' said Ren.

'What?'

'Your floor is wet.' She reached a hand up to her head. 'My hair is all . . . weird.' She pulled her hand away. She was breathing properly for the first time since they started kissing. *Oh, no. Something is wrong.*

Billy reached over and turned on the lamp. They both looked at Ren's hand. It was covered in blood. Billy looked past her. His eyes shot wide.

'What?' said Ren. 'What's the—'

'Don't,' said Billy, reaching out to turn off the light. 'Do not . . .' He tried to pin her legs down with his other arm.

Ren was gripping his hand, distracting him with the blood that covered it, prising his fingers away. She moved to flip her body over. But then she stopped.

'Oh, Jesus,' she said.

Beyond Billy, reflected in the giant mirror he had promised her, she could see the blown-apart body of Peter Everett . . . and his blood, soaking into her hair and dripping down her bare shoulder.

52

Ren sat on Billy's bed, looking tiny, dressed in his sweat-pants and hoodie. She had taken a shower and tied her wet hair in a knot in the back. Her face was gray.

Billy crouched in front of her, holding her hands. 'Well, have you made a decision, yet?'

'Peter Everett is lying dead in a house rented by Billy Waites, a man who has been linked to many crimes, and who is linked to Special Agent Ren Bryce . . . who is linked to Dr Helen Wheeler. Who is dead. Who is linked to Peter Everett who is dead. Who is linked to Ren Bryce. Who, let's face it, is dead.'

She laid back on the bed. 'I feel like I'm in one of those movies where someone runs through all the back gardens and takes all the washing lines with them.'

Billy got up and sat on the bed beside her. 'So . . . are you going to call work?'

'Yeah, I'll call in sick.'

He smiled.

'I am being attacked,' said Ren. 'And I have no idea why. What do we do about this – do we walk away from this crime scene, shut the doors and hope none of the neighbors get the smell? And when they do, then what? I can't ever have been here. I have no reason to be here. You and I have zero working relationship.'

'Here's some good news,' said Billy. 'This house is not registered in my name. No one can connect me to here. Not right away, anyhow.'

Ren glanced around the room. 'But . . . your stuff.'

'My stuff is that,' said Billy, pointing to a half-open sports bag in the corner. 'Remember?'

'You live like someone on the run.'

'At least I can admit it.'

'Whoa,' said Ren. 'Where did that come from?' She stood up and walked over to the window.

'Where broken-hearted Billy lives.'

Ren turned back to him. 'Stop. I hate that.'

'I'm trying to keep it light.'

'Everett hadn't been here long, this was all recent,' said Ren.

'And he was killed here.'

'So say your lovely blood-spattered walls.'

'What do we do?' said Billy.

Ren let out a slow breath. She watched the falling snow and the white lights sparkling across the city. And then she noticed red lights. And blue lights. And they were flashing. And there was a siren to go along with them. And they were coming towards the house.

Ren turned to Billy. 'We get the hell out of here.'

The narrow lane that ran behind the houses had barely been cleared of snow. Ren was a strong, fast runner, but she was barefoot on rough, icy ground and being hauled along by someone bigger and taller than her with strides twice the length of hers. She stumbled, and he whipped her arm up in the air like a child's to keep her from falling.

'Jesus Christ, Billy. Slow down. Please.' Ren stopped and pulled up the track pants with one hand. 'These are huge on me.'

'Ren, I don't care if you're half-naked. We have to run. As soon as they find that body in there, they'll be spreading out like flies. Why am I even telling you this? Someone has obviously sent them this way. And for now, we don't know if it's the person who killed Everett or a neighbor who heard it, so we don't know if the police already have you and me on their radar. And we sure as hell can't stick around to find out. Let's hope it was a neighbor.'

They started up again.

'At least we don't have to run through gardens and washing lines,' said Billy.

Forty-five minutes later, Billy was carrying Ren on his back across the rough, glass-strewn grounds of an apartment complex in Five Points.

'Where are we going?' said Ren, stopping, catching her breath.

'We are going to pay a visit to my friend, Stray Eddie.'

'I'm guessing he was not christened Stray.'

'No, nor was he blessed at birth with the gift of a good aim or a steady hand.'

'You have to be kidding me,' said Ren. 'I am going to the home of a guy who has a known reputation for shooting people.'

'Yeah, but he misses . . .'

'You can't tell him what I do.'

Billy glanced over his shoulder at her. 'No shit. I'd say it would be the first time he might hit his target.'

'What are you going to tell him?'

'The truth, the partial truth and nothing but the partial truth. We're fleeing the po-pos. You're my bitch. That's all he needs to know. He'll let us hang out. And he has cars. If we need one.'

What has happened to my life?

'It's cool,' said Billy. 'He's a good guy.'

'Sure, maybe missing his targets is his way of high-fiving Jesus . . .'

Stray Eddie's apartment looked like what would happen if a nightclub exploded and penetrated the wall of a historic apartment block. Eddie had left the door open, so he could go back and sit on his sofa. Ren could see Billy waiting for her reaction. He had been here before. She looked at him and smiled. The walls and ceilings were made of some strange white glossy resin. Unsynchronized mood lighting pulsed different colors in different rooms. Ren expected to see two hot lesbians wrapped around each other through an open doorway.

'In here,' said Eddie, calling them into the living room.

Eddie was tanned and fresh from the shower, with his black hair slicked back. He was dressed in gray Calvin Klein loungewear. *Nice.* Ren found herself drawn to the last place she should have been. Stray Eddie *had* been gifted with something at birth.

'Well, hello there,' he said.

'Hello yourself,' said Ren. She could not tell if he had noticed her stare.

'This is Ren,' said Billy.

My real name? Excellent.

Eddie gave a thoughtful nod. 'I used to date a girl called Ren . . . not. What the hell kind of name is that?'

'I don't know, Stray Eddie.'

'Ha,' said Eddie, re-arranging himself. 'So, what's up?' he said to Billy. 'What do you and your shoeless friend here need? Your feet are bleeding, by the way.'

Ren looked down, then back at the smudges of blood she had left on the floor. 'I am so sorry,' she said.

'If you're going to shed blood, it's the right surface for it,' said Eddie.

'A fresh body is lying in my house—' said Billy.

'Oxymoron dot com,' said Eddie.

'Hey, we didn't kill the guy. Someone is fucking with us.'

'Riiight,' said Eddie. 'But I could still—'

'No cleaning required. The cops are all over the place,' said Billy. 'Here's what we need: to hang here for a while and to borrow a car. And probably some money.'

'Hang here, yes,' said Eddie. 'Borrow a car? Not so much.'

'Shit, why?'

'They're all out.'

'They can't all be out,' said Billy.

Eddie shrugged. 'They might be back in a little while, I don't know.'

'Well, screw you,' said Billy. He was smiling.

All of you go screw yourselves. Is anyone taking this seriously?

Billy saw her face. 'It will all be cool,' he said.

'I'd love to know how.'

'So,' said Eddie, shifting again in his seat. 'Looks like the lady here is in deeper shit than you, Mr Waites.'

'The shit is rising to the exact same point on both our necks,' said Billy.

53

Ren stood up. 'Eddie, do you mind if I . . . is there a quiet room I could use?'

'For what?'

'I just need to think.'

'Sure, sweetheart, go across the hallway.'

She caught him glancing at Billy. *What's with your crazy friend?*

Across the hallway was a bedroom, like a modern hotel bedroom. There were four light settings. Ren chose pink. The bed was perfectly made. Ren was brought back to Domenica flipping out at the maids.

'*Si quieres hacerla en este país cada cosa la tienes que hacer perfectamente. Yo no estaría aquí si no fuera por eso.*' You want to succeed in this country, you do every job to the best of your ability. Look at me! I wouldn't be where I am today if it wasn't for that!

Ren paused – she had made a mistake. Domenica hadn't said 'eso' – I wouldn't be where I am today if it wasn't for that! She had said 'esto': 'if it wasn't for *this*'. This, meaning the job of being a maid?

Ren went back across the hall. 'I need to make some calls. Where can I go?'

'You need a phone?' said Eddie.

'No, no.' She waved her cell phone at him.

'I mean a throwaway,' said Eddie.

Duh. 'Yes. Thank you. Thank you. What time is it?'

'Eleven,' said Billy.

Stray Eddie watched her. 'I read that Bernie Madoff wore two Rolexes – one with the time in New York, the other for London time.'

'You don't miss a trick,' said Ren.

'Where are you calling?' said Eddie. 'Who are you calling? Will they be in bed? Or will they be having breakfast?'

Ren looked to Billy and back to Eddie. 'OK, Sherlock,' said Ren, 'being that I know you all of a half-hour, I'm going to guess you will not know who I am calling, no matter where in the world they are.'

'I just like to know things,' said Eddie. 'It's who I am. Any things.'

'I'll think of something exciting for when I get back,' said Ren. 'Is there a room I can use?'

'Sure, go straight across the hallway. What's that one up to?' said Eddie when she had left.

'My focus right now,' said Billy, 'is getting a car, Eddie. And getting the fuck out of Dodge.'

'Relax, relax. It's not under control.'

Billy stared up at the ceiling.

'But seriously,' said Eddie, 'flipping out isn't going to make this happen any quicker. We'll chill, watch a movie. No one knows where you are.' He slapped Billy's knee. 'Whoa. Is that a steel plate? My hand.'

Billy followed Ren in out into the hallway. He found her

in one of the rooms. She batted him back out with her hand.

Sorry Billy. Sorry. But you really can't know any of this.

'Ferris Bueller,' said Eddie, pointing at the screen when Ren walked back in.

'Go piss up a flagpole,' she said.

'Everyone remembers that line,' said Eddie. 'And look – Bueller . . . Bueller. Are you done talking to Taiwan?'

'Yes,' said Ren. 'They've just finished making the remaining square inch of glossy white surfacing to complete your apartment.'

'Great,' said Eddie. 'That's the bit behind the toilet that's been bothering me.' He patted the seat beside him. 'Sit down, Renaldo.'

Ren sat beside Billy.

'I don't think I ordered the Billy sandwich,' said Eddie.

'Well, I don't think Ren ordered a side of Italian,' said Billy.

Ren directed her gaze toward the television. She saw a flash of their reflections in the screen.

How did we all get here? Three people, lined up on a sofa watching a movie that reminds us of a time when the worst thing you could do was skip school.

The car was driven to the back of Stray Eddie's apartment complex. It was a limousine with a driver. Ren looked at Billy. *Is this for real?*

'It's cool,' he said. 'Eddie's got drivers with different limo companies . . . for when people are desperate.'

Ren turned her back on the car. 'We're not that desperate,' said Ren. 'I'm not dying to get ID'd here. There is no way that some random driver is going to lay eyes on me. So you get him out of that car and into Eddie's or wherever the hell he wants to go, but I am not sitting in a car being ferried around by a stranger. Is Eddie insane?'

Billy lowered his voice. 'You're forgetting Eddie doesn't know your day job. We are all partners in crime in his eyes. Not partners in crime-fighting.'

'Just, please do something.'

Twenty minutes later, Billy was at the wheel of the car.

'OK – what the hell was that all about back there with the secret phone calls?' said Billy.

'I'm sorry, Billy, but . . . will you trust me?'

'Dammit, Ren. I am right in the middle of all this. I *have* been as soon as you asked me for my help and now that the shit has really hit the fan, you go sneaking off making phone calls – in my buddy's house, on my buddy's phone – and you won't tell me what's going on? Does that not strike you as unfair? In any way?'

'Yes, it does.'

'And if the tables were turned, there is absolutely no way you would accept that from me.'

True. 'Of course I would.'

'Don't be ridiculous.'

'Look, there's nothing else I can do, so can we drop it?'

'Of course we can. Not a problem. Let's bury it.'

Ren stared out the window. 'I need you to drive back to your house.'

Billy stared at her. 'You have to be shitting me.'

'No. I need to check something out.'

'No way,' said Billy. 'I am not going near that place. The whole of Denver PD is there.'

'Hey – keep your eyes on the road. *You* don't have to go back to the house,' said Ren. 'I just need to check something out. I may have dropped something in the garden out back.'

'Your sanity,' said Billy. 'And the ability to come up with convincing excuses. I'd say you'll find them both there in the snow. With the cops.'

'It will be fine,' said Ren. 'You just need to drop me three blocks away—'

'And you're going to do what?' said Billy. 'Walk back to the house?' He looked down at her feet. They were slipped loosely into a pair of Eddie's sneakers.

'At least I won't leave prints,' said Ren. 'Just drag marks. They'll be looking for a man with two limps.'

'Why are you doing all this?'

'Why do you *give* a shit?'

Billy could barely speak. 'I'm going to do three things right now. One is to bear in mind that you are under huge pressure here—'

Ren looked at him.

'The second thing is that you are bipol—'

'I cannot believe you just said that, you . . . that is the answer to every—'

'And the third thing is to ignore that reaction,' said Billy. *Screw you.*

'I am trying to help,' said Billy. 'I . . . am not sure you are thinking rationally.'

'Thanks, Billy. Thanks for that.'

'I'm sorry . . . but this is unreal. Why have we spent the last few hours holed up in Eddie's only to come right back to the scene of the crime? It's insanity.'

'That's what it is,' said Ren. 'Please, just take me where I need to go.'

'And then what? Wait for you?'

'Yes. Wait for me for one hour. And if I don't show, get the hell back to Stray Eddie's.'

'An hour?' said Billy. 'But how do you know that's going

to be enough time? And what will you do if it isn't? Hitch a ride?' He gave her a kind look. 'Have you thought any of this through?'

'Billy, come on. Yes. Of course I have.'

'Jesus, Ren. Should I be stopping you doing this?'

'No.'

So Billy did as Ren asked. And two hours later, he forced himself to start up the engine and drive back to Stray Eddie's alone.

Billy Waites sat across the table from Stray Eddie in a cramped diner on a busy corner on Colfax. It was day time, but felt like night. A strange parade of people walked by the window, drawing Stray Eddie's gaze more than Billy's.

'You OK?' said Eddie.

Billy nodded and called the waitress over for more coffee. He picked up the sugar dispenser and started hitting it with the palm of his hand, trying to dislodge the lumps. Eddie grabbed it from him. He reached over to the next table and handed Billy the dispenser from there.

Eddie turned back to the window and the night-time people dressed in clothes not fit to be seen in winter daylight.

'Are you banging her?' said Eddie.

'Who?' said Billy, glancing out the window.

'I'm not talking about some random chick from outside. Miss Ren.'

'No, Eddie. No.'

'You want to, though.'

Billy smiled.

'She looks dirty,' said Eddie.

'You say that about every woman.'

'I don't notice women who aren't dirty. Who is she?' said Eddie.

'If I could work that out . . .'

'Women are fucked up.' Eddie leaned forward in his seat. 'Yo, check it out,' he said, pointing past Billy's shoulder to the television. Billy turned around. A photo of Peter Everett was in the top right-hand corner of the screen.

'*In a shock update on the disappearance of missing tycoon, Peter Everett, an FBI agent with the Rocky Mountain Safe Streets Task Force was taken into custody this evening following the discovery of the body of a fifty-three-year-old male at a house on Walker Street. The agent, who has not yet been named, was arrested at the scene—*'

Eddie stared at Billy. 'That's your body, isn't it?'

'Shhh.' Billy held a hand up to silence Eddie.

The rest of the report focused on Peter Everett's life.

'That's your body,' said Eddie. 'I'm right, aren't I?'

Billy's face was white. He nodded.

'Did your future wife do that? All that blood on her feet . . .'

'That was her own blood,' said Billy. 'She'd been running barefoot.'

'No wonder you were running,' said Eddie. 'If there was a dirty Fed in the mix.'

'Yup,' said Billy.

'Or were you and your fiancée in cahoots with the guy?'

'No.'

'Fucking Feds, always protecting their own,' said Eddie. He took a drink of coffee. 'My name, photo and the location of the last toilet I shat in would be scrolling along the bottom of that screen if I were found hanging around a dead body. It's one of theirs? No names given, nothing. Total shutdown. Case closed.'

'Case closed, I guess,' said Billy.

54

The warehouse floor echoed as it had when Ren Bryce crossed it to find the dead body of Javier Luis. Catherine Sarvas walked past the same door, glancing inside, recoiling at the blood stains, the twisted crime-scene tape, the grim sense of decay. She was dressed in a long, padded cream coat, clutching her black leather purse strap, moving through the cold white air of her breath. Further down the hallway, she stopped and took a right into a large room with gray walls and gray floors that carried the faint markings of a basketball court.

Domenica Val Pando sat on a chair in the far right-hand corner, one leg crossed over the other, a lit cigarette and a cardboard coffee cup gripped in her right hand. She stood up and sat against the edge of the table.

Catherine walked across to her. They shook hands.

'Gregory told me you were unaware of his . . . position . . . with us,' said Domenica.

'He was my husband,' said Catherine. 'He told me every-thing.'

Domenica smiled; a slow smile, held too long to be genuine. 'You must have had a difficult time with the FBI.'

'I knew that Gregory had hidden everything well,' said Catherine. 'I knew that they couldn't trace anything to him. And if they could find my sons for me . . .'

'Well, that's my job now, I believe. I have something you want, you have something I want.'

Outside, the wind was building. Catherine glanced up at the row of rectangular windows that stretched across the wall above Domenica. The snow was hitting the windows at an angle and had gathered halfway up the panes at the corner, bright white, untouched.

Ren Bryce sat alone in the darkness on a battered steel bench. The room stank. The floor was filthy, the walls shedding flakes of paint. It was rotting from the inside out. Ren's mind was racing. She had barely slept in three days.

Helen's voice came back to her: 'Ren, you need to be aware of your triggers for mania: you need to avoid stress, get a lot of rest, reduce your caffeine intake . . .'

Uh-oh – if you know your triggers, you don't just know how to avoid them . . . you know how to seek them out.

This time, the mania had slowly built – late nights, fear, stress, travel, caffeine . . . and then, she knew. Her mind sharpened, her thoughts sped. Connections jumped off the page, her fingers worked quicker on the keyboard, she drove faster, she got everywhere quicker. She got here quicker.

This is the end. It's all over.

Domenica dropped the cigarette butt into her coffee cup and pushed it out of her way.

'You can hand your husband's files over,' she said to Catherine. 'I will organize to have your son returned to you and . . . and then we can say our goodbyes.'

Catherine felt a surge of anger that lit up her eyes. 'You were responsible for that . . . man . . . raping me.'

'He was not meant to rape you,' said Domenica. 'He was meant to intimidate you, he was meant to wait until you and your husband were in the house together . . . without your children. He was sent to get a message across to your husband, to warn him how unwise it would be to co-operate with the authorities. Oh yes, I knew as soon as he made his first move in that direction, but I was giving him a chance to rethink. But Erubiel Diaz acted like an animal. You were never going to forget the face of the man who raped you. And it would be easy for you to ID him when his face appeared on a Most Wanted list. If Diaz had done as he was told, your husband might still be alive, you and your sons would not have been harmed, I would not be in this position. No one would be any the wiser. Erubiel paid for that error with his life. Your error was to call in the FBI. You complicated everything for yourself, getting involved with Agent Ren Bryce.'

'I needed to find out what happened to my family.'

'The sequel to that message.' Domenica's face was impassive. She shrugged. 'After Diaz' visit, we expected your husband to change his ways. When he made his next move, it seemed he was defying us. How were we to know that Erubiel Diaz had failed to deliver the message? He didn't tell us that he raped you, that he never even saw your husband.'

'Where is my son, Michael?'

'I don't know.'

'Yes, you do. Of course you do.'

'I'm not in that . . . world.'

'Of course you are!'

'I meant that low down,' said Domenica. 'I could maybe get people to see if anybody knows anything.'

'Why would that be good enough for me?'

'Good enough for you? If you give me what I want, nothing more will happen to you – that is as good as it gets for you.'

'Do you think there is anything more that can happen to me?' said Catherine. 'After what you've done already, what's left?'

'You want to be here for Michael, if he shows up. You're that kind of mother.'

'Every mother is that kind of mother.'

Domenica said nothing.

'You can't even promise me Michael,' said Catherine. 'Why would I give you anything of Gregory's?'

'But what if I do find Michael?' said Domenica. 'I am the only one in a position to locate your son. You certainly can't. The FBI wouldn't know the first place to look. So you will give me what I want. Because, if I do find Michael, what might I do then?'

Catherine's heart pounded. But she had nothing to say. There were no words for a woman like Domenica.

The door beside Ren opened without a sound, without a crack of light. Ren could make out Gary Dettling's face in the darkness. Then Colin. Then Cliff. Then Robbie. Then the rest of Safe Streets. They were all there. She held a finger up to them. *Not a word.* She sat back on the bench and pulled off the headphones she was wearing. She handed them to Gary. He nodded.

Ren smiled. Her heart was soaring. The world was beautiful. Everything was under control. She was as controlled and focused as she had ever been. She stood up and walked past everyone. They all nodded to her. Robbie squeezed her arm.

She smiled wider. *I love you guys. I love my job. I love the whole fucking world right now.*

Ren knew she was wired . . . and she wouldn't have it any other way. She got to the door. God bless stress, coffee, starvation, Red Bull, the white light coursing through her brain, making everything clear . . .

I'm sorry, Helen. But this one's for you.

Domenica stared at Catherine. 'Here's what I need to know.' She reached inside her jacket and pulled out a gun.

Catherine's legs went weak. She thought she was going to pass out. 'Please, don't,' she managed to say.

'I need to know,' said Domenica, 'exactly how your husband was co-operating with the Mexican authorities. I need to find out exactly when his betrayal began and how much they know.'

Catherine felt as if her heart was about to explode. She didn't know anything about betrayal. She didn't know that her husband had spoken with the Mexican authorities. She hadn't got all the facts. She was in a room with this crazy woman and she hadn't all the facts.

'Shit,' said Gary. The Safe Streets team looked at each other. No one had known this part. No one had any idea that Sarvas had made contact with the Mexican authorities. Catherine Sarvas would never have been sent in if they'd known Gregory Sarvas had committed the ultimate sin as far as Val Pando was concerned: betrayal. And, thanks to them, Catherine Sarvas had managed to convince Val Pando that she knew about everything her husband did.

'Go, go, go,' said Gary.

*   *   *

Ren burst through the door into the room where Catherine Sarvas and Domenica stood.

Domenica's face went through a series of readjustments.

'Drop your weapon,' said Ren. 'Drop it.'

Domenica glanced back and forth between the two of them.

'Drop it,' said Ren.

Domenica did as she asked.

'Catherine,' said Ren. 'Please leave.'

'I want to know where Michael is,' she screamed at Domenica.

'Let me take care of that,' said Ren.

'No she won't,' said Domenica. 'She doesn't give a shit.'

'Catherine, go,' said Ren. 'Please.'

'Ask her,' said Domenica. She jerked her head at Ren: 'Why don't you tell Mrs Panzón your little history—'

'Shut the fuck up.' Ren turned to Catherine, her eyes pleading.

Catherine looked at her. *Don't screw this up.* She had the courage to walk away from the only two people who could help her find her youngest son.

Ren waited until Catherine was gone before asking: 'Tell me where Michael Sarvas is.'

'I presume you heard me say that I don't know,' said Domenica.

'Who killed Helen Wheeler?' said Ren.

Domenica smiled. 'I don't know who Helen Wheeler is.'

'Whether it was Javier Luis or James Laker or Erubiel Diaz, the answer, ultimately, is: you,' said Ren.

Domenica shrugged.

'Fuck you,' said Ren. 'You didn't need to go near Helen.'

'But I didn't.'

'You fucking bitch!'

'You slept with James Laker and Javier Luis,' said Domenica. 'You let Luis escape to commit all the crimes you wanted to arrest him for. So you had to kill him. And you had to kill Douglas Hammond to stop your files being accessed. And then you killed Peter Everett—'

'Who is Peter Everett, Domenica?' said Ren.

Domenica smiled slowly. 'Everyone knows who Peter Everett is.'

'But not everyone knows what you saw him do, that you were the illegal Mexican nanny who gave Mia Hammond a little too much cough syrup to make sure she went back to sleep after all that commotion her daddy and Peter Everett made when they killed her mother.'

Domenica frowned. 'What the—'

'I know, Domenica. I know you gave Gavino cough syrup to make him sleep and keep him out of your way. And I know your first little kick of leverage was walking in on Douglas Hammond and Peter Everett. That was how you got them to do what you wanted all these years later. Peter Everett could doctor Helen's files to make me look unstable, to make everything I ever had on you look like fiction. Douglas Hammond was roped in to make sure it all had the legal seal of approval. That didn't quite work, though, did it? You were underestimating his guilt at what he had done to his wife. I'm betting he didn't want any more blood on his hands. He knew what your next step would have been if my files weren't released. He was trying to do me a favor.'

'You are mentally ill,' said Domenica. 'You don't know what you are saying, you are insane, you are paranoid. I have never even heard of these people.'

Ren moved toward her.

'You came into my home, my life, my son's life . . .' shouted Domenica.

'Which is more than you did.'

'Oh, now look who is the little nanny.'

'I was doing the job I was employed to do,' said Ren. 'What about you?'

'He was *my* son.' Domenica sobbed the last part. Domenica slammed a hand on to the table. 'My son, you bitch. You broke the heart of a six-year-old boy.'

You have to be fucking kidding me. 'You're the one who's insane,' said Ren. 'Did you not know that I was there in the woods when you ran from the compound with Gavino in your arms? I was there, you delusional bitch. I saw you look him in the eye . . . your seven-year-old *son* . . . and you tried to leave him behind. Alone. Alone.'

'That's not true.'

'Oh my God,' said Ren. 'This is unbelievable. Do you really believe that? Do you? Have you re-written his entire childhood? At one point, you told me that he was the biggest mistake you ever made.'

'I never said that.'

'Then I've clearly come back late enough into your life for the edited version to have over-ridden the truth,' said Ren. 'Does Gavino even believe that shit?' Ren walked away. 'Why do I care?'

'A little part of you loves my son,' said Domenica.

Ren turned again. She was about to deny it but changed her mind. 'And what if I did, Domenica? What if I did? Do you think we're the same? Is that it? You are so fucked up.'

Domenica's eyes shone with anger. 'I won, Ren. You lost.' She shrugged. 'You lost your mind.'

Ren punched her – hard, fast relief. Domenica's head

snapped back and hit the wall behind her. She half-staggered to her feet, but collapsed on the floor. Blood was streaming from the split skin under her right eye.

And I do not care. Ren stood over her. Blood was dripping on to Domenica's shirt, running from the back of Ren's hand. *And I do not care.*

Ren was transfixed. Domenica locked eyes with her. They were streaming. No emotion, just salt water. Domenica didn't speak. She struggled to her feet.

Ren turned briefly away. *I can't stand watching weakened people.*

'How pathetic it is that you have no control over your emotions,' said Domenica.

Ren smiled. 'The rollercoaster always has the longest lines.'

'And the most dramatic drops.'

'Oh, I think you had the most dramatic drop, Domenica.'

'You have nothing, Ren. No one. You are wired for a lifetime of pain. You will always be discontent. And every day, you are aware of that. And every day for the rest of your life you will be aware of that.'

'You have no clue,' said Ren. 'None.'

'I read your file,' said Domenica.

'Do you know one thing psychiatrists always say?' said Ren. 'That they are not mind readers. They know only as much as the patient tells them. And with someone like me? Half an hour every few weeks? When what I say depends on the mood I'm in? You know nothing, Domenica.'

'You took away the father of my child,' said Domenica.

'"Father of your child" – you make it sound so worthy. And . . . well, untrue.'

'James loved me,' said Domenica.

Insane. 'Domenica,' said Ren, leaning forward, 'James Laker was raped.'

Domenica went to slap a fat hand across Ren's face. Ren blocked it.

'James Laker loved me,' said Domenica.

'Don't be ridiculous.' said Ren. 'You haven't got a clue. James Laker feared you. He couldn't leave the compound. You were the warden he was your prisoner – that was your relationship. I helped him leave, so he could at some stage be a proper father to Gavino and have a chance at a decent life once you were put away.'

'You did all that, yet you didn't love Gavino?'

'James Laker wanted to get as far away as possible from you,' said Ren. 'Can you understand that, Domenica? You crossed the border to get what you wanted, didn't you? You understand what it's like to do that to get what you want? Well, he did the same. He got the fuck away. Maybe you should have learned from yourself; maybe you should have patrolled your own borders a little better.'

55

A door opened to the right of Domenica and Gavino Val Pando walked in. The task force had gone through the building earlier, but no one had been assigned to cover that door, because it appeared to lead into a locked room.

Ren remembered the building plans. *The skylight. There was a skylight.*

The last time Ren had seen Gavino Val Pando, one year earlier, he was as handsome as she had always known he would become. He'd worn his hair short, he'd been fit, tanned, dressed well. He'd looked as if he'd stepped straight from an Abercrombie doorway.

Oh my God. What happened to you?

Gavino looked unwell. Mentally. Ren and Domenica glanced at each other and for a moment, shared something human. Gavino stood there, his hands by his side, his eyes moving back and forth between the women.

What is going through your head right now?

'How fucking dare you,' he roared at Domenica.

Domenica recoiled with the volume, the force of his anger. 'What do you mean?' she said.

'Oh, Jesus. What do I mean?' said Gavino. 'What do I mean? *You*, you lying bitch! I mean *you*. How fucking dare you?'

Domenica raised her hands. 'I don't know what you're talking about.'

'That's because there are so many things I could be talking about,' said Gavino. 'That's how screwed up this all is. You have no idea what I'm talking about because it could be any number of millions of things you have done to me over my whole short life.'

Ren watched him. He looked medicated.

'Is he on medication?' said Ren, without turning directly to Domenica. She kept her voice low. But not low enough.

'What?' said Gavino. 'What did you say to her?'

'I asked your mother if you were on medication.' Ren kept her tone even.

Gavino stared up at the ceiling and started laughing. 'Yeah, like she'd have a clue. Ask her what my favorite TV show is. What music I listen to. Who my best friend is. Oh, hold on, I don't have any.' He looked at Ren. 'Funny, isn't it – she is my mother. Yet you're the one who worked out that I'm on medication and it took you, oh . . .' he checked his watch, 'thirty seconds. Well done.' He turned to Domenica. 'See that, Mother? She's good. Yes, Special Agent. I am medicated. Because of that bitch.' He pointed at Domenica.

She rolled her eyes. 'Why do kids always blame their parents for everything?'

Shut the fuck up, you stupid, stupid woman.

Gavino's eyes flared. He looked at Ren. She shook her head, tried to plead in some way, but not quite sure what she was pleading for.

'Here is why,' said Gavino, continuing his own train of thought, as if Domenica's comment had not been said. 'All my life, I had a cold, heartless mother and an asshole father.'

Domenica rolled her eyes again and looked away. Ren was mesmerized by her ignorance as to what was unfolding.

'Augusto was a prize prick,' said Gavino. 'And my mother was clearly insane. And violent. Who has a violent mother, for Christ's sake? Probably point zero five per cent of the population. Lucky fucking me. Anyway, blah blah, I was a kid, I was unhappy, blah blah. Then I got a little older and something really screwed up happened. My father began to notice I was alive—'

'Oh, for God's sake—' said Domenica. 'Where is this going?'

Shut up. Ren spoke to Gavino. 'Your mother will listen to you, Gavino. She will.' Ren looked at Domenica, willing her to see. *Really see what's going on here.*

Domenica looked confused.

You don't control the room now, bitch.

'Go on, Gavino,' said Domenica.

'My father noticed I was alive and started to involve me in things,' said Gavino. 'And so did you.' He pointed at his mother. 'And I liked being given a shit about. I really did. And then I fucked up. I broke his remote-control Ferrari. I stood on a toy car. And Augusto gave me the beating of my life. Mother just ignored me completely – worse than before. If you can actually ignore someone in degrees, that's what she did. I was eleven years old.' His shoulders slumped. 'I will never forget that feeling.' He paused. 'It wasn't what you think: I wasn't feeling rejected or unloved. I was thinking "I am a freak of nature. I am the product of these two terrible people."' He spaced out for a moment.

'Did you know that Ted Bundy had a child?' said Gavino. 'He got married when he was on Death Row and had a child with his new wife. Somewhere out there is a girl whose father is a serial killer and whose mother was a fucked-up bitch who wanted to marry a serial killer. How would that make you feel? But I kind of know how that could make you feel or what that could make you do. That could make you, at eleven years old, go into some shitty-ass barn, pick up a knife and . . .' Tears filled his eyes. 'I knew where babies came from . . . and I knew that I never wanted to—'

Holy shit. No.

Domenica's hand shot to her mouth. 'Did you . . . oh my God . . . you didn't . . .'

Ren turned to her, amazed. *How can you not know the answer to that, you crazy bitch?*

'I started,' said Gavino. 'I did enough that I still . . . but there was so much blood, I passed out. When I woke up, I was bandaged in my bed. And one of the compound wives was sitting beside me.'

'Where was I?' said Domenica. Her voice had shrunk away.

'Oh my God, who cares where you were?' said Gavino. 'Don't you see? There was no point to you any more after that. Apart from making me get obsessed with the future of the fucking universe if I was in it. So for years, I wanted to die, I just wanted to die, but I was too chickenshit. Then last year, I go flash some stolen money about and you go ballistic. And the big irony is that I was trying to impress the chicks – the only way I know how. Some guys get girls drunk, so they can have sex with them. I need to get them drunk enough not to notice my . . . problem. I can turn off the lights, tell the girl she's too drunk, and that I have too much respect for her to take advantage of that. Then at least I have something, I have someone beside me, even if it's only for a few hours.' He glanced at Ren as if she was the last person who had ever been beside him.

Ren's heart flipped. *Oh, Gavino, you poor boy.* He looked young and raw and heartbreaking.

'Now,' said Gavino. 'It turns out that all those however many years being tortured, being in agony every day, none of that shit needed to have happened. If you—' he stabbed a finger at Domenica '—had told me the truth, that you had hand-picked a man to be my father because of his genes. Do you have any idea what it was like to hear that? James Laker – good-looking, intelligent, kind, an athlete. I mean, it's ridiculous. I'm half of that. I'm not half of Augusto Val Pando. Where is he now, Mother? He is as useful to you as you were to me that day in the barn.'

Gavino raised the gun. 'I want this so bad, it aches,' he said. He pointed it at Domenica.

Don't do it. Do not do it. Live your life. Live your life.

56

'Please, no,' said Domenica, falling to her knees. 'Santa Maria—'

'Who do you think is listening to your prayers?' said Gavino. He walked over to her and pulled her up by the hair. She screamed.

'Stand up, stand up, you bitch.'

Domenica stood in front of him. Gavino was six inches taller than her. He brought his arm up and put the barrel of the gun into her mouth. 'I want this so bad,' he said. He smiled. 'But do you know what I want more?' He looked around.

Ren stood, rooted. *Please not me. I did love you. I did not want to abandon you. I had no choice. Please not me.*

Images exploded from somewhere in the dark attic where she had buried them; wide-eyed Gavino, holding her hand, singing nursery rhymes . . . images that seemed so starkly innocent against the backdrop of Domenica's world.

Please do not do this.

'I loved you so much,' he said to Ren.

Oh, God.

Ren's heart started to thump. She knew her eyes were giving away her fear.

'And do you know what?' said Gavino. 'That's never really gone away. I still love you.' He pushed his mother to the floor. 'Because what you were doing to us, well, you were just doing your job. Your job was to destroy her business. But when it came to me, you were not doing your job – you were doing the opposite of that. You were just being you. Your job was not to betray a seven-year-old child, was it?'

Ren shook her head. 'No.'

'You were being kind,' said Gavino. 'You just couldn't help it. You couldn't stand by and watch how they treated me. You really cared for me.'

'Yes,' said Ren. 'I did. But I shouldn't have let myself . . . because I always knew I would have to leave. I'm sorry.'

'It's true, though – it is better that I have loved and lost,' said Gavino.

He looked at Ren. 'Can you come over here?'

Ren walked towards him. Gavino stood facing her, the gun in his hand. He stared at her, his pupils huge, his eyes filled with tears. He took a step towards her and reached out his arms.

Oh, God. You're not going to kill anyone. Ren put her arms around him, held his shaking body. 'Thank you,' he said. 'Thank you for everything.'

'I'm sorry,' said Ren. 'It's OK.' She stroked his back. 'Everything's going to be OK. I can help you now. I'll do anything I can to help you.'

'*What* do you want more?' said Domenica, getting up from the floor. 'What did you mean when you said that there was something you wanted more?'

Gavino pulled back from Ren and looked over her shoulder

at his mother. 'I meant that I don't want to kill you. I could do that right now. But instead, I imagine you sitting at a table beside some defense attorney who has crumbled under the weight of all the documents the prosecution has, signed by one of the best witnesses they could have – the son of the accused. Detailed accounts of the life and works of Domenica Val Pando. A mountain.'

Domenica's face was a mess of emotions.

He's got you, Domenica. We've got you. You. Are. Done.

'Your father is dead,' said Domenica.

They both looked at her. Gavino walked over to her and shoved his face into hers. 'Nice try. But I'm still not going to shoot you.' Gavino put the gun back in his pocket. He turned to Ren. 'You can do the rest, right?'

Ren cuffed Domenica. 'Gavino, give me the gun.'

He shook his head. 'Not until she's gone.'

'Gavino, I am not walking away from you while you have a gun. That's just not going to happen.

'Don't you trust me?' he said. He looked so hurt.

'Of course I trust you,' said Ren.

'He'll kill me if we turn our backs on him. He will kill me,' said Domenica.

And?

'I'm doing the worst thing that I can possibly do to someone like you,' said Gavino. 'Killing you would get you off the hook.'

'Gavino . . .' said Ren. 'Just walk with me.'

He shook his head. 'I want to see her go.' He paused. 'Is there anyone here – do you have back-up?'

Ren nodded.

Domenica suddenly bucked against the restraints and slammed her heel hard against Ren's shin. Ren half-buckled. Gavino caught his mother by the arm and yanked her forward, dragging her toward the door. Ren followed, gripping Domenica's wrists tightly, pulling them up too high for her to risk the pain of moving.

'I'll walk with you,' said Gavino. 'I'll wait by the door. But . . . I couldn't bear you to be the one who has to take me away. Can you send one of your colleagues instead . . . ?'

'Sure,' said Ren. 'Not a problem. You are going to be OK, Gavino. I'll get you help. And . . . I'll ask my friend Robbie to come get you. He's right outside.'

Ren pushed through the door. Gary and Colin moved toward Domenica. Ren pushed her their way. She turned to Robbie. 'Could you go get Gavino? He's—'

Hold on a second. Why had Gavino prepared a whole stack of documents? Why wouldn't he just testify in court? He could do it by video. He didn't need to – Oh no. Oh shit, no.

Ren turned back to the door, reached out her hand. The blast was deafening, instantly ringing in her ears. *Oh my God.* She was about to push the door in. *Please, let this be something else.* Gavino's last sentence hit her: 'Can you send one of your colleagues instead?'

Oh, God.

Ren stopped. She leaned against the wall, her head hanging. Robbie and Cliff had rushed past her through the door. Robbie had stood against it on the other side. Ren looked up. His back was blocking the window.

'Who's back there?' said another agent, running up to Ren. 'We had people at all the exits. We searched the building.'

'Gavino Val Pando,' said Ren. 'He's alone.' She turned and walked away from another room that held another tragic death behind its door.

57

When Ren got back to the office, there was an email waiting for her: the legal attaché in Prague asking her to call urgently. She Googled the time zone – it was eight a.m. The leegat answered the phone right away. Ren listened and took notes. She thanked him and put down the phone. She let her head fall to the desk and said a prayer. She didn't know if Daryl Stroud would want to be disturbed at three in the morning, but she didn't care.

When he answered, she could hear the sound of his bedclothes brushing against the receiver.

'Daryl, it's Ren. I just got a call from Prague. This could be it.' She waited for it to register.

'Ren? OK . . . go ahead.'

'They've got a Jakub Kral, now sixty-one years old, convicted pedophile who was released from a Czech prison in 1978, which means he was a free man in 1981, the year Louis Parry disappeared. He worked as a roadie – if that's the word – for the orchestra. Kral was back inside again from '82 to '87 and '89 to '93. He's been a free man since then, but as of two hours ago is sitting in a cell in Prague awaiting questioning.'

Ren could hear Daryl readjust his position in the bed. 'Jesus, Ren. Let's hope it's him.'

'And let's hope he remembers Louis Parry,' said Ren.

'Yes.'

'I'm sorry for calling so late,' she said.

'Don't worry about it. I know how much it means.'

Ren put down the phone. She expected that the Czech authorities were currently listening to the sound of silence. What had Kral to gain by admitting to crimes he had gotten away with almost thirty years earlier? He would claim he was being victimized by the police, he would talk about his human rights, the fact that he was a changed man, the fact that he was in his sixties now, an old, broken man. *The usual bullshit.*

Ren let out a deep breath. *Please, God. Please let him be the one. And please let him own up to that.*

The next morning, an update came in on the Sarvas case. Gary was about to make the call, but Ren told him no. 'I'll do it,' she said. 'Continuity of care, remember?'

Ren went straight to her desk and dialed the number. Catherine Sarvas answered on the first ring.

'Catherine, they've found Michael,' said Ren. 'And I'm afraid the news is not good. He passed away yesterday.'

Catherine let out a terrible moan. 'What happened to him?'

'He was in Tijuana. He was found by two young boys . . . he had collapsed on the street. He had a bacterial infection from a contaminated needle.'

'Needle?' said Catherine.

'I'm afraid so,' said Ren. 'That's what the cartels do. Get people hooked on drugs.'

Through her sobs, Catherine's voice turned to ice. 'Greg did this. My husband did all this.'

*　　*　　*

Ren left Catherine Sarvas to her grief. She put the phone down gently and rested her head on the desk. After a minute, she looked up.

'Imagine your son is missing eight months and you hear that he died,' she said. 'But that it happened the day before – you don't hear he was killed as soon as he was abducted or four months later. You are told, "Your son died yesterday." He would feel within reach. It would have to make you feel like you could have done something or that you could still do something. That would fuck with my head. And also that it was your husband's fault.'

'Catherine Sarvas, right?' said Cliff.

'But how could you not know what your husband is doing?' said Ren. 'Wouldn't you see papers lying around? Didn't he talk about his work? Wouldn't you know? I mean, Gregory Sarvas got up in the morning, ate breakfast with his wife and sons, drove them to school, came home, went downstairs to his home office – hello? – and worked as an accountant and lawyer for a top Mexican cartel. How could you be so out of touch with your husband's job?'

'I'd say she knew,' said Colin.

'But she didn't,' said Ren. 'She had no idea. You should have seen her face. It was awful. Hey – I'm just flying in here from Denver to tell you that your husband was a liar, oh, and he clearly didn't give a shit about you or your kids and whoops, he sucked you all into one of the most dangerous situations on the planet—'

Colin looked up. 'Ren, stop trying to put yourself in other people's positions: that whole "God, if it was me, I'd . . ." thing. It's not you, it's never you, and you don't know how you'd react until you're in a situation.'

'Woo,' said Ren. 'No, I don't.'

'So . . . Gregory Sarvas was lying about one part of his life. It sounds like he was a good husband to this woman, right? She loved him, right?'

'Yes, but how could she not be—'

'Maybe that's all that mattered to her,' said Colin. 'That she had a husband who loved her and was good to her. Not every woman is so lucky.'

Ren shook her head slowly. 'Oh my God. Have you ever had a conversation with a woman that didn't begin and end with "Nice rack"?'

Colin said nothing.

'You have no clue,' said Ren. 'Please – stay away from women.' She called out. 'Run, Naomi, run. Save yourself!'

'El Coyote Panzón,' said Cliff, drumming his fingers on the table.

'Funny, isn't it?' said Ren. 'Gregory Sarvas wasn't who his wife and children thought he was. He wasn't who we thought he was. He didn't even work as a coyote. He was good, very good.' She paused. 'He *was* fat, though. The big guy with the gray hair and the big beard that reminded someone somewhere of a coyote.'

'I don't get how it worked,' said Robbie. 'Sarvas was lawyer for the Puente cartel.'

'Yes,' said Ren, 'He knew everything inside out, how the business worked, who the players were, blah blah blah. So he could also see the vast amounts of money coming through. He's obviously being paid a small fortune to do this job, but it's nothing compared to what he could be making. He lines up Domenica Val Pando, who's been sniffing around; he's seen what she's done before, but knowing her mistakes he knows how she can avoid making them again. He recruited Domenica Val Pando, not the other way around.

'But at the same time, Sarvas had hooked up with the

Mexican authorities, planning to get safely out the back door of the Puentes – under their protection. The authorities think Sarvas is on their side, but his only interest is in dismantling the cartel. Because waiting in the wings is his very own operation with Domenica Val Pando, who will keep it running in his absence. He does the front-of-house good-guy shit.

'The problem with these cartels is that, as soon as the authorities chop off one head, a new head grows back – an uglier one. The rest of the drones scuttle off into the darkness, then come out again and regroup. They may have learned some lessons, they may not, but no matter what, things will have to change and the cops are going to have to start looking at them again from scratch. I mean, what else can they do, but arrest and jail the kingpins? It's just that there are queenpins and jackpins and straightpins . . .'

'So,' said Robbie, 'Sarvas is getting out of one cartel knowing exactly how it operates. He quietly sets up his own organization to rival it and has all the inside information he could possibly need to beat them—'

'Yup,' said Ren. 'I mean, he may have decided that would be enough, that that would be all he needed to trump them. But I'd say when things got really intense down there over the past few years, he went for overkill – trying to bring the Puente cartel down and get rid of the competition before he even started trading, selling them out and setting himself up as the good guy to the authorities.'

'What was he thinking?' said Colin.

'That he was invincible, that he was smarter than any of them,' said Ren.

'Why would Domenica want to play second fiddle to Gregory Sarvas?' said Colin. 'I mean, whatever about agreeing to it – realistically, could she follow through?'

'He was a mine of information,' said Ren. 'He effectively

had eleven years on her – so much had changed while she'd been gone. He knew how everything worked along the border. And he had a list of the players living in the pockets of the kingpins.'

Colin shook his head. 'He was crazy to think he could get away with that.'

'These people don't live in the real world, or at best they've one foot in it. They're permanently on the edge, they just push themselves further and further until there's nowhere else to go.'

Gary walked into the bullpen. 'The lab just got in touch. The reason Safe Streets got that call to that warehouse crime scene was because someone knew the victim was on our Fifty Most Wanted – DNA matched our number four – Javier Luis.'

Ren's heart started to pound.

58

Ren's cell phone rang as she was turning the key in the lock of Annie's front door that evening. She hit Answer and heard the voice of the Czech legal attaché.

'It was Jakub Kral,' he said. 'He's confessed.'

Kral had given police a gas station marker fifty miles west of Catskill and a vague set of directions from there. But almost thirty years on from a random decision on a hot, dark night, no one held out hope much that what remained of Louis Parry would be returned to what remained of his family.

Ren walked into the hallway and stepped on to a small white envelope with her name on it. She picked it up and opened it. She had never seen the writing before. It was beautiful.

Dear Ren
I can't do this any other way, because it's too hard. I wish I could take whatever you give me, but, from you, I need more. I don't know if I'll ever find someone who'll give me one hundred per cent and whether, if I do, she'll be wonderful enough that I have the same amount to give back, but that's a risk I'm going to have to take. Because this is killing me. I

*don't think you know how much it hurts. And it's worse
because I know you are a good person and that you mean
everything you say to me and everything you do.*

*But when you look at me, there's guilt that goes along with
it and I just want to make it go away. But I know I can't.
And I can't be the guy in the shadows, because with someone
as amazing as you, it feels wrong to hide.*

*Please know that no matter happens, I'm here if you need me
. . . just not in the same way.*

Love always

Billy x

Billy no longer Waites. Ren put the letter down. She felt sick.
She walked over to the window and looked out. Billy was
gone. Billy had left her. Her heart raced. *I am not ready for
this.* She let herself drift away with the falling snow, running
through everything she and Billy had together, how perfect
and fucked-up the whole thing was.

Screw this. She grabbed her keys and ran to the Jeep. She
jumped in, started the engine and headed for Five Points.
Billy had to have dropped the car back to Stray Eddie. Or
maybe he had let Billy take it wherever he needed to go.
Stray Eddie would know.

Ren drove through town, thinking of throwing her arms
around Billy and being held there and being kissed and loved
and never let go. A multi-colored stream of city lights washed
over the windscreen. *Bright shiny things.* She felt free. Her mind
was filled with what they would do and where they would go.

My whole life is Billy Waites.

Her heart was traveling fast, her body felt light. She couldn't
let him go. She would tell him to stay, promise him one
hundred per cent. *We'll go out tonight, find a hotel room, drink
champagne, have sex all night . . .*

She kept her foot on the accelerator and sped into the turn-off for Five Points.

Billy will be here. Everything will work out. I can not be alone. I can not be alone.

She pulled into the parking space outside Stray Eddie's. *I cannot be alone.* The car was gone. *I cannot be alone.* She looked up at the dark window of the apartment. *Where are you Billy? I cannot be alone.*

Tears welled in her eyes. She had been here before. The drama of breaking up with someone and wanting them back. The high of pursuing them. The motivation that, when stripped away, was wrong and was the one that was ringing clearly in her ears. Not *I love Billy.* Not *I cannot be with anyone except Billy.* Not *Billy, I want to spend the rest of my life with you.* Just *I cannot be alone.*

And Billy Waites deserved more than a damaged woman not wanting to be alone. With tears streaming down her face, Ren turned on the engine and reversed out.

I want a man whose rings I will wear for the rest of my life. My own Edward Lowell. A man with a yellow tie.

Two thousand miles away, investigators unearthed the skeletal remains of Louis Parry in a deep grave, fifty miles west of Catskill. Two hours earlier, his mother, Rita Parry had passed away.

Ren lay on her bed that night, imagining what could have happened on June 20th, 1981: Louis Parry walking down the shaded path from his parents' house and into the bright sunshine. In his pocket was a folded-up flier: *The Czech National Orchestra Plays Haydn. Performances 4 p.m., 6 p.m., 8 p.m.* Louis had piano practice with Beau at 4 p.m. And he had to be at home for supper at six. And he might have decided that he would risk being late. His mother would think his class had overrun – he had an exam the following week – but that he was safe with the Bryces. He was right – that was exactly what Rita Parry had thought.

Desperate to see the performance, Louis went to the park with no money in his pocket. Instead, he climbed a tree by the tent and was going to settle for listening to it . . . until Jakub Kral came outside to adjust a tent peg. He looked up and smiled when he saw the little blond boy. He called him down, told him he would get a better view from a small nook at the side of the stage, as long as he didn't move a muscle. Louis Parry was thrilled. He was even happier when, afterwards, Kral solved another problem – knocking ten minutes off Louis' journey home. He had pulled his van right up outside the back of the tent to sneak Louis out from under the tarpaulin and give him a ride right back to his front door. Ren imagined Louis, smiling and enthusiastic and grateful, giving precise directions to a man who had no intention of ever doing anything this little boy asked; no intention of stopping the van, of letting him out, of stopping hurting him, of letting him live.

Kral had locked away each detail of the twenty-nine hours he had held on to Louis Parry, while strangely, not recognizing the little boy's face when he was shown his photograph. What Kral remembered was the evening's performance.

The world is so fucked-up.

Ren cried.

Stop. Crying. Jesus.

59

Ren walked into Gary's office before allowing the knock on the door to register with him. He jumped.

'God . . . I'm sorry,' said Ren. 'I wouldn't normally just barge in.'

Gary looked up at her. 'It's not that.' There was a struggle behind his eyes.

Ren sat down in front of his desk. 'Is everything OK?' she said.

Gary slid open the top drawer and pulled out a pamphlet. He threw it down in front of her. 'Take a look at this.'

There was a horse on the front, rearing up on its hind legs. And above it was written in curly script: *Can You Rise Up To Your True Height?*

Bizarre.

Ren opened up the folded card. There were several photos of pretty, smiling teenagers. Across the top of the page was a banner that read *Who you are is what is right*.

Ren looked up at Gary. 'It's the Messiah of the Most Wanted? Jim-Jams?'

'Jonah Jeremiah Myler,' said Gary, nodding.

'Well, he hasn't lost his creative touch,' said Ren. 'He is truly nuts. Why do these kids respond to such insane images and language? Is this what the disenchanted youth is looking for?'

Gary struggled to speak. 'Do you want to know where I found it?'

'Yes. Where?'

'Claire's book bag . . .'

Oh my God. 'Your daughter Claire?'

Gary nodded.

Holy shit. 'But . . . people are always handing out fliers,' said Ren. 'She probably just—'

'Let me skip your niceties,' said Gary. 'There's a cell phone number on the bottom of that. Claire has called it. Four times. And texted a boy called Ruben five times.'

Whoa. 'Did you confront her?'

Gary was staring into space. 'So,' he said as if he didn't hear her, 'it looks like sometimes the disenchanted youth is sitting across the breakfast table from you.'

'Did you say anything to her?' said Ren.

'I would have had to defuse years of landmines to get close enough.'

'Oh.'

'Yes,' said Gary.

'But . . . what are you going to do?' said Ren.

'Start by bringing down this fucking freak,' said Gary, taking the flier back. 'Sick son-of-a-bitch . . .'

'Teenage girls can be so innocent,' said Ren. 'Even these days. They're oblivious to danger. She was probably flattered by the attention. Teenage girls—'

'—should be happy and secure enough not to be sucked into . . . this,' said Gary. 'And it's my responsibility to take care of that. It is a father's job to make his daughter feel loved and respected and safe, so she isn't looking to some dirtbag older man to do it in the wrong kind of way.'

'It wouldn't have come to that,' said Ren. 'She wouldn't have got that close to him. Claire's a smart kid.'

'She's a kid, period,' said Gary. 'And having this pamphlet in her book bag is already too close.'

'I know. You're right,' said Ren. 'What are you going to do?'

'Kill him if we find him. Kill him.'

'Let's hope it doesn't come to that . . .'

'I would have no problem doing it.' Gary shook his head. 'You see me here. I'm not exactly . . . I'm not an emotional person. I . . .'

'But—'

Gary looked up at her. 'Ren, it's not like I come home at night and turn into Wonderdad, OK?'

'Gary, you're not this horrible father,' said Ren. 'You know that. Kids need to accept that parents are people too. They have their own shit going on. It's just that my parents' generation or yours gave the impression that everything was OK in the world and that they had no problems.'

'My father slept with two of my friends' moms and asked me to cover for him on three separate occasions . . .' said Gary.

'Alrighty, then.'

He smiled. 'But thanks anyway. So, you knocked on my door. What did you want?'

'I was just coming in to ask you for some of those giant rubber bands to flick at Robbie.'

'And the fate of the nation rested with one woman . . .'

'Do you have any?'

Gary shook his head slowly. 'On the filing cabinet.'

'Thanks,' said Ren, waving a handful at him.

'There's one more thing,' said Gary. 'There is one little undercover job I'd like you to take care of.'

'Uh-oh. What?'

'I told Claire you might help her with her Spanish . . .'

'Ah . . .' said Ren.

'She won't talk to her mother about boys or anything like that. But she might talk to you. To someone like Claire, you would appear cool.'

'What do you mean just "to someone like Claire"?' said Ren. She nodded. 'Sure, I'll do that. No problem.'

'I appreciate it,' said Gary.

'But she still knows you're my boss, she mightn't say a word.'

'I don't know – be conspiratorial. Make up something shitty I did to you.'

'"Make up"?' Ren smiled.

Gary's phone rang. Ren took it as her cue to leave.

That evening, Ren pulled into the parking lot of the Jefferson County Cold Case Unit and dialed Janine Hooks' number.

'Janine? Hi, it's Ren Bryce. I'd just like to apologize again for everything.'

'There really is no need,' said Janine.

'I know, but still . . . I'd like to . . . make amends. I'm outside your building and—'

'What?' said Janine.

'Yes,' said Ren. 'Can you spare a minute?'

Janine paused. 'OK, but—'

'If you could come out to the parking lot, I'd like you to meet someone.'

'You can bring them up to my office,' said Janine. 'That's not a problem.'

'I can't. Please, it'll only take a minute.'

341

'OK,' said Janine. 'This is a little strange.'

'That's how I roll,' said Ren.

Ren got out of the car when she saw Janine crossing the lot. Janine was already looking into the car. She frowned at Ren.

'She's on the floor,' said Ren. She opened the back door and Misty stood up.

'Wow,' said Janine. 'She's beautiful. Hello, girl. You are beautiful,' she said, crouching down. Misty threw herself at Janine.

'I saw the dog photos in your office,' said Ren. 'All over your office.'

'What, and you bought me a dog?' said Janine. 'You must be riddled with guilt.'

Ren laughed. 'Yes. And no, I did not buy you a dog, I brought you a . . . colleague.'

'What?'

'Meet Misty,' said Ren. 'She's my cadaver dog. A warm friend to cold cases. We are at your service. If you'd still like to search those possible burial grounds you mentioned.'

Janine stood up. 'Are you serious?'

'Yup.'

'Do you think she'd be any use?'

'You bet,' said Ren. 'She's very well trained.'

'Thank you so much,' said Janine. 'I've always wanted to work with a cadaver dog.'

'Well, here we are.'

'I really appreciate it,' said Janine. 'I might take the hex off you, now.'

Ren laughed. 'OK, well, we better get going. Send me an email and we'll go from there.' She turned to put Misty back in the car.

'Ren,' said Janine. 'My first case here, there was this

woman, she was eighty-two years old, one of the nicest little old ladies you could meet. And I believed that her son had killed his pregnant girlfriend in 1972. He had disappeared the same day the body was found. No trace of him since then. So I called to this lil ol' lady's door, pretending I had gotten lost in the neighborhood. She was so blind, she thought I was about nineteen years old. She brought me in, made me tea. I called back with flowers, I took her grocery shopping another day . . . ' Janine paused. 'Look, her son's in jail now because of my finest efforts. He had gotten back in touch with her when the dust had settled. He would call her, visit if he could. And I took him away. I get what it's like to do what you have to do—'

'Wow,' said Ren. 'You played an old lady? You are one mean bitch. Stay away from my dog.'

They laughed.

Ren's cell phone rang. 'It's my boss,' she said. 'I better take this.'

'Sure,' said Janine. 'I'll be in touch.'

'Cool,' said Ren. She hit Answer.

'Ren, get into the office. Now.' He hung up.

Half an hour later, Ren was walking down the hallway registering the barely contained fury on Gary's face as he stood in his doorway with his arms folded.

Oh shit.

Ren paused in front of him. 'What's this ab—'

'Grab your coat. We're going to Stout Street.' Stout Street was the FBI's federal building in downtown Denver.

'Why?' said Ren.

'A man called James Laker has just walked in there with footage of Javier Luis' murder, saying Domenica Val Pando was responsible.'

Oh my God. James Laker is alive?

'Aren't you going to ask me why you're coming with me?' said Gary.

'I guess we both know why I'm coming with you.'

'I don't think *you* know. Laker is saying he was forced at gunpoint to falsify information about Special Agent Ren Bryce on the same tape. He wants to make a sworn statement to the contrary.'

Oh, thank God. Thank God.

Gary glanced at her. 'I don't know what's on this tape. All I know is that you have nine lives, Ren Bryce. And you are running through them faster than anyone I have ever met.'

THE CALLER

NYPD Detective Joe Lucchesi is on the trail of a killer locked into a dark fantasy world that has come crashing into reality with devastating results… and a rising body count. People are being murdered in their own apartments, their faces savagely beaten, their bodies discarded in their hallway for a loved one to find.

Back on the job after a year out and a terrifying ordeal at the hands of a psychopath, Joe finds himself the reluctant lead in another high-profile investigation. And his problems don't end there, battling with physical pain and overwhelmed by friction in the task force and at home, Joe throws himself into his work. But just when he feels close to making a breakthrough, the investigation is rocked by tragedy and another victim's life is hanging in the balance.

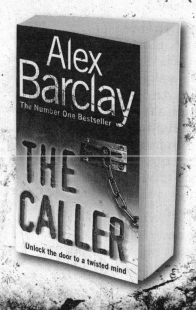

DARKHOUSE

In 1985 in a North Texas backwater, two teenage boys made a chilling pact that would unite them forever in a dark and twisted loyalty.

Now one lies dead. And the man responsible is going to pay.

When a routine investigation comes to a violent and tragic end, Detective Joe Lucchesi takes leave from the NYPD and moves with his wife and son to a quiet village on the south east coast of Ireland. They're happy. They're safe. And they're about to enter a nightmare more terrifying than the one they left behind.

When a young girl goes missing and the village closes ranks, Detective Lucchesi sets out to find the truth and uncovers a sinister trail that leads from the other side of the Atlantic and cuts directly to the very heart of his family.

His wife is lying. His son is lying. And a killer is lying in wait.

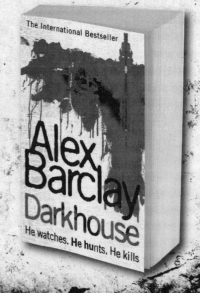

The International Bestseller

Alex Barclay

Darkhouse

He watches. He hunts. He kills